Iron Tigers

David Neil Drews

Harb and Russell Media

Edited by Sally Boyington
Cover design by Momodou Lamin Barrow
Interior formatting by Jason Anderson, Polgarus Studio
Published by Harb and Russell Media

ISBN: 979-8-9881718-0-5

For my wife, Hilary Taylor Drews

Preface

My passion for sports history and American history led me to the 1899 Sewanee football team. Consisting of heirs to the Old South, this team brazenly barnstormed across 2,500 miles to battle five college football Goliaths in six days. Their courage, endurance, audacity, and achievements inspired me to write this historical novel, *Iron Tigers*—an account of these extraordinary and daring late nineteenth-century athletes amidst their historical moment and the South's as well.

I chose fiction as my vehicle instead of nonfiction for several reasons but primarily because I wanted to ride on the train with these players and see them up close on the distant gridirons they visited. I wanted my reader to be with them, too.

In *Iron Tigers*, the Sewanee team's accomplishments are solidly based on the public record. Newspaper accounts of the games inform much of the on-field play I depict. The fictional characters that inhabit *Iron Tigers*, in varying degrees and ways, connect to aspects of actual Sewanee 1899 players as well as the manager, coach, and trainer. This book's characters have external and internal conflicts, thoughts, and discussions that are inventions of my imagination, fictional elements threaded through the actual story and settings.

Among the many pleasures I experienced writing this book was researching 1899 football rules, conventions, and equipment. As an aid for modern-day readers, here is a summary of these particulars:

If a player were to exit a game, he could not return to action. As a result, players played both offense and defense. The starters were collectively referred to as "The Eleven." Forward passes were prohibited until 1906. These rules—playing both ways and only being allowed to pitch or hand off the football—are the two most striking distinctions between the nineteenth-century game and today's.

Starting in 1882, offenses were given three downs to achieve a first down, which was five yards instead of the ten-yard requirement established in 1906, the same year forward passing was initiated.

Points awarded for scoring were five points for a field goal, which could be scored by place-kicking or drop-kicking; five points for a touchdown, which was followed by a kicked extra point attempt; and two points for a safety.

In today's game, offenses strive to avoid punting. Not so in 1899. Because no forward passing was allowed, gaining field position was a major objective. Due to the importance of field position, punting skills were highly valued, and teams would sometimes punt on first or second down.

Part of the joy of going to a nineteenth-century football game was to witness the aerial show of long arcing spiral punts. A team might have moved into a punt formation or executed a quick kick, which is when a ball handler feigns a run or pitch and punts instead. A punt receiver was allowed to signal for a fair catch by making a divot in the turf with his heel. He would then punt the ball back to the opposing team, or if within field goal range, the return man might place-kick or drop-kick the ball.

Further underscoring the strategic emphasis on field position, when a team scored, the opposing team kicked off—not the scoring team. Kicking off was seen as advantageous.

Whether it be an end around, dive, buck, mass play, or punt, the team's captain called the plays. Coaches were not allowed to call out signals or instructions from the sideline.

If a modern football fan traveled back in time to, say, the 1899 Sewanee versus the University of Texas game, they'd see players clad in long-sleeved shirts under lace-up canvas vests, quilted moleskin pants, shin pads, soft leather boots, and a few in leather head harnesses to protect their ears. When play commenced, the fan wouldn't see a quarterback dropping into a pocket of blockers and throwing the ball downfield. However, the fan would experience much more action and drama than "three yards and a cloud of dust"—the cliché often applied to pre–forward pass football.

I have attempted to put the flesh on the bones of this epic tale. I hope you enjoy the ride through the 1899 American South with the most daring college football team of all time.

Iron Tigers

Chapter One
Sunday, November 5th, 1899

With only moonlight for guidance, Patch Mercer ran up a narrow mountain path from Monteagle, Tennessee. The short and wiry football player hurdled embedded rocks and dodged exposed tree roots. He stumbled a few times but kept his balance until the trail dipped. Staggering forward, Patch leapt into a handstand. His legs teetered, so he walked his hands back and forth to steady himself. Then he sprang to his feet, bowed, and bolted up the path, cutting and darting at each turn.

Patch skipped over a brook, stopped, and rested with his hands on his knees. He coughed a few times, then unbuttoned his suit coat pocket and pulled out his watch. In the darkness, he could only guess the position of the watch's hands. If his approximation was correct, the Sewanee football team curfew was in twenty minutes.

Facing the town of Monteagle below, Patch stared into the black and imagined the girl he had just held in his arms. She was probably brushing her hair in front of a mirror—her soft, long, strawberry-blond hair. He could be in that room with her for the rest of the night, with the window cracked, the fall night cooling the intense heat from the room's steam radiator. He could get up at dawn and hustle up the mountain in time for chapel. Patch had missed many previous curfews, always to extend his time with a young lady.

He leaned against a tree and folded his arms. "I can spend the night in my dorm room or in Iris's bedroom." He shook his head and chuckled. "That's an easy one." He began walking back toward Monteagle.

As he hiked down the mountain, he pictured Woody, his roommate and teammate, already in bed. The team trainer taking an equipment inventory. The team captain modifying plays. The team manager fine-tuning the financial details for an epic and deranged journey. On the following day, the 1899 Sewanee Tigers would begin an odyssey over 2,500 miles of rail to play five college football teams in six days.

Patch stopped and turned back uphill. Glancing over his shoulder, he blew a kiss to his Monteagle gal, then ran hard up the path to Sewanee.

He reached the edge of the woods and saw the silhouettes of the six Gothic buildings that constituted the small Episcopal college. For a few seconds, he stood gasping for air. Then he lowered his head and sprinted down a cinder path.

Five yards from his dormitory's steps, he tripped over a low, taut wire spread across the path. He landed and slid facedown. "Dammit!" Lying motionless, Patch heard cinder crunch under approaching steps. He lifted his head and saw the shiny but well-creased cowboy boots of the football team's captain, Titus Scott "Turl" Turley from Brazoria, Texas.

Patch raised himself onto his knees and looked up at the captain.

Turl bent down and held his pocket watch in front of Patch's face. "You're six minutes late. You'll carry water for this. Look at you, you've spent yourself down there in town—I might just put a scrub in for you for the first half."

"Ah, Turl. Don't sub me out."

"Why shouldn't I?"

Patch shrugged his shoulders. "I almost beat the curfew."

"*Almost* is for losers."

"Turl, I'm just saying—"

"As great as you are on the field, you lack much as a teammate."

"I care about my teammates, Turl."

"Tennessee game. We were lined up to kick off, and you came running down the hill. You'd been with some girl and—"

"Yeah, but I scored three touchdowns, including a spectacular fifty-six-yard—"

"It was dazzling, Patch, but it doesn't have a damn thing to do with what I'm talking about. You miss curfews. You show up late to practice. Why? I'll tell you why, it's because you put your lustful desires before your team. Tonight, you cared more about humping that wagtail down in Monteagle than spending time with your teammates on the eve of our departure."

Turl's ungentlemanly comment surprised Patch—the Sewanee captain was rarely crass. Before Patch could challenge the remark, a freshman tripped over the wire and landed on Patch, slamming the 125-pounder back to the ground and knocking the wind out of him. The underclassman scrambled after his strewn books and quickly moved down the path.

While Patch tried to recover his breath, Turl helped him get up. Chest heaving, Patch said, "Hell. Damn med ghouls. Why don't they tell us when they've laid wire for the freshmen?"

Turl swept cinders off Patch. "You okay?" Patch nodded his head. "Let's go upstairs so you can catch hell from everyone and then we can all get to bed."

After climbing a flight of stairs at Saint Luke's Hall, the two young men walked into Patch's dorm room, which he shared with Sewanee's right tackle, Woodward "Woody" Partridge Barnwell of Galveston, Texas. Woody had earned his B.A. at Kenyon College, where he was captain of the football team. He was now a Sewanee Seminary student.

Patch found Woody lying on his bed reading. Under his breath, Patch said, "Typical." When not playing football, sitting in class, studying, or attending chapel, Woody was reading the Bible or the Episcopal Book of Common Prayer.

At the other end of the room, Alfie Melville and four Sewanee football players sat at a round table, playing poker and drinking Jack Daniel's. Standing at attention behind Alfie was Joseph Hill, a fourteen-year-old black servant and the football team's assistant trainer. He was dressed in a dark jacket, a white shirt, and an off-white silk puff tie. When one of the students wanted a drink, Joseph drew the liquor from a keg in the corner of the room.

Alfie was the perpetual dealer. He admonished any card player who delayed the game or didn't keep his cards facedown on the table. A senior with large blue eyes and jet-black hair, Alfie spoke with a carnival barker's cadence, and he ran the Sewanee team just like he ran a poker table, with gravity.

Alfie, without looking up from his cards, said, "Joseph, no more whiskey for Finn or Peck, here."

Patch noticed that Finn was swaying in his chair, and Peck was slurring his words.

Joseph said, "Yes, Mister Alfie."

Patch caught a glance from Alfie. The manager said, "Mister Mercer, how collegial of you to join us this evening."

"And what a den of virtue you're orchestrating here, Mister Melville," Patch said.

"Why, we are merely gaming, leisurely conversing, moderately sipping, and momentarily we will be sleeping."

Addressing Patch, scrub Finn Grayson said, "You got your refreshment horizontally—we're getting ours upright." The poker players laughed, and Alfie let out an exaggerated guffaw. Two of the players clinked shot glasses and threw back whiskey.

Patch said, "Look at these guzzle guts." Finn offered him a drink. He waved it off. "Clear out, men, I'm to bed."

Alfie said, "Your own, I trust."

Finn chimed in with, "Gave her the green gown, did you?"

Patch became angry—that was twice a teammate had disrespected his Monteagle girlfriend. He scowled and walked toward Finn. Turl firmly placed his hand on Patch's shoulder and redirected the star right end toward his bed.

The captain broke up the card game, and he and Alfie Melville shooed everyone to their rooms. On his way out, Finn offered Patch a handshake. Patch shook his hand after a slight hesitation. Then Patch unlaced his boots, kicked them off, and sprang backward onto his bed, doing a full twist and landing perfectly.

The visitors had all left except Turl and Alfie. Turl asked Patch, "Do you like that girl down in Monteagle?"

Patch raised his eyebrows. "Iris."

"Iris."

"She has many fine qualities."

"I apologize for my vulgarity earlier regarding her."

"Apology accepted. And I won't miss curfew anymore."

"You're still carrying water in Austin."

"I know."

Turl then looked at Alfie. "Well, manager, did you win enough money to cover our travel cash deficit?"

"Just enough for my own pocket change," Alfie said. "But don't worry, captain, I'll get everyone out west and back."

Turl said, "You might have to pitch in that pocket change and more."

"Goodnight, fellas," Patch said.

Woody Barnwell looked up from his book for the first time since Patch had come in. "Captain," he said, "may God send angels to guard your sleep, fortifying your health and spirit so you may run like a devil over the next five games."

Turl nodded his head and said, "May God hook up our train with a caboose loaded with angels."

Alfie said, "Sleep soundly, boys. Tomorrow we ship out for war." Turl and Alfie left the room. Woody returned to the book he had been reading.

Patch asked, "Not up for a bedtime chat?"

Woody kept his gaze on the page he was on. "This trip might be the best adventure of our lives. An opportunity to bring glory to God, our school, and each other. Yet you couldn't forgo carnal pleasure for even one night. We are about to travel over two thousand miles and do battle five times in six days against large universities—a colossal challenge. Before we even leave the Mountain, you have diminished our cohesiveness."

"That is a patent exaggeration."

"Without team unity and comradery, how will we compete with these teams? We're lighter, and we will become increasingly ragged from continuous travel while stuffed in a sleeper car."

"Why must you lecture me, on the eve of a trip that you said might be the best of our lives?"

"When we are priests we will reflect—often—about our time on this mountain, our time with these men. I foresee you having many regrets, wishing you could have tempered your appetite for seduction and flesh."

"And I prophesize that you, too, will have regrets. You will wish that you had pursued young ladies and sought various other forms of leisure. Our teammates relax together playing cards, sipping whiskey, laughing, and you, you're in bed reading . . ." Patch sat up and grabbed Woody's book. "*Bishop Philander Chase's Reminiscences!*"

"The seminary is more rigorous than undergrad. You'll find that out next year. Unfortunately, I won't be here to mock you."

"Seminary. My grandfather, my father, and now you have my whole life laid out for me."

"Tidy, isn't it?"

"Stiflingly so."

Patch's father was a Sewanee Seminary graduate and a priest, and Patch's grandfather was the Bishop of Georgia and a noted theologian in the Anglican world. In his nineteen years, Patch had attempted to please them, while he also worked to drown out their voices of disapproval. At Sewanee, he found himself in the same paradox with his best friend. When they had roomed together in boarding school, Patch had thought Woody was a very dedicated and devout student, but not judgmental—of himself or Patch.

Woody asked, "Is it the vocation of priesthood that scares you? Is it fidelity to a wife? Or something else?"

"I don't know if I can genuinely lead a flock. And, honestly, I have wild oats to sow, and I don't know how long I'll be sowing them."

"You're trapped."

"Exactly!"

"I mean you're trapped by your devotion to conquering female hearts and bodies."

"You have also trapped yourself. You've installed a tiny Cotton Mather in your brain. He judges you moment to moment."

"My faith has grown and my behavior has followed suit."

"You worship piety more than you worship God." After a brief pause, Patch cleared his throat. "I wish I hadn't said that, Woody. You know I have great respect for you and your devotion."

"I forgive you, and please don't worry. We've both been too sharp with each other."

"I hate to watch you miss out on so much. So much fun. Fun specifically designed for young men like us. Leave Puritanism in the history books. I'm not suggesting you live recklessly like me. Just let Woody Barnwell enjoy more than just football."

"And I am afraid you'll deny yourself your inheritance as a great leader in the Church and all of the rewards that will accompany a lifetime of pastoring."

"We're trying to protect each other from future regrets."

The two young men lay quietly for a few moments.

"Goodnight, Patch."

"Goodnight, Woody." Patch turned off the lamp between their beds.

Chapter Two
Monday, November 6th, 1899

At 7:00 the next morning, the three hundred men of Sewanee sat quietly in Saint Augustine's Chapel. Twenty-one of the worshippers played football for the Sewanee Tigers. They sat with Alfie Melville and Coach Hobart "Hobie" Lourie. These twenty-three young men were six hours from boarding a private Pullman sleeper that would take them to Austin, Texas. There would be one more passenger, the team's trainer, or rubdown man, Henry Jordan, who was not at Saint Augustine's for morning prayers. He was not allowed to worship at Saint Augustine's.

Henry was at home sipping coffee and warming a leftover biscuit. He was staring at the empty chair across the table, where his wife, Emma, used to sit. On the table in front of her seat were chemistry and anatomy textbooks. Henry placed the books there whenever he wasn't reading them.

A half mile behind the Sewanee campus, Henry lived alone in a cottage that sat in a ravine along with twelve other small houses. Sewanee's white people referred to this neighborhood as Happy Hollow. Its residents, all black, called it The Cut. All of the town's black people resided there. Like Joseph Hill, those thirteen or older worked for Sewanee as low-wage servants. The university reserved the higher-wage service jobs, like launderer, for local whites. When Henry was not working with the team, he drove the campus garbage wagon for two dollars a week.

As Henry ate his biscuit, he thought of Joseph. On game days, Joseph's principal jobs were to set up medical supplies, carry water before the games, serve water to the players during the games, sponge-bathe them afterward, and clean wounds. When time permitted, Joseph observed his mentor studiously, watching Henry employ a variety of rubdown techniques.

Joseph deeply desired to go on the trip, and Henry had asked Alfie Melville to include the boy. Alfie had told Henry that there were not enough funds for Joseph to travel with the Tigers. After receiving the manager's decision, Henry had gone to the Hills' cottage. Henry sat with Joseph and his parents, Silas and Rose Hill, in the family's kitchen. Henry said, "Y'all, Mister Alfie told me there's not enough money to carry Joseph on this trip."

Everyone was quiet until Joseph lifted his gaze from the floor and said, "Mister Alfie might let me go on the Auburn–North Carolina trip after y'all get back from whippin' them teams out west."

Henry said, "He sure might, Joseph."

After leaving the Hills' cottage, Henry had regretted that he hadn't convinced the team manager to bring Joseph along, and not just for Joseph's sake. It was going to be difficult to perform both his and Joseph's tasks.

Henry finished his breakfast, put on his Sewanee baseball cap, and hiked to the gymnasium. On the training table, Henry had three crates filled with large brown bottles of his latest liniment concoction and four crates of bandages. He unscrewed the top of one of his bottles and sniffed the contents. He smiled.

Henry enjoyed being the Sewanee football trainer. It was an honored position, and he was driven to keep his men on the playing field. He loved mending people, and he loved Sewanee football. And almost the entire campus—students, professors, and staff—adored Henry. He tended to the school's young athletes' bodies, their minds and spirits. People on his garbage route often came out and greeted him when he arrived to remove their trash.

Football was a contest of perpetual body-on-body collisions. A man like Henry Jordan was invaluable. He treated the boys' lacerations, stiffness, jammed fingers, contusions, sprains, pulls, spasms, concussions, and minor fractures.

Henry took another whiff of his liniment. Breathing in the fragrance, he identified a few of its individual components: witch hazel, peppermint oil, and ginseng. Henry had grown up helping his grandmother Rebecca pick, boil, and mix mountain herbs for both common and uncommon ailments. He dreamed that one day he would be a certified doctor and combine modern medicine with Grandma Rebecca's remedies and methods.

On mild days, Henry sometimes sat on a bench outside Thompson Medical Hall. The windows were open, and he would listen to the confusing words the professor used. He hoped one day to be privy to their meaning and importance.

Most of all, Henry wished he could go back in time as a doctor and save Emma, who had died three years earlier from typhoid. They were both eighteen when they married and twenty-six when she died.

Emma was Henry's first academic tutor. Emma had taught him how to read using the worn and discarded books he salvaged from the garbage wagon. Henry's rescued book collection included slightly dated college textbooks, like the two on his kitchen table. Another was an astronomy book, *The Heavens on Earth*, which had vivid descriptions and swirling depictions of the sun, planets, moon, stars, and Milky Way. Henry had read this book to Emma and showed her the illustrations while sitting by her bedside during her final days.

His only way to bring her back, in any sense, was to honor her. If he became a doctor, Emma would beam with pride from her star in heaven. And he would feel her radiance. He knew this without doubt. If Henry could save lives, perhaps, with time, he could forgive God for taking his Emma. Perhaps then his pain would ease a bit.

He had no idea how to pay for or find a medical school that would accept him, but for the past two years he had frequently read the old anatomy textbook and chemistry textbook he had plucked from the trash. Until he figured out how to advance his education, he had his memories of his beloved, his books, and his Sewanee charges.

***

Hours before their departure for a week of brutish struggles across the South, three of Henry's athletes led the procession at Saint Augustine's. The remainder of the team sat together among faculty, clergy, and fellow classmates. Patch and Woody were next to each other, as they always were in chapel. Woody was focused on his teammate and fellow seminary student Telfair "Prayer Bear" Embree, who led that morning's procession. Prayer Bear, the choir cross-bearer, carried a metal Celtic cross mounted on a staff.

A native of Jonesborough, Tennessee, Prayer Bear was blind in one eye, over which he wore a black patch. He was one of the larger football Tigers at six feet and 200 pounds, and he had extraordinary innate strength, both physical and spiritual.

Woody played next to Prayer Bear on the Sewanee line. He admired his fellow seminary classmate as a team leader and passionate Christian. Although a terrifying guard for opposing linemen to face, Prayer Bear was a gentle soul who saw the Episcopal Church and Sewanee as pathways for him to ease human suffering and spread the gospel.

During games and scrimmages, Prayer Bear and Woody worked in tandem, joined by their joy of football, but Prayer Bear carried his joy beyond the football field while Woody struggled to allow himself happiness off the field.

The congregants pulled down their prayer kneelers, and the chapel priest led the recitation of the General Confession:

Almighty and most merciful Father; we have erred and strayed from thy ways like lost sheep. We have followed too much the devices and desires of our own hearts. We have offended against thy holy laws . . .

The opening lines of the General Confession often distracted Woody, as they did in chapel that morning.

The line *And there is no health in us . . .* echoed in his mind.

From rote, he continued the recitation while he obsessed over this line, convinced that there was *no health* within him. He failed to absorb the remainder of the prayer, which asks for God's mercy.

Interrupting Woody's thoughts, Patch quietly said to him, "Five games in six days. Melville is crazy."

Woody hushed him, then whispered, "The vice-chancellor approved it."

"He's also loony."

"Are you packed?"

"I will be."

"Please don't try to bend the clock to Patch's will."

"I'll be ready, don't fret."

After the Lord's Prayer was recited, Prayer Bear went to the altar and read Psalm 133: "Ecce quam bonum et quam iucundum. Habitare fratres in unum!" Prayer Bear paused, looked at his teammates, and then recited the remainder of the psalm.

When he finished, he looked at the chapel priest, who cued Prayer Bear to continue. "Today, my teammates, manager, coach, trainer, and I begin an odyssey. A quest for many facets of glory for ourselves, for Sewanee, and for the Lord. We wear the purple proudly, for we know the mightiness of our small school, a beacon in the wilderness that forever burns and glows, just like our faith. We will carry that purple fire on behalf of all of you. We will carry it to Austin, Houston, New Orleans, Baton Rouge, and Memphis; it will never be snuffed out. We will bring our seminal torch back to the Mountain, where it will send light out into darkness unimagined."

The father said, "Thank you, Telfair, and Godspeed to you and the other men. Please rise as the Augustine Choir leads us in 'Gloria Patri.'"

***

Just before 1:00 p.m., the team, coach, manager, and trainer stood on the Sewanee depot platform. They faced a crowd of four hundred supporters: fellow students, village residents, faculty members and their families, boardinghouse matrons, administrative staff, and servants from The Cut. The student orchestra played "Dixie," "Ta-Ra-Ra Boom-de-Ay," and the "Star-Spangled Banner." The crowd sang along.

Between songs, the students chanted cheers, progressively louder with each one:

Everywhere we go
People want to know
Who we are
So we tell them
We are the Tigers,
The mighty, mighty Tigers!

Next, they yelled out one of Sewanee's favorite cheers:

Born on a mountain top
Raised by a tiger
No time for a dandy fop
I'm a Sewanee fighter
Sewanee, Sewanee we run farther
Sewanee, Sewanee we drink harder!

Carrying a basket full of biscuits and working her way to the front of the enthusiastic crowd was Miss Cecilia Fontaine, one of the sixteen Sewanee matrons and, at twenty-four, the youngest. Miss Cecilia owned and ran the Hiawassee boardinghouse. She was the granddaughter of a Civil War widow who had originally built and run the Hiawassee House.

Miss Cecilia reached the platform and went down the line handing each team member a biscuit wrapped in a light purple cloth napkin. On the final napkin, the initials "B.A.M." were embroidered with gold thread. She handed this one to Patch, who, without smiling, mouthed, "You look lovely." She responded with a quick, flirty smile.

After the songs and cheers, the Sewanee captain thanked the supporters, who promptly interrupted him, chanting *Turl, Turl, Turl . . .* Appreciative but embarrassed, Turl motioned with his arms to quiet the gathering. The crowd complied, and the captain said, "During this journey we promise you no less than the glorification of the true sportsmanlike manhood of Sewanee!"

At these words from this widely admired young man, the crowd roared. The supporters again chanted *Turl, Turl, Turl . . .* The captain grabbed and lifted fullback Kimbrough Lowndes's hand. Quickly the whole team likewise clasped hands and raised them above their heads.

The crowd began to chant *Henry, Henry, Henry . . .* Turl spun around to find the trainer and saw him quickly move behind Coach Lourie and Alfie. Turl gestured for Henry to join him in the front. Slowly Henry moved forward. Turl raised Henry's hand. The chant for Henry gained volume, then slowly faded out. Another cheer gathered power:

Tigers! Tigers! Leave 'em in the lurch!
Down with the heathens!
Up with the church!
Yea, Sewanee's right!

This cheer reached a crescendo by its fourth recitation, at which point the team members touched their hearts and blew kisses to the crowd. Then they boarded the train.

The massive, shiny black locomotive, the Mountain Goat, slowly pulled out of the station and began the seven-mile descent down the mountain to Cowan, Tennessee. The windows were up, yet the team could still hear the giant farewell party. Moved by the support, the players crowded around the train's windows to watch the gathering.

Alfie Melville didn't look out a window. Instead, he sat and observed the spirited faces of the Sewanee Tigers. He wondered if he had underestimated how grueling the trip would be for the players. Would the money last? What if the Mountain Goat were to break down? At a whisper, he asked himself, "Are the odds too high?"

Chapter Three
Monday, November 6th, 1899, Goat Hall

The Mountain Goat rolled rapidly down the mountain and chugged over flat terrain for the final mile of the short trip to the Cowan depot. At the station, a telegram awaited Alfie Melville:

```
TEAM BOOTS ARE COMING
WAIT IN COWAN
```

On the eve of departure, without Henry's knowledge, Joseph had dragged home two duffle bags stuffed with the team's cleated boots. He stayed up until dawn cleaning and polishing each pair. Then he slept until 1:30 p.m., when his mother woke him.

"Get dressed and wash your face, your daddy's waiting for you."

Joseph rubbed his eyes.

"He needs your—wait, what's that you just wiped on your eyes?"

Joseph looked at his hands and saw black shoe polish smudged on his fingers. Panicked, Joseph said, "The train!" He sat up, put on his shoes, and began tying his laces.

"What train? And what's in these two sacks?"

"Momma, I gotta go."

"Yes, you're goin' to help your daddy with the Wilson barn."

Joseph slid on his coat and grabbed the two duffle bags of boots. "Love you, Momma." He flew out the front door and into the cottage's front yard, where his father grabbed him and said, "Hold on, son, hold on."

"The Tigers' boots—I shined 'em—Gotta get to the depot!"

Silas Hill had hitched a mule to his wagon, which was loaded with lumber and carpenter tools. Joseph slung one of the bags over the wagon's sideboard and onto the lumber. "Please take me, Daddy. I can't run and carry these sacks that far, and I'd miss the train even if I could."

"Son, I think the Tigers' train is gone."

Joseph hoisted the other bag of boots onto the wagon.

Silas looked at his lumber, then at Joseph. "All right, let's go. Maybe they got held up at the sendoff."

Silas drove his fourteen-year-old son to the Sewanee depot. The station agent was alarmed that the Sewanee team didn't have their football boots. He gave Joseph a round-trip ticket for the next train to Cowan and telegrammed the Cowan station. Thirty minutes later, Joseph hugged his father.

Silas stepped back and gripped Joseph's shoulder. "Now, don't miss the train coming back—expect you at dinner."

With twenty-one pairs of nicely polished and softened cleated boots, Joseph climbed aboard the train to Cowan.

***

While waiting for Joseph, Coach Lourie asked Turl to lead the squad in calisthenics on the station's lawn. The air on the plateau was refreshing, and the exercise made the time pass quickly for the starting eleven and ten substitutes. The team then sat on the lawn and ate chicken salad finger sandwiches and drank lemonade. Prayer Bear said, "Remember, it is kind to feed the bears in these parts—just in case one of your little tummies get full." He received a chorus of boos, which made him laugh.

Alfie and Henry stood in the boxcar and inspected its contents. Alfie pointed to the partially closed boxcar door. "Henry, let's get some more air in here."

Henry slid the door all the way over. "Mister Alfie, I did inventory this morning. I don't know how—" He stopped himself, then continued. "It is my fault, sir, for being careless and missin'—"

"Hold on, looky here," Alfie said.

Dragging two bags, Joseph approached the boxcar. Alfie and Henry lowered themselves to the ground. Joseph pulled out a pair of boots tied together by the laces and held them out like he was presenting a gift.

Alfie took the pair from Joseph and ran his hand down the side of one of the boots. "Why, you rubbed these to a fine shine. You softened them, too."

Henry said, "Joseph. You didn't tell me you were gonna shine these boots?"

"I wanted to surprise you at the depot, but I slept through the morning, tired from shinin' all night."

Alfie patted Joseph on the back. "Well, it all came out in the wash. Here's fifteen cents. Now go see the stationmaster and buy a ticket back to Sewanee. Get yourself a sandwich and lemonade with the change."

Joseph hesitated and then held out his hand for the coins. "Thank you, Mister Alfie."

"You're welcome, Joseph."

The engineer walked up to Alfie. "Mister Melville. Please ask everyone to stay clear from the tracks." He pointed at a shiny Pullman sleeper. "Time to—"

"Isn't she pretty, Henry?"

"Yes, Mister Alfie. She's a beauty."

"Wait until you see inside," Alfie said.

The engineer cleared his throat. "As I was saying, Mister Melville."

"Yes. Please, go ahead."

"I gotta swap out cars."

Alfie shouted at the team, "Y'all stay on the lawn! Swappin' cars."

After the Mountain Goat, sleeper car, and boxcar were connected, the team loaded on and examined their new home. For some, this was the first time they had been on a luxury sleeper car; for others, it was the first time they had seen one this nice. As the boys sat in the opulently adorned, roomy, cushioned seats and felt the upholstery's soothing velvet, they rhapsodized over their accommodations. Alfie said, "Nothing's too good for Sewanee men."

Prayer Bear said, "I christen thee 'Goat Hall'!"

Several players responded, "Amen!"

There were upper berths and lower berths. On each side of the aisle, a pair of seats faced each other with a collapsible table in between. Alfie demonstrated how to properly extend a seat to form a bed.

Above the seats were shellacked cherry wood compartments. "Men, you pull this upper berth down like this." He patted the upper berth's mattress. "And you've got as comfortable a bed as the bottom ones. Coach Lourie and I have laid claim to the front berths on the left. Divvy up the others, and whichever you pick is where you'll rest your noggin for the next nine days."

The car's curved ceiling had Tiffany lamps down the middle, floral inlaid designs, gilded metal panels, and stained-glass portal windows above the upper berths. At the front of the car was a dinette, and in the rear was a restroom. The car had not been wired for electricity, but its gas fixtures fully illuminated the car's interior.

Alfie sat down across from Coach Lourie. "What do you think of this elegant hotel on rails?"

"Comfortable. Might somewhat mitigate the grueling effects of five bone-crushing contests over six days."

The Mountain Goat started hissing steam, and the conductor pulled the whistle to let Alfie know the engine was ready. Shouting over the whistle, Alfie asked, "Where's Henry?" A few heads turned in the manager's direction.

Finn Grayson looked at Alfie and said, "In the boxcar. That's where he'll ride. Why wouldn't he be there?" Alfie stared at Finn, who turned his head and snickered in the direction of his friends, James Bristol Coffey and Thompson Peck. They both grinned.

In a seat across the aisle from Finn, Coffey, and Peck, Prayer Bear had settled in and was resting his eyes when he heard Finn's comment. He hadn't paid much attention to Finn when they were in boarding school together, but as teammates at Sewanee, Prayer Bear frequently heard Finn express his petty meanness and bigotry. Finn was a devotee of the Lost Cause, along with his friends Coffey and Peck. Prayer Bear viewed the Lost Cause crusade as an anti-Christian ideology. He followed the New South movement, of which his father, Union Captain Ellis Embree, was a leader. The Embree men, all from upper East Tennessee, had fought for the North. It delighted Telfair Embree that this fact outraged Finn.

"Finny, did you hear that crowd loving on Henry, back there, what, just two hours ago?" asked Prayer Bear. "After we come home victorious, do you want to be the one known to have made Henry Jordan sleep on equipment, baggage, and whatever else we've got piled up back there?"

Finn squinted his eyes and pursed his lips.

Prayer Bear enjoyed watching Finn seethe and laughed when he puffed up his chest. "Now go on, Finny. Be a good Finny." Smiling, the seminary student got comfortable in his seat, folded his arms, and closed his eyes.

Coffey and Peck turned their attention to their textbooks. Finn paced up and down the aisle. On a seat in the back row of the Pullman, he saw a duffle bag, which he thought might be Henry's. Two books rested on the adjacent seat. He picked up one of them and read the cover: *Human Anatomy by Claude Sinclair.* The book slipped from his grip, but Finn caught it as some loose pages floated to the floor. He collected the pages and inserted them in the back of the book. He opened the front cover and saw *Property of Henry Jordan* written in a pleasing style of cursive. He grabbed the other book. Henry's signature was inside its cover as well. Fuming, he glanced to be sure no one was watching, then took the tomes into the Pullman's restroom. He stashed the books in a latched cubbyhole that held a box of baking soda, white vinegar, and a toilet bowl brush.

***

Still upset over not checking for the shoes, Henry was in the boxcar taking another inventory. He heard whistling and footsteps, so he looked out the boxcar door and saw Alfie approaching.

"What are you doing, Henry? The boots are right there." Alfie pointed to the two duffle bags Joseph had dragged to the boxcar.

"I want to make sure everything else is here, Mister Alfie. Being careless, I already made us late. Only got the back third of the car to count."

"Never mind that. Jump down here." Henry did as he was asked. Alfie grabbed the boxcar door and slid it closed. "Go take your seat up there in Goat Hall."

"Goat Hall, Mister Alfie?"

"That's what Telfair named the sleeper car."

Henry boarded the train, and Alfie went to tell the conductor to pull out of Cowan.

***

The Mountain Goat rolled through valleys and over ridges for two and a half hours. As the train moved through Nashville, Henry was looking out a window. Alfie Melville sat across from him, a gesture Henry appreciated. He knew the manager was trying to reassure him that everything was all right.

A large Victorian building alone on a hill came into view. Soaring above the four-story structure was a turret capped with a conical roof. Alfie said, "What a stately building."

"That's Fisk University, a negro college, Mister Alfie."

"I've heard of Fisk. Their football and baseball teams are supposed to be good."

"They are. My cousin Louis is the trainer for both teams."

"Well, that explains their success. Healing talents and team devotion must run in the family."

"Thank you, Mister Alfie."

The manager returned his gaze to the passing scenery, as did Henry, who wondered whether a man like Alfie Melville secretly wanted white schools to play black schools. Henry thought how much he would like to pit his Sewanee eleven against Fisk's best eleven.

The Mountain Goat coasted through central Nashville and came to a stop at Union Station. Some of the team members filed off the sleeper, while others stayed aboard and queued up in front of two barrels of Tremlett Spring water, which was the University of the South's main water supply.

Alfie stood up. "You know, Henry. That was an ace idea to bring our own water along."

"Thank you, Mister Alfie. Can't risk no dysentery. Also thought it was good for the players to quench their thirst with something from the Mountain."

"Even in dry Texas, the Tigers will be restored and refreshed by Sewanee's lifeline. Hmm. I'm going to use that line in my first dispatch to *The Purple*."

Henry and Alfie got off the train. The manager went to talk to the engineer, while Henry quickly walked back to the boxcar. For peace of mind, he wanted to finish the inventory he had started in Cowan. After sliding open the door and hoisting himself up into the car, Henry gasped when he saw Joseph Hill sleeping on top of the players' luggage. Joseph had barricaded himself in the back to avoid detection in Cowan. Henry tugged on the young man's feet. "Joseph, wake up! Wake up!" Joseph kept sleeping, and Henry kept pulling on his feet. "Boy, you need to get up!"

Joseph woke up startled. "What's wrong?"

"You! You're what's wrong! Boy, is your daddy going to whoop you back at The Cut."

"I'm your assistant. You need my help."

"Follow me."

At the end of the platform, Henry found Alfie. The manager was smoking a pipe and coughed when he saw Joseph. He cleared his throat. "Mercy, wait till your daddy takes hold of you."

Henry wagged his finger at Joseph. "That's what I told him, Mister Alfie."

Alfie said, "Sure enough!"

"I'll talk with the stationmaster, Mister Alfie—see when the next train to Sewanee comes through."

Joseph started to follow Henry to the ticket counter, but Alfie stuck out his arm in front of the stowaway. "Hold on. You stand here with me, little Houdini."

Henry returned. "The next train to Sewanee is tomorrow morning."

Alfie drew Henry out of Joseph's earshot. "Got any ideas? We can't leave him here all night."

"No, sir. Someone evil might give him trouble."

"That and he might hop a train to Houston or New Orleans and wait for us there." They both glanced at Joseph, who was shuffling his feet. "Lord Almighty." Alfie clucked his tongue. "At least now you'll have some help."

Alfie sent a telegram to Sewanee, addressed to Silas Hill:

```
JOSEPH STOWED AWAY WITH US
WE WILL TAKE GOOD CARE OF HIM
```

SEE YOU IN NINE DAYS
ALFIE MELVILLE TEAM MANAGER

The team boarded the train and found their seats. Soon, half of the players had books and writing tablets on the tables in front of them. Joseph and Henry sat next to each other in the back, where Henry assigned his helper tasks for the upcoming games.

Midway up the aisle, Patch and Woody sat facing each other with their books open. They were both looking out the window as the Mountain Goat slowly gained speed. The roommates were distracted by Nashville's two-year-old Parthenon. The structure was the exact dimensions of the ancient temple in Athens.

Patch said, "I wonder if there is a golden Athena inside there."

Woody said, "I don't know, but what a prodigious building."

"She represents everything a Sewanee man is supposed to be."

"Martially strategic, wise, moral, learned—"

"Maybe she is the guide and protector of our football odyssey and we are her men of Ithaca."

"Odysseus's men did not make it home to their mountain alive," Woody said. "Only Odysseus did."

"True. Okay, so we are Odysseus, collectively."

Woody nodded.

Patch twirled his hair and thought of Cecilia Fontaine. He compared her to Athena, thinking that, like the goddess, Cecilia was wise, moral, learned, and beautiful. Softly he said, "Louisiana's Athena."

"What did you say?"

"I was just thinking about Athena." Patch reclined his seat and closed his eyes.

By 9:00 p.m., the Mountain Goat had the Sewanee Tigers near Jackson, Tennessee. The Goat was at full throttle and the cotton fields flew by, undetected below a dark fall sky.

Two hours later the team was settling down for dinner at the Memphis Union Station diner. Henry examined the diner's menu and wrote down what he wanted the players to eat: one pork chop, three to four boiled red potatoes, two servings of green beans, one serving of carrots, one buttered roll, and a large glass of milk. He gave the list to Alfie. Henry regretted that they were eating so late, but he was pleased that the diner served items that were on his training menu.

Joseph and Henry ate in a small roped-off section. A sign dangling from the rope read "Colored Seating." An elderly black couple was eating there as well.

After dinner, the Sewanee group gathered on the train platform. Alfie had just lit his pipe when Henry asked him if they could speak in private. The two stepped away. Henry said, "Mister Alfie, it might cause trouble with Joseph and me staying at night in the sleeper with y'all."

Alfie glanced over at Turl and Coach Lourie, who were talking football. Then he looked back at Henry. "Naw, nonsense. You tuck him in on the berth above yours, in the back row."

"Thank you, Mister Alfie."

The Tigers loaded back on the train, and the Mountain Goat was soon chugging over a bridge that stretched across the Mississippi River. Patch and Woody sat facing each other with a table between them. Woody contemplated the river below. The Mississippi was an inky swath that expanded beyond Woody's field of vision.

Patch was penning a letter to his summer girl, Miss Julia Giles Harding. The summer girls were young ladies from well-established families who sent their daughters to Sewanee for the month of July so they could enjoy the mountain air and meet well-bred young men. The summer girls stayed with host families and attended social mixers with the men of Sewanee.

Woody grabbed the letter and looked at the addressee. As he handed it back, he asked Patch, "Why do you demonstrate affections to several girls at one time?"

"They're all so charming—to be close to them electrifies me."

"A rationale as rich and tempting as a butter cake."

"Why not a Kentucky bourbon cake, brother?"

"Have you forgotten Iris so soon?"

"There is room in my heart for an Iris, a Julia, and more. In a few years, I will commit myself to a single young woman and will be cast out of the garden. In the meantime, I will enjoy every delightful flower in the manner of familiarity each craves and allows."

Woody smiled wryly at his friend. "That's a barrel full of horse dung. You know that, don't you?"

Patch shrugged his shoulders and returned to writing. "Prophet Solomon had seven hundred princesses and three hundred concubines."

"So it's Princess Julia of Shelbyville and Iris the Concubine from Monteagle."

"Recite a spot of scripture where relations before marriage are prohibited."

"Mark chapter seven, verses twenty to twenty-three: 'What comes out of man is what defiles a man. For from within, out of the heart of man come evil thoughts, fornication—'"

"Hold on right there. The Greek word is *porneia,* which does not mean fornication as you mean it."

"Fornication is illicit sexual intercourse."

"Where in the Old or New Testament does it explicitly state that—"

"—fornication is illicit sexual intercourse?"

"Yes."

"It is implied in several places."

"Implied?"

"Yes, implied."

"My Classics professor taught us that although *porneia* does mean fornication, to the Greeks fornication meant adultery and incest—that was how Saint Paul and his fellow Greeks defined it. Priggish translators expanded the definition to turn sex before marriage into an evil act." Patch reached across the table and opened Woody's Bible. "Let's go to Leviticus chapter twenty, verse ten, where the directive is not implied at all but clearly and unequivocally stated. Quote: 'If a man commits adultery with the wife of his neighbor, both the adulterer and adulteress shall be put to death.' So, why don't we execute adulterers? We don't execute adulterers, because it would be barbarous to do so, just like it was to burn so-called witches at the stake, acts justified and carried out by the Puritan Church. And as you know, many of those witches were fornicators, in your sense of the word."

"Perhaps after your B.A. you should read law instead of attending the seminary."

"Don't tempt me."

"I can't." Woody grinned. "I don't wear a dress and bonnet."

"Try to understand that God, the King of Kings, gave me a robust sexual appetite; therefore, it must be holy."

Woody stared out the window and left his friend to his letter. After a few moments, he said, "After you copulate, do you believe your spirit and soul are elevated or degraded?"

"Without any trepidation, dear old friend, I can tell you it never fails to be an uplifting experience."

"Do you ever worry about word of your activities reaching a priest or a faculty member?"

"No."

"Why not?"

Patch leaned forward and in a hushed voice said, "What is a Southern Episcopal college and seminary going to do to the grandson of the internationally acclaimed Bishop of Georgia?"

"I hope no one tests your theory."

"Someone will let their jealousy or zeal get the better of him." Patch looked over Woody's shoulder toward the front of the car, where Finn was strumming his banjolin, while singing with Coffey and Peck, all glee club members. "Like Finn," he said.

"Finn?"

"Yes, Finn. He wants to be one of the eleven. He wants my position."

"All good scrubs should want to join the eleven. Competitiveness is a good, manly trait that benefits the team."

"Agreed, but a Christian man—in fact, a Sewanee man—roots for the eleven, works hard to improve the eleven, and fairly fights to join that eleven, without treachery."

"Why do you think he will break ranks?"

"His father was an end on the '78 undefeated Princeton team. This is

Finn's last year to make dear old dad proud. Finn Grayson is sneaky, too. And he tries to get people's goat."

"Last night you let him get the best of you, but he apologized."

"Yeah, because Turl and Alfie were standing there."

Woody nodded in agreement. He turned to watch Finn.

In addition to being on the football and track teams, Finn was glee club president and a medical student from Richmond, Virginia. Finn's parents had wanted him to attend his father's alma mater, but Finn had insisted on attending a Southern university.

Most of the Sewanee men were Southern-raised and romanticized the Old South and Confederacy. It was a way to show respect to their grandparents and parents and to celebrate—specifically, drink excessively on days like Confederate Memorial Day. Finn and his friends Coffey and Peck took their heritage much more seriously. The antebellum South was a sacred era and its values had to be resurrected.

Turning their attention away from Finn and his fellow troubadours, Woody slid out of his jacket's breast pocket a soft leather-covered book, and Patch started proofing his letter to Julia. Woody slowly turned the almost translucent pages of his pocket-sized book. "Have you read your grandfather's latest?"

"No, what's the title?"

"*The Triumph of Faith*."

Patch looked up, smiled, and said, "Let me see it." Woody handed him the book. With an index finger, Patch traced the embossed title. "*The Triumph of Faith*. That is a weighty title—sounds like a religious *Wealth of Nations*. I'll read it over winter break, for he will test me at Christmas dinner, no doubt." Patch opened the book to a random page and began reading out loud: "To become a person who is like the personality of God—that is our aim—not enjoyment and not sorrow. We shall not debase nor despair. Man shall be delivered by his own choices, and he shall climb to the princedoms of God or tumble into an odious swamp of degeneracy, ignobility, and self-pity."

He slowly handed the book back to Woody. "That's Granddad's austere voice, all right." Patch then returned to the subject of girls. "What about you,

Woody? You were corresponding with Miss Rebecca Stanley. Why did all that business end?"

"She deserves better."

"Out of all the Sewanee men her interest was in you, and out of all the summer girls, only she captured your attention."

Woody looked out the window. The train was passing a pine forest. Woody noted that the forest appeared to be endlessly deep. He closed his eyes. In his mind, he saw rows of trees. Woody imagined himself among the pines. Rebecca Stanley appeared. She had her back to him. He began to unlace her corset. Alarmed by the fantasy, Woody tried to suppress it.

Patch said, "Woody?" There was no response. "Barnwell!"

Woody looked at his friend and said, "Yes?"

"Do you want to change the subject?"

"Yes."

"All right."

Woody nodded, and then they both turned their attention back to Finn, Coffey, and Peck, who had begun to sing:

Hello, ma baby, hello, ma honey,
Hello, ma ragtime gal

A few of the players began singing along with the three glee club members.

Send me a kiss by wire
Baby, my heart's on fire . . .

Henry, along with almost everyone else, was watching Finn's trio. Henry was particularly interested in Finn's banjolin. When he was around Joseph's age, Henry had observed a man playing an odd tiny banjo tuned like a mandolin. The man rewarded Henry's curiosity by handing him the instrument. Henry quickly found the chords and picked melodies from there. He had grown up playing a pump organ in church, where he developed his already naturally gifted ear. Sometimes when the organ in Saint Augustine's was not in use, Henry sat down at it and played hymns and even fragments of classical pieces he had heard.

Henry switched his focus from Finn's instrument to the song.

If you refuse me
Honey, you lose me
Then you'll be left alone, oh baby
Telephone and tell me I'se your own . . .

The tune was familiar to Henry because people all over Sewanee were humming or whistling it. Henry started to hum along, but he noticed Joseph was looking up at him with a furrowed brow. Henry was about to ask him what was wrong when the next line caught the trainer's ear:

Then some other coon will win her

Henry bristled at the word "coon." He wanted to respond to the slur but wasn't sure how. He knew what Silas Hill would do—walk up to Finn Grayson, snatch the banjolin out of his hands, take its peg head, and twist it off like he was wringing the neck of a Christmas goose.

After finishing "Hello Ma Baby," Finn retuned his banjolin. Once he had it in tune, he hit a note repeatedly while Coffey and Peck harmonized with it. They began singing "All Coons Look Alike to Me."

Henry ground his teeth as he listened to the song's lyrics, but the trainer remained seated. Then he and Joseph were subjected to the chorus:

She'd no excuse, to turn me loose, I've been abused, I'm all confused,
'Cause these words she did say, "All coons look alike to me, I've got another
beau,
You see, and he's just as good to me as you, nig! ever tried to be . . ."

Henry put his hand on Joseph's shoulder, then pressed down on the arms of the seat and stood up. His temples pounded as he walked up the aisle. The wind swayed the train, so he had to grab the back of the seats for balance. Prayer Bear stood in Henry's way. "Let me take care of this." Prayer Bear stomped to the front of the Pullman car.

Turl waved Henry over. "Anyone gives you or Joseph some guff—come straight to me or Prayer Bear. Don't try to settle it on your own."

"Yes, Mister Turley. I understand." Henry appreciated Prayer Bear and Turl's consideration for him and Joseph, but it was humiliating at the same time.

With a scowl, Prayer Bear stood over Finn.

"What's wrong, Telfair?" Finn asked.

Prayer Bear ripped the banjolin out of Finn's hands. "We all need to get some sleep. Besides, that is not a song for a Christian man to sing."

"Why? 'Cause a coon wrote it? Coons write a lot of great songs these days, Telfair."

Prayer Bear pulled his eye patch up onto his broad forehead. He stared at Finn and said, "The merciful man does goodness for his own soul, but he who is cruel troubles his own flesh. Proverbs eleven seventeen." Finn pulled back from Prayer Bear's milky eye. Prayer Bear lowered his face to a couple of inches from Finn's. Menacingly he said, "No more minstrel shows around this team. You can quit school and take your act on the road, but I better not see or hear it again."

As Prayer Bear stepped back, Finn made a shooing-away gesture with his hand. Prayer Bear lifted his fist. Finn sat down.

Prayer Bear went to the back row and handed Henry the banjolin. Henry tinkered with the instrument and quickly found the melody he had in his head. He played and sang, in his natural baritone:

> *Wade in the water*
> *Wade in the water, children*
> *Wade in the water*
> *God's gonna trouble the water*

After a few verses he said, "Goodnight, Tigers."

In unison, most of the team responded, "Goodnight, Henry."

Finn whispered, "Traitors."

There was little talking as the passengers collapsed tables, extended seats into beds, and opened and climbed into upper berths.

Lying on his back in his upper berth, Patch spread out on his chest the napkin covering the biscuit from Cecilia. He rubbed the monogram and admired Cecilia's stitch work. The biscuit had a folded piece of paper resting on top of it. He started eating the biscuit while staring at the note and contemplating its message. He and Cecilia had stolen several furtive moments of time alone over the past year. These had to be executed very carefully, with code names when they wrote to each other.

As far as Patch knew, even Woody had no idea of these encounters. In public, Cecilia and Patch played the proper roles. Patch, Woody, and Turl liked to visit the Hiawassee for dessert and tea, after which Miss Cecilia played her cello and treated her guests and boarders to Brahms, Vivaldi, and Bach, with the Tigers' quarterback, Ham DuBose, accompanying Miss Cecilia on piano.

After finishing his biscuit, Patch unfolded the note, which had writing on one side and a hand-drawn map on the other:

Charlton,

When you return victorious from the campaign, I will be in a celebratory mood and prepared to honor a certain Sewanee man, an intellect and a warrior.

The map to my humble sylvan abode is on the opposite side of this note. Until we reunite, may God watch over you and the others, on and off the field of play.

With you in heart,
Esplanade

The pseudonyms, "Charlton" and "Esplanade," referred to the streets on which he and Cecilia had been born: Patch in Savannah, and Cecilia in New

Orleans. She had picked the names. Patch thought they were clever. He turned the paper over and deciphered the map to Cecilia's hideaway. Seeing, on paper, the path to this secretive rendezvous thrilled him. He slid the map into his suit coat's breast pocket. Patch draped the napkin over his pillow and changed into his nightshirt.

Patch pictured Cecilia's face when she handed him the biscuit at the depot, the Mountain Goat hissing as it built up steam. The image pleased him. He smiled.

He wondered how it was possible that the Mountain Goat left Sewanee in the early afternoon and already they were nearly halfway to the University of Texas. The sound of the train wheels hitting the seams between the rails created a rhythm that slowly lulled Patch to sleep.

Chapter Four
Tuesday, November 7th, 1899

Just after dawn in Texarkana, Texas, the men from Sewanee filled tables at the Bluebird Dining Room and Hall. After the host had seated the white members of the breakfast party, he came back to the register and escorted Henry and Joseph to the kitchen, where the staff fed them breakfast. Coach Lourie said, "Orange juice and milk for everyone."

There were some sighs and Finn said, "I want a cola."

Mockingly, Patch said, "I want a cola."

Over the laughter, Prayer Bear yelled, "Ha!"

Coach Lourie loudly clapped twice. "Henry's orders, men, orange juice and milk!"

After breakfast, the Tigers were back on the train, nineteen hours into the first leg of their trip. Prayer Bear and Woody led an abbreviated chapel service—Alfie Melville had promised the vice-chancellor that daily chapel would be observed over the nine-day absence from the Mountain. Then the men studied, napped, played cards, talked, and teased each other. Using water instead of alcohol, Ham DuBose and Kimbrough Lowndes were developing a drinking contest they called Skippers. The general premise was to set a cup of beer on a table two feet in front of a player, who would take a half dollar and attempt to bounce the coin into the cup.

Ham slid a half dollar across the table to Kimbrough. "You go first."

Kimbrough bounced the coin into a cup half filled with water. "What happens now?"

"You skipped it into the cup, so you pick the drinker."

"I pick you."

"There is no one else to pick, I was speaking hypothetically."

"Well, I didn't bounce it in there hypothetically, so drink up."

Ham curled his lip and drank the water.

"A skipper bounces until he misses?" Ham nodded. Kimbrough landed his next four attempts and insisted Ham drink all four cups of water. He bounced the next one over the cup.

Ham smacked his hand down on the table. "Man alive! You missed."

Kimbrough slid the empty glass across the table. "So how does a contestant win?"

"Not sure."

"Here it is. The last man still able to drink is the victor."

"Perfect."

They decided to start a competitive club for Skippers as soon as they returned to the Mountain. They imagined beer as the essential component but were open to the club's democratic selection of the right libation.

Another fourteen hours of riding in Goat Hall, broken up by two forty-five minute stops along the way with limbering calisthenics and light refreshments at each break, and the Sewanee group pulled into Austin, Texas, and ten minutes later the University of Texas campus.

The Texas football manager, Billy Sims, was standing at the depot when the Mountain Goat arrived. He and Alfie Melville, Coach Lourie, and Captain Turley shook hands and exchanged introductions.

Alfie said, "And this is our trainer, Henry Jordan, and his apprentice, Joseph Hill." Henry took his hat off and said, "Honor to be here, sir."

Billy said, "Now, Mister Melville, I remember you writing me about Henry, but I don't remember mention of a junior rub-man."

"Well, we didn't know that Joseph was going to join us until . . ." Alfie looked at Coach Lourie. "Where did he pop out?"

"Nashville," Coach Lourie said.

Billy smiled. "Oh, a stowaway."

"You don't have to worry about Joseph. He is a devoted Sewanee servant and a fine apprentice trainer," Alfie said.

"Is that right, Joseph?"

"I am here to help Henry, sir. I'm no trouble."

"All's well then. We'll put you with the same negro family where Henry's going to stay. Calvin Burrows is our campus groundskeeper, and his wife, Ida, will be thrilled to host an extra guest."

The Tigers grabbed their bags, and Billy Sims escorted them to their overnight accommodations—a three-story former student residence hall that the university maintained for campus visitors. Then Billy took the team to the university dining hall, where the team ate fried ham, mashed potatoes, boiled okra, pickled tomatoes, and preserved apples with cinnamon. On stools inside the kitchen, Henry and Joseph ate the same dinner that the team ate. Henry was impressed with the quality of the meal and quantity of its portions. He asked one of the waiters to pass a message to Coach Lourie, requesting the coach to please encourage the men to ask for refills of milk but discourage them from seeking a second plate of food.

By 10:00 p.m., all but two of the Sewanee team members were either preparing for bed or in bed. Captain Turley and his roommate, Ham, were in their room with Coach Lourie and Alfie Melville. Sitting around a table, the four talked about the Texas game. It was only fourteen hours before kickoff. Coach Lourie said, "I played baseball at Princeton with a fella named MacGregor who teaches Latin and coaches baseball here."

Ham leaned forward. "The lanky guy you were sitting with at dinner?"

"Yes. Mac told me that the Texas eleven doesn't have a player who isn't at least a hundred and eighty, and each lineman is five seven to five nine, so they're solid and steady."

Turl said, "Well, then they're slow."

Coach Lourie shook his head. "According to MacGregor, for their build they're surprisingly quick."

Ham grinned. "Our line will give them hell."

Coach Lourie looked at Turl. "When we have the ball, we need to outfox them. They've played three games, won them all and only had six points scored on them."

"So? We've won four and haven't given up any points," said Ham.

After a moment of quiet, Turl asked Coach Lourie, "What's the plan?"

"We buck the line."

Turl got up and walked to the window. "But you're telling us they're a wall of stone."

Coach Lourie said, "Initially, first downs will be difficult, but we'll accomplish—"

"Grinding down Turl, Kimbrough, Franklin, and me," Ham said. "By halftime you'll have crippled all four of your backs—whether we stay in the game or not we'll be of no use."

"Ham, let coach finish," said Turl.

"I'm not going to send you and the other backs on a suicide mission. We'll have body leverage on them. They're too stout to hit lower than we can. Between our low-driving blocks and Kimbrough's long punts, within ten to fifteen minutes, those thick Texas legs will be like waterlogged tree trunks. Then we switch things up on them."

Ham smiled. "Run outside them."

Coach Lourie said, "Exactly, let 'em chase the likes of Patch Mercer around the corner."

They all nodded in agreement with the coach. Then it was lights off and Alfie and Coach Lourie made their way to their room.

Alfie said, "What did your friend Mac think about our chances?"

"He said for me not to take it as a slight, but he had placed a wager of five dollars on Texas, giving up three to one."

"What did you say to that?"

"I told him I liked those odds and bet him five dollars."

Chapter Five
Wednesday, November 8th, 1899

After Mrs. Ida Burrows treated the three to a breakfast of flapjacks, fatback, molasses, and coffee, Henry, Joseph, and Calvin walked thirty minutes to Clark Field. It was 9:00 a.m. The Texas football field sat at the top of a sloped berm. Along one edge of the field was a covered wooden grandstand like one might see at a midsize horse track. It stretched from one 35-yard line to the other and had twenty rows of wooden benches. The timber was clean and plumb. The university had built the structure just before the previous season.

There were low clouds and no sight of the sun. It was fifty degrees.

Calvin took the Sewanee trainers to a large shed near the field. Inside was the University of Texas trainer, Victor Garcia, who was struggling with a large, rolled-up white canvas tent. Victor had weathered skin. Over his seventy years, the Texas sun and wind had cut deep crevices into the former cattle herder's hands, face, and neck. Calvin introduced Henry and Joseph to Victor, who said, "I am sorry you all have come so far to be sent home unhappy."

Everyone smiled. Joseph started to laugh, then covered his mouth.

The three men carried the cumbersome tent up to the field. Joseph dragged the sledgehammer. Over a training table that Victor had lugged to the Sewanee sideline, the men mounted and secured the tent. The Sewanee trainers were bivouacked.

Victor pointed to a cart hitched to a donkey tied near the field's shed. "Pedro over there will help you with your load."

Henry said, "Thank you, both. I hope we can be as helpful to y'all if you ever come visit our mountain."

Victor said, "You live on your own mountain?"

Calvin explained, "The Sewanee school is up on a mountain."

Victor said, "Football is going to be really big, so I am sure our coach will want to play you again and go east to do it." Victor looked directly at Joseph and said, "That is, if you give a fight today!"

Joseph said, "We will." The men laughed and Joseph smiled.

Toward the three men and Joseph, Texas team manager Billy Sims was walking quickly across the field while holding his hands behind his back. Victor noticed him first. "Ah, problema."

The three others saw Sims approaching. Calvin quickly looked away.

Victor called out, "Good morning, Mister Sims."

"Good morning, everyone." He stopped and addressed Henry. "I'm sure Calvin and Ida took fine care of y'all."

"Yes sir. They were very kind to us."

"Good, real good. Calvin, I'm glad you're keeping company with our guests, but there is plenty of field prep to do. Wouldn't you agree, Calvin?"

"Of course, Mister Sims. I'm sorry for loafin'. I'll run over an' start rakin' our sideline right now, sir, then I'll do the Sewanee side." Calvin gave Henry a furtive smile. "Excuse me, y'all." He jogged toward the grandstand.

Sims nodded at Henry, smiled at Joseph, and walked away.

"Mister Sims rides Calvin hard even though the man makes the field look like velvet." Victor made a sweeping gesture, and Henry and Joseph scanned the turf. "Well, Henry, let me know if you all need anything. Calvin and I will help with the tent after our men win." They all smiled, and Victor shook Henry's hand and rubbed Joseph's head.

Henry turned to walk away but stopped. "Victor." Henry reached into his pocket, pulled out a dime, and held it up. "Maybe we should make a small bet."

"Even odds? And Joseph holds our dimes."

"Agreed."

Joseph led Pedro to the Mountain Goat, which sat on a railroad spur a quarter mile from Clark Field. Henry and Joseph unloaded supplies from the boxcar and loaded them into the cart.

Henry said, "Let's make sure we've got it all. Call out what's in that big crate."

"Bandages, gauze, splints, liniment, smelling salts, headache powder, laudanum, and plaster." Joseph named the rest of the cart's cargo, reassuring Henry that they had everything.

They filled four buckets with Tremlett Spring water, and each carried a shoulder yoke attached to two buckets. Henry led Pedro back to the football field and Joseph followed from behind, struggling to keep water from sloshing out of his buckets.

Inside the tent, Henry and Joseph unpacked and arranged their supplies. When they finished, Henry gestured toward the training table. "Let's sit up here and catch our breath." There were a couple of minutes of quiet, during which Henry noticed his nerves had released butterflies in his stomach. He went through ten minutes of this before every game, no matter how weak or mighty the opponent.

Joseph said, "Mister Henry."

Henry was about to give Joseph license to refer to him as just Henry when he remembered that Silas Hill required his children to address black adults in the same manner they addressed white adults. "Yes, young man."

"You and my daddy ain't like the other men from The Cut."

"Nope, we ain't."

"Why not?"

"We're not from plantation negro folk. Our people were escaped slaves who hid up in the Cumberlands to stay free."

"Daddy says he's known you since you were both little."

"That's right. Fished together almost every day when we were your age."

"Mister Bedford from plantation folk?"

"Yes, everyone livin' in The Cut is except your family, mine, and the Elliots."

"Why're plantation folk different?"

"'Cause most of their people went from being a slave straight to Sewanee, so these black folks been free over thirty years, but they're still smilin' and bowin' like another day on master's farm. You ain't never goin' to see your daddy or me conduct ourselves in that manner."

"The eleven come from people who owned slaves?"

"Most. Most of the scrubs, too."

"Mister Finn's people had a plantation?"

"I hear a big ole one in Virginia—bigger than all of Sewanee."

"When you stood up to set Mister Finn right, what were you going to do?"

"I'm not sure. I do know that if Finn Grayson is ugly like that again, he's goin' to face this black child of a wrathful God."

Henry and Joseph stepped outside the tent and found the Texas team forming four well-spaced rows. Henry's butterflies had calmed down but started flapping again when he saw the size of the Texas players.

Coach Lourie and Alfie walked up along the sidelines and stood next to Henry and Joseph. The four of them silently assessed the Texas team. Alfie took his pipe and tobacco pouch out of his suit coat pocket, stuffed the bowl with loose leaf tobacco, and lit the pipe. The Texas eleven ran through plays, with light contact, against their scrubs. Then the eleven and the scrubs did some slow jogging around the perimeter of the field. The entire team ran except four players who practiced field goals, dropkicks, and punts. The Texas quarterback drop-kicked several goals from thirty and forty yards. Coach Lourie said, "Where is he from, Australia?"

Alfie took a long draw on his pipe, exhaled, and said, "What do you make of these boys, Henry?"

Henry thought for a minute. "Well, there's size and then there's skill and speed, so my money is with our varsity eleven."

Alfie said, "How much did you wager?"

Henry didn't know if Alfie was teasing him or not. The two men exchanged glances while Joseph purposely looked straight ahead.

Then Alfie slapped his knee, laughed, and said, "Cat got your tongue, Henry?"

Henry smiled and shook his head.

Coach Lourie laughed but quickly refocused on the Texas team. He said,

"I always heard Texas had stout bulls, but I didn't know they suited them out for football."

Alfie said, "Thick, they are thick boys."

Coach Lourie walked to the tent. He opened the entry flap and looked inside, then said, "Looks like you're all set, Henry."

"Ready for win number five, sir."

Coach Lourie looked at Joseph and said, "Probably good you jumped aboard, Joseph."

Joseph said, "Here to follow Henry's orders, Coach Lourie."

"Good, 'cause this is going to be war," the coach said.

Coach Lourie knew gridiron combat firsthand. As Princeton's quarterback in 1898, he'd played against Yale and Harvard. When any of those teams met, they injured each other—it was a matter of course. As coach, he appreciated the fight inside the Sewanee eleven, but here in Texas he saw the physical prowess of a gifted foe. He had planned on forgoing a pep talk, but he changed his mind. He said, "Mister Melville, let's go talk to our men."

Alfie and Coach Lourie walked across the field toward the grandstand. Midway they met the Texas coach, Sam Beaumont, and the game's referee and umpire. The five shook hands and briefly exchanged football backgrounds. The referee, Morgan Jones, who had played for Army in 1896, had heard of Princeton's Lourie. The referee handed Coach Lourie the game ball. He examined it and tossed it to Coach Beaumont. Both men approved of the ball and wished each other luck. The Sewanee coach and manager walked over to the grandstand.

The crowd was already at eight hundred. A third of the spectators were young women in tightly corseted dresses that covered up all except the neck and above. The male spectators, mostly young men, were dressed in fine three-piece suits, bow or puff ties, and hats, mostly derbies. This group represented students, faculty, staff, alumni, lawyers, and other professionals working in the Texas capital city. There were also men who worked manual jobs and enjoyed football and gambling.

Four men in the stands stood out sharply from the crowd. They wore casual slacks and vivid purple varsity turtleneck sweaters. They made eye contact with Alfie, who waved for them to come down to the field.

Coach Lourie said, "We don't have time, Alfie."

"Just a quick thank you—remember, we're building a movement."

After questioning the fans, Alfie quickly learned the four were Sewanee alumni. Two had played on the 1894 Sewanee football team, while the other two had played Tiger baseball the same year. They were partners in a law firm in Austin. Alfie took down their names and their firm's address and promised he would put them on the mailing list for the school's student newspaper, *The Purple.*

Coach Lourie and Alfie continued on. Behind the grandstand they walked by two Texas male cheerleaders, one of whom had a pitbull on a leash. The dog was clothed with a burnt-orange blanket draped over him and tied off underneath him. The cheerleader restraining the dog said to the other, "Did you feed Pig this morning?"

"Yes, why?"

"He looks hungry."

The cheerleader gestured his thumb over his shoulder and said, "He smells tiny purple tigers. Makes him lick his chops."

The two men from Sewanee ignored the cheerleader's taunt and kept walking.

Twenty yards behind the Clark Field grandstand, they found their team gathered in a gully. The Sewanee Tigers were in their quilted football pants and purple game jerseys. They had their cleats strapped on.

Coach Lourie briefly paced. He stopped and focused on the faces of each of his eleven. A few caught his glance and nodded. After his quick survey, he determined some of them knew what they were about to face and the rest were still at the Bluebird in Texarkana.

Typically, the captain would deliver the pep talk, yet the coach felt compelled to do it on this particular day, even though inspiring other men with words was not something Coach Lourie enjoyed doing. He didn't feel like he was good at it. However, words had been stacking up in his mind and heart since the previous night. Coach Lourie looked over at the large campus building called the Main. This Victorian hall was so tall and wide that even though it was forty yards away it loomed over the gully. Coach Lourie launched his message.

"Men, we are over a thousand miles from the Mountain, but we're not. We are the Sewanee vanguard. Think of this, too: The University of Texas has over one thousand men from which to select a football team. We have three hundred. And the truth is, I'd put our scrubs up against any varsity eleven we've played this year. Sewanee only needs three hundred men. We've played four games this year and scored a hundred forty-four points, and our opponents, none. So, these are the truths you deploy to stomp out any doubt that might creep like a rotten snake into your mind. And remember, snakes can be underfoot and we don't know it until it's too late." The coach turned and looked in the direction of the football field, then back at the players. "Turl, take these men up to the field."

Turl led the team scrambling out of the gully. They sprinted up to the bottom of the berm. He held his hand up, and they all stopped, Prayer Bear right next to Turl and the rest gathered close behind.

Looking up at the field, Patch said, "My God, they're titans."

Prayer Bear said, "Yes indeedy." He turned and smiled at his teammates. "Boys, today we slay pagan giants. How's that sound, Woody?"

"It sounds like God's glory, Prayer Bear, pure glory."

"Amen, brother. Everyone come in close and take a knee. Lead us in the Lord's Prayer, Mister Woody, if you would, please, sir."

Woody said the Lord's Prayer in a quiet but intense manner.

It was noon, there were two thousand spectators in attendance, and the grandstand was full. Five yards behind both sidelines was a rope barrier that ran the entire length of the field. The Texas side was three-deep with fans behind the ropes. Sewanee had only forty people on their side of the field, but Alfie was thankful for them and let them know it.

In awe of the packed grandstand, Alfie wished he had a minimum plus gate percentage deal with Texas and the trip's other four opponents. However, the Sewanee vice-chancellor had insisted on a ledger with fixed revenues and expenses. After turning in his budget, Alfie's instinct was to go back and secretly renegotiate the deals, but he was afraid that if he were caught the vice-chancellor would cancel the trip.

The sky had broken up a little. Above was a mixture of gray and white clouds with a few slivers of blue appearing and disappearing. The noon sky cast a soft light on the scene, giving the field, jerseys, and bows on the ladies' hats a sharp brightness that full sun would have washed out.

Turl led his team in calisthenics. After exercising, the team ran some offensive plays with the scrubs standing in their positions instead of defending. They ran a dozen plays, and then Coach Lourie sent three scrubs to replace Kimbrough Lowndes, the fullback, Patch, the right end, and Turl, the left halfback.

These three members of the starting eleven practiced their kicking. Patch and Turl were solid punters and dropkickers, but Kimbrough was probably the best punter, placekicker, and dropkicker in the South. Patch and Turl sailed their punts and dropkicks and Joseph shagged the balls. Kimbrough hit nine straight field goals from the 30-yard line. Then, from the 40 and on the run, he booted five out of six dropkicks through the uprights.

Meanwhile, on the offensive side of the ball, the team ran their practice plays at full speed. On each snap, they shot out of their stances and sprinted five yards with their shoulders lowered. It was on one of these plays that Woody stepped into a slight depression in the field and twisted his ankle. He hobbled a few steps, then knelt and tightened his boot. He got up and jogged around. Turl said to Woody, "You ready?"

"Ready, captain, ready."

The umpire blew his whistle. Turl and the Texas captain, quarterback Andrew Dudley, met at midfield for the coin toss, which Sewanee won. Turl elected to kick, and Texas chose to defend the south goal.

Turl returned to the sideline, where he had the Tigers form a circle, put their arms around each other, and yell:

> *Tigers! Tigers! Leave 'em in the lurch!*
> *Down with the heathens!*
> *Up with the church!*
> *Yea, Sewanee's right!*

The Sewanee eleven sprinted onto the field and got into position. At midfield, with his teammates lined up to his left and right, Kimbrough

Lowndes made a divot in the turf with his heel. He placed the ball in the nick, backed up five steps, and kicked the ball high and with carry. Forty-six hours after leaving their mountain campus, the Sewanee Tigers were flying down the gridiron to engage a formidable foe.

On the Texas 20-yard line, the ball landed in the hands of John Coolidge, Texas's 220-pound fullback. The son of the Texas Limestone King ran straight down the center of the coverage. He encountered his first Sewanee defender at the Texas 40-yard line. Sewanee's right halfback, Franklin Dill Brownlow, at 170 pounds, lowered his shoulder into the prodigious Coolidge. The collision flipped Brownlow onto his back and knocked the wind out of him, and Coolidge just missed stepping on Brownlow's head. The contact slowed the Texan for a fraction of a second, which gave Patch the opportunity to grab Coolidge's jersey from behind. With two hands, Patch fiercely held on to the burnt-orange shirt while making his 125-pound body go limp. This slowed Coolidge enough for three more Tigers to reach him, ram him, and drag him to the turf. Coolidge yelled, "Down," and the referee blew his whistle. The Texas faithful loudly cheered their fullback and team, who already had the ball at midfield.

Turl helped Brownlow get into a crouched position and encouraged the halfback to breathe slowly in through the nose and out through the mouth. After a couple of minutes, Brownlow was still winded, yet he took his position in the defensive back line.

Prayer Bear had the toughest assignment of all the Sewanee eleven. The previous season, Walter Camp named only one Southern college gridironer to his prestigious All-American team: the Texas left guard, Joe Abbott. Prayer Bear knew all about Mister Abbott's accomplishments and reported ferocity, all of which thrilled and motivated the Sewanee theology student. He was elated to line up across from Abbott. They both got in four-point stances and stared at each other. Abbott's gaze fixed on his opponent's black eye patch. Prayer Bear ripped the patch off, threw it behind him, pointed at his blind eye, and said, "Got this last time out." The ball was snapped. Prayer Bear sprang into Abbott, jammed his fists under the bottom of his rib cage, drove him onto his back, and landed on him. Texas tried to blast through the

Sewanee right side but were stopped at the line of scrimmage. Prayer Bear stood and said, "Buck as you may, gentlemen, the purple wall is impregnable." He extended his hand to help his opponent stand up, but Abbott rejected it. The Texas guard slowly rolled over and stood on his own.

Equally excited for battle, the teams set up for the next play. Three yards back from the Texas center, Dudley bent at the waist and held his hands in position to receive the snap. The quarterback called out the signals: "493–493 Chaz play up 49—" Dudley was interrupted when, jumping the snap, Joe Abbott shot from his four-point stance and delivered a forearm shiver to Prayer Bear's throat. On the ground, Prayer Bear rolled back and forth clutching his neck. The referee blew his whistle, issued an unnecessary roughness penalty of twenty-five yards against Texas, and warned Dudley that next time Abbott would be ejected from the contest.

Abbott said, "What about that maniac?" while pointing at Prayer Bear. The referee ignored him.

Henry and Joseph rushed onto the field and attended to the injured Sewanee guard. Woody and Turl propped up Prayer Bear, who was unable to speak. Joseph had a bottle of Henry's homemade liniment and a water bucket with an ice block in it.

With extended cupped hands, Henry said, "Joseph, pour a good bit of liniment in my hands." Joseph did so, and Henry carefully spilled the liquid on the front of Prayer Bear's neck. "Now, this rub is gonna open your throat back up, Mister Embree. Try to relax and let me give it a gentle smear." With his fingers, Henry lightly massaged the liniment over Prayer Bear's throat. "That's right, now take slow deep breaths and let 'em out the same as they come in." Henry pointed to the bucket, and Joseph chiseled a chip of ice and handed it to Prayer Bear. "Just let that melt in your mouth, Mister Embree, and we'll give you another one."

Henry nodded at Joseph. The assistant trainer gave Prayer Bear another piece of ice. "Here you are, Mister Embree."

Prayer Bear swished the ice around in his mouth, and when it was almost melted, he smiled, shook his head, and playfully wagged his finger at Abbott. After the Sewanee captain and Woody helped their teammate to his feet, Turl said, "You're still locked in with us, right, Prayer Bear?"

The guard shot his captain a look that implied he had asked an absurd question. In a soft raspy voice, Prayer Bear said, "You need much more than a slingshot to put down a bear."

Anxious to get busy again, the two sides lined up for Texas's second down. On all fours, Abbott and Prayer Bear awaited the snap and glared at each other, their faces the length of a football apart. Abbott said, "Welcome to Texas, boy. I rope steers. I'll have no trouble with a one-eyed Tennessee teddy bear." Prayer Bear grinned.

An offense had three tries to gain five yards to earn a first down. Texas only had two remaining downs to advance thirty yards, so they decided to punt. The Texas center snapped the ball to Dudley, who quick-punted the football, which wobbled through the air but still carried well. It fell from the sky, bounced, and rolled to the Sewanee 15-yard line. A Texas end reached the ball first and downed it.

With his team backed up near their own goal line, Coach Lourie decided to abandon his original strategy. Instead of rushing the Texas line, wearing them down, and making them chase his speedsters around the outside, he would rely on his fullback's stellar punting abilities. Kimbrough Lowndes was the best kicker Coach Lourie had ever seen, and the coach was willing to pit Kimbrough against any team's punter in a field position battle.

To communicate the new game plan to Turl, Coach Lourie stood on the sidelines with a football next to his foot. Coaching from the sidelines was prohibited, so Coach Lourie had to employ coded signals for Turl, which he displayed subtly because if a coach broke this rule, the umpire would eject him.

Turl glanced at the Sewanee sidelines, then jogged over to Ham and Kimbrough. "Coach wants us to mark for a fair catch and punt until I like our field position." Turl pointed at Kimbrough. "Punt it and don't go downfield—I think Dudley is going to try to outkick you."

On first down, Kimbrough punted. With the ball high in the sky, the Texas quarterback made a divot in the turf with his heel while Patch raced toward him. When Dudley fielded the punt, Patch stopped and gave him the required ten-yard free kicking zone.

From the Sewanee 47-yard line, Dudley kicked the football to Kimbrough, who made a fair catch mark and punted back to Texas. Over the next six possessions, Sewanee and Texas each marked for fair catches, fielded, and punted the ball. The crowd cheered in appreciation of the aerial show, especially Kimbrough's kicks, which flew five to ten yards farther than Dudley's. As a result of the Sewanee fullback's performance, the Tigers had Texas backed up to their own 20-yard line.

Before Dudley could call the next play, his coach yelled, "Victory, victory, men!"

Dudley called out the Texas signals for a mass wedge play, "10–6, 12–8 muleskin." The Texas halfbacks and fullback shifted their positions to the right side of the ball and lined up in a row adjacent to Dudley. The quarterback barked, "Hut—hut!"

The Texas quarterback caught the snap, his right and left ends pulled into the backfield, and, with Coolidge at the tip of the attack, the ends and backs formed a V. Clutching the football with both arms, Dudley nested inside the V. Coolidge led his five teammates as they rammed through and past the Sewanee defense. Patch chased Dudley from behind the V. Sixteen yards down the field, Patch wrapped up Dudley's legs and twisted him to the turf.

Texas continued to march down the field. Occasionally Dudley ran the ball from inside the V formation. Mostly he handed the ball to Coolidge, who alternately charged the left and right sides of the Sewanee line. The Texas center, guards, and tackles got under their opponents and drove them backward. All-American Joe Abbott was winning the fight with Prayer Bear, and the Texas left tackle was pushing Woody around.

When Coolidge and his blockers busted through a hole, the Sewanee backs swarmed the stout fullback and his escorts, slowing them down enough for Sewanee linemen to catch up and try to pull Coolidge down from behind. Then the rest of the two teams' eleven would join the scrum, shoving and yanking each other. On each play of the drive, Texas gained four to ten yards before Sewanee could take a Texas ball carrier to the ground.

Alfie said to Coach Lourie, "Our line is battered just twenty minutes in."

"I underestimated Texas's conditioning."

"Seems like your man MacGregor should have mentioned that."

The coach looked at Alfie and turned back to watch the game.

Texas reached the Sewanee 46-yard line and, on second down, attempted their first end-round play of the game. Dudley pitched the ball to his left halfback. In front of the play, running interference for the ball carrier, Coolidge angled toward Patch, who planted his feet and braced for impact. As Coolidge went low to hit the tiny end, Patch vaulted over him, scrambled to the ball carrier, and slung him to the turf for a four-yard loss.

Alfie pumped his fist in the air. "Thank you, Patch Mercer!"

Coach Lourie nodded.

Rather than punting, Texas lined up to attempt a first down. They had six yards to gain. Coolidge shot the gap between Prayer Bear and Woody but gained only four yards, so the ball went over to Sewanee.

The Tigers charged at different points of the Texas rush line, but they could never buck through for decent gains, and Coach Lourie saw no evidence of any significant fatiguing effect on the Texas linemen. He turned to Alfie. "Fighting above our weight class is wearing us down."

"Our backs still have spunk, just bruised and scratched. And Patch looks as spry as ever."

Coach Lourie walked over to a duffle bag stuffed with footballs and pulled one out. He stood on the sidelines holding the ball under his arm. Turl glanced at the Sewanee bench and saw his coach's signal. The captain grabbed quarterback Ham DuBose and said, "Pitch Patch, pitch Patch."

Third down and on their own 40-yard line, the Tigers got in punt formation. The two halfbacks, Turl and Brownlow, were split, and the fullback, Kimbrough, was ten yards back from the Sewanee center, Otay Carter. Patch was positioned wide on the right wing.

Ham yelled, "292–292 Jack star!" Center Otay Carter long-snapped the ball to Kimbrough. Ham and Brownlow ran interference for Kimbrough, and the three backs swept right. Patch took three steps off the line of scrimmage and into the Sewanee backfield. Ham crashed down on the Texas left end, Brownlow blocked the left halfback, and Kimbrough pitched an underhand spiral to Patch, who cradled the ball to his chest and dashed up the field. He looked to his left and saw that he only had to contend with Andrew Dudley, the Texas quarterback, who had been standing on his own 30 to field a punt. Patch veered to the sideline and ran like a hare, but Dudley was also fast and had charted a precise angle. He drove Patch out of bounds at the 12-yard line and pounced on the Tiger. Face down, Patch winced as a sharp pain shot through the bottom of his rib cage. He forced a smile and popped up to his feet.

The Sewanee players sprinted to line up, but the Texas linemen moved slowly, winded from the struggle and chase. The referee set the ball. Ham took the snap and pitched the ball toward Brownlow. Patch was at the halfback's right hip and watched the ball bounce off Brownlow's arm and hit the ground. Patch dove on the ball and was quickly buried under three Texans. He yelled, "Down!" While Patch was squashed under a quarter ton of dead weight, a fourth Texan threw himself on the stack, triggering stabbing sensations in Patch's already tender ribs. Pinned to the turf in half darkness, Patch took measured breaths and imagined himself in a canoe by a waterfall with Cecilia. Woody and Prayer Bear started peeling Texans off their buried teammate. The fumble cost the Tigers four yards, putting them on the Texas 16-yard line, but the umpire called a piling-on penalty against Texas, which moved the ball to the 1-yard line.

Off to the side, Ham grabbed Brownlow and said, "You can't stick your arms out in front of you like that and cleanly catch the pitch."

Brownlow said, "Why don't you try to send it low like you're supposed to, and I won't have to stick my—"

Turl separated his quarterback and right halfback. "Men . . . we need to score a touchdown, so shake hands like the Christian gentlemen we know you are." They shook hands. Turl said, "Good. And by the way, you're both right."

With two minutes left in the half, Tigers and Texans faced each other on the Texas 1-yard line. Ham quickly barked out the signals: "96–96 bear woodchuck, 96–96 bear woodchuck." Otay snapped the ball to Ham. Turl shot toward the gap between the Sewanee center and left guard, Ham pitched him the ball in stride, and Turl plunged straight into the line. He couldn't push through. The heavier team surged and leaned into Sewanee, and Turl was driven backward and downed on the 3-yard line.

On second down, Ham called Turl's number again. Brownlow led the interference and smacked into and knocked heads with a Texas tackle. Turl followed Brownlow and advanced to the 1-yard line, where he stalled behind Otay, Prayer Bear, and Woody, who were grappling with Texans. Kimbrough pushed Turl from behind but was unable to shove him through the Sewanee line. Players from both sides joined the fray. With the two teams locked in a scrum, Kimbrough grasped Turl by his pants waist and hoisted him up onto the scuffle. Woody reached overhead and gripped the captain under the arms while Prayer Bear grabbed his hips. Pumping their knees high, the two of them carried Turl over heads and shoulders and shot him forward. Turl tumbled over the goal line and onto the turf. Sewanee five and Texas zero.

At the Texas 15-yard line, Ham held the ball in place for Kimbrough's point-after-touchdown attempt. Starting four steps back, the fullback approached, cocked his foot, and drove the football over the crossbar and through the goalposts. Sewanee six and Texas zero.

Texas chose to receive the kickoff, which they fielded on their own 30-yard line. The kick returner gained five yards before Turl swung him to the ground. They ran an end-around play for two yards, and the timekeeper fired a shot into the air, ending the first half.

The Sewanee substitutes left the bench so the starters could sit. Five of the eleven sat down, and Joseph served them water. The other six were in the training tent with Henry and Coach Lourie. Woody was on the trainer's table. His ankle was swollen and red. Henry said, "Did you hear a snapping or cracking sound?"

Woody said, "No."

"Did it feel like a crack or snap?"

"No, just a dull ache and some throbbing."

"For how long?"

"Since I twisted it, during warm-ups."

Henry wrapped a chunk of ice in a towel and placed it on Woody's ankle. "Hold it right here, Mister Woody."

Patch had his jersey off. The bottom left side of his rib cage was purple and maroon. Henry examined the bruised area. Patch said, "No cracking or snapping sounds. Only thing I heard was the crowd's roar."

Henry said, "Take some slow, deep breaths, Mister Patch." Patch drew air in and out. "Does that hurt the ribs?"

"No."

"Well, good. They're bruised, not busted. We'll ice them now and directly after the game, and then we'll go with my liniment for the pain."

Coach Lourie said, "I'll ice him, Henry."

"Thank you, coach. I'll tend to these other men."

Halftimes were only ten minutes long, and Henry had four more Tigers crowded inside the trainer's tent. In addition to Patch, there was center Otay Carter with a jammed thumb, Ham DuBose with a bruised ear, Turl with a two-inch gash above his hairline, and Prayer Bear, who needed more liniment for his neck. Equipped with iodine, gauze, and medical tape in his hands, Henry turned to the captain first.

Turl said, "Take care of the others, Henry."

"Yes, captain."

Henry proceeded to apply first aid and measured reassurance to his players. He performed quickly but calmly. He then went out to the bench to examine the other five to be sure they weren't hiding any injuries and their spirits were strong. Kimbrough Lowndes was rubbing his wrist. Henry walked over to him and said, "You all right, Mister Kimbrough?"

"Just a little strain. It'll be fine."

Henry squatted, supported Kimbrough's forearm, held his hand, and gently rotated it in one direction, then the other.

"Joseph, fetch me a bottle of liniment, please. How's that feel?"

"No worse," Kimbrough said. "Might be loosening it up a bit."

Joseph returned with the bottle of liniment, and Henry lightly massaged the medicine into Kimbrough's wrist. Henry said, "I'd like to put a little wrap on it."

"We can't do that, Henry. I've got to catch snaps and pitches."

"Please let the captain know if it gets bad. It's a long road to December. Got to keep you right."

"I know, and I will."

The team huddled on the sideline. Coach Lourie said, "We're going to keep running around the end. When they have the ball, stay patient and in position. Watch out for trick plays."

Alfie said, "Go finish them off, Tigers."

The team members let out rebel yells, and the eleven took the field. Turl hung back to get a final directive from Coach Lourie.

The coach said, "Turl, I have a strong hunch that they will dropkick early in the downs—it's their only legitimate chance."

Turl said, "That doesn't mean they'll make them."

Pointing across the field at Dudley, Coach Lourie said, "Alfie and I saw that quarterback hit three out of four dropkicks from forty yards. Keep an eye on him." Turl nodded and ran to join his teammates on the field.

Texas chose to receive the second-half kickoff. Sewanee's Kimbrough missed the sweet spot on the ball and made a short kick of twenty yards. Texas's John Coolidge bobbled the ball, which fell to the turf. He leaned over and picked up the ball. As he rose, Patch crashed into the 220-pound fullback. The collision flattened Patch on his back and left Coolidge standing. Fifteen yards upfield, Sewanee mob-tackled Coolidge and brought him down.

Patch got to his feet and wobbled toward the line of scrimmage. Halfway there he raised his arms and flexed his biceps in a strongman's pose. Relieved, Henry and Coach Lourie smiled at each other and shook their heads.

The teams pushed each other back and forth for twenty-five minutes. Sewanee mostly alternated between mass plays into the interior line and quick pitches around the ends to take advantage of the Sewanee eleven's superior speed. At halftime, Coach Lourie had instructed Turl and Ham to mostly go to the left side of the line because Prayer Bear at right guard, Woody at right tackle, and Patch at right end were all hampered by injuries. Ham called about one play to the right per every three to the left.

Texas kept hitting the Sewanee rush line hoping to wear down the lighter foe. However, Sewanee scrapped, numbed their pain, and pushed past their fatigue, allowing Texas only four first downs with ten minutes left in the game.

On second down, Texas had the ball at the Sewanee 40-yard line with four yards to go. With the Texas fullback, Coolidge, at the quarterback spot and Dudley, their quarterback, lined up as a fullback, Turl yelled "Kick, kick!" and sprinted to the goalposts behind him. The snap went to Coolidge, who pitched it five yards back to Dudley. The Texas backs sealed the ends, and Dudley held the football extended in front of him at a downward slant. He took a step with his right foot, then his left, and dropped the ball. As soon as it hit the ground, he struck it with his right foot. Prayer Bear jumped and stretched his arms to the sky and watched the drop-kicked ball go end over end just past his fingertips.

The ball started its descent. Still with his back to the play, Turl, at full speed, was approaching the 5-yard line. The ball flew over his head, hit the crossbar, and fell toward the field of play and into his arms. Turl secured the football and circled back toward the Texas goal line, ninety-five yards away. Turl was streaking up the field before the players, on both sides, understood what was going on. Several Sewanee and Texas players were on the ground. A few had wrapped their legs around their foes' legs. The standing Texas players sprinted toward Turl, but the Tigers threw hard and skillful blocks with their shoulders and hips, knocking some opponents down, slowing or diverting others. They interfered so effectively that the only Texan to break free and chase Turl was Dudley, the dropkicker and quarterback and fastest of the Texas eleven.

As Turl raced down the Texas sideline, Dudley was eight yards from cutting him off. Then he put on a burst of speed that closed the gap. Within three yards of the Sewanee captain, Dudley dove at Turl's heels, but he made no contact and slid face-first on the field. Turl sped past the grandstand. He had never felt this kind of elation in his life. He crossed the goal line, came to a stop, placed the ball on the ground, collapsed, and rolled over onto his back. He was so exhausted he felt light-headed. His teammates reached him and lifted him to his feet. They shook his hand and put their arms around him while getting him onside for the kick after the touchdown. Kimbrough made the one-point kick. Sewanee twelve and Texas zero.

The two teams played a tug of war for the final eight minutes. The bruises continued to mount on both sides, but each set of eleven reached the final gun without any member having to leave the game.

The two schools' coaches, trainers, scrubs, and starters congratulated each other on a fine contest, largely played within the rules of the game. Joe Abbott shook Prayer Bear's hand and said, "Are you from Texas?"

"No, sir. Jonesborough, Tennessee."

"You sure are gritty like a Texan."

"You're gritty like a Tennessean."

Victor Garcia jogged over to Henry and Joseph, who were breaking down the tent Victor had loaned them. The three managed to roll the tent up and carry it to the shed.

Victor said, "Henry, how are your men?"

"Well, they definitely saw battle today, but I think they'll be fit for Texas A and M tomorrow afternoon."

"I hope so."

"How about your men?"

"I'm afraid our right tackle, Julian Sullivan, pulled a hamstring. I've got him walking it, and tonight I'll ice him."

"That's what I would do, too."

"We play in a week. I'm sure everyone but Julian will be ready."

"Hope he heals up soon."

"Don't know how you all will manage five games in six days."

"We'll do our best and leave the rest to the good Lord."

"Amen."

"Amen."

"So, enjoy that dime you took off of me, Henry, and here's a nickel for you, Master Joseph."

"Thank you, Mister Garcia. What for?"

"Every time I looked across, you were working fast and smart, like a sharp quarterback. Isn't that how he performed, Henry?"

"Sure enough. I couldn't have done the job without him."

Joseph smiled.

Henry extended his hand to Victor, who shook it. Then Victor shook hands with Joseph.

Coach Lourie's former Princeton baseball teammate, Jack MacGregor, came down from the stands to congratulate his friend. Coach Lourie said, "What did you think, Jack, old pal?"

"Well done, Coach Lourie, well done."

"Thank you, Jack. I've got the horses."

"You do at that. That little guy—"

"Patch Mercer."

"He darts around like a mongoose."

"He's the best tumbler for Sewanee."

"Ah. Well, Hobie, here are your winnings." MacGregor handed Coach Lourie five dollars. "And here is another five to place on my behalf. I'm picking Sewanee over A and M. Actually, let it ride all the way back to Sewanee."

"But you don't know the odds."

"I don't care. I've seen Sewanee beat the finest team in the Southwest. And I know the Sewanee coach very well—it's safe money."

"Good seeing you, Jack."

"I'll see you at the '03 reunion. Bring my winnings."

"Will do. Good luck with your baseball team."

The former teammates clasped hands.

Texas football manager Billy Sims had sent word to Alfie Melville to meet him in the box office under the grandstand. Through a barred window, Alfie saw Sims standing at a captain's desk counting bills. Alfie tapped on the window, and Sims waved him in. The door was locked, so Sims got up and opened the door for him. Walking back to his stacks of money, Sims said, "Congratulations, Melville. Your eleven out-finessed ours, simple as that— well, that and y'all's speed."

"I imagine if we played again in five days, we might very well see a different outcome."

"Well, by God, let's do it—you go play your game in Houston, load your men in your sleeper, and come back and play us."

"You're serious."

"Hell yes! See these stacks—biggest gate in the history of Texas football. I've already got your take in bank bags." He pointed to three bank security bags on the floor in a corner. "You might want to fetch your one-eyed guard and big ole center to escort you to your Pullman. There's seven hundred in there, per our agreement, and in further appreciation of Sewanee's contribution to our athletic department, I've made arrangements for your team to bathe and recoup at the Austin Club before tonight's German Society Ball." Sims took out of his vest a jeweler's envelope. Inside were twenty-three guest membership cards to the prestigious men's club. "I think they'll enjoy lounging in the grand study. Oh, and there will be barbecue in the courtyard. I'll send our men over to socialize with yours." Sims gently tossed the envelope to Alfie.

"Mister Sims, you are extremely generous and kind, but we can't come back after Houston. We have three games after that before we return to the Mountain."

"Forfeit those games and I'll give you five hundred dollars plus a fifty-fifty gate split if you play us again in four days."

"Forfeit? This team is going undefeated."

"All right, Melville, I'll guarantee you eight hundred dollars—guaranteed. You know you can't guarantee an undefeated year. Take the cash. Y'all are a small school up on a jungle mountain. I imagine a crowd of two-fifty is big for y'all. You need capital more than you need an undefeated season."

"We need both." Alfie tucked one of the bank bags under his arm and grabbed the other two by their handles. "I'd never forgive a team that didn't show up against us because they got a better offer, so I'm not about to do that to any eleven."

"I know you're a church school, but there's no need to get sanctimonious."

"I'll see you at the German. We'll have a drink."

"Or several."

Alfie went directly to the Pullman, counted the cash, and locked it in the car's strongbox. He stepped off the train, took his pipe and tobacco pouch out of his suit coat pocket, stuffed the bowl with loose leaf tobacco, and lit the pipe. He leaned against the Pullman and smiled.

Inside the Austin Club, the Tigers soaked in warm baths. Then the club's staff rubdown men massaged the Sewanee eleven and scrubs. After dressing for the ball, the Tigers joined the Texas players, coach, and student manager in the club's grand study. Later, in the courtyard, the men ate barbecued brisket and drank beer together.

At eight o'clock the two teams arrived at the ball, sponsored by the University of Texas German Society, of which nine Texas football players were members. Among the attendees were the Texas Women's Tennis Team and the school's Ashby Literary Society, an all-women's club.

While others waltzed to Brahms with Texas coeds, Patch and Woody stood drinking whiskey sours with the Texas left tackle and left end.

Patch said, "You men do not know how fortunate you are to have so many lovely ladies in your midst at school."

Rit Forrester, the Texas left end, said, "After five years at boarding school, I knew I was going to a college that accommodated the fairer sex."

Patch gazed at the girls dancing with his teammates and other men. "I don't really know what I would do. There are so many—just here, tonight."

Woody said, "You? You would do nothing other than chase skirts—morning, noon, and night."

At that, Patch downed his drink, handed the glass to Woody, and walked over to a pretty petite tennis player whose eyes Patch had already held a few times that evening. Patch and April Scott danced and ate desserts together.

Rit Forrester introduced Woody to Lillian Lewis, a freshman from Woody's hometown of Galveston, and her cousin Edwin Towns, a Texas medical student from Houston.

Lillian said, "Mister Barnwell, our families are well acquainted, yet I don't believe we've ever formally met."

"No, I have not met you, Miss Lewis, but I do remember a little girl named Lillian Lewis running around with my younger siblings at church picnics."

"I am one and the same, except a lady now, which means I don't run, I walk. That is, unless I am playing tennis."

Edwin said, "Lillian rarely runs when playing me in tennis. Instead, she sends me running back and forth."

"Walking, running. How about dancing?" Woody felt embarrassed and immediately regretted his gambit.

"Only with handsome and athletic gentlemen." She extended her hand.

Woody hesitated, then took Lillian's hand. "Excuse us, cousin."

Edwin smiled and raised his glass of bourbon.

The Tigers flirted, danced, snacked, and drank, though Coach Lourie and Turl cut off each player's imbibing at two drinks. Alfie drank whiskey sours, and Billy Sims kept his new friend's glass refreshed. The Sewanee man liked Billy and thought he was an exemplary host, yet he wondered if Billy was working him. He waited for another offer for a Texas game, but it never came. Billy did tease Alfie, though. "Admit it, Melville, you don't have the stomach for a rematch—you don't think your eleven can stand up against our longhorns twice in a week."

"Longhorns? That's good. The Texas Longhorns."

"It is! It just popped into my head. I think I'll pitch that to our administration."

"Good luck—it's a muscular and musical nickname."

As the Tigers' curfew approached, many Sewanee men and Texas women exchanged addresses, including Woody and Lillian. Patch did not commit his love to April of New Braunfels, Texas, but he did pledge to write her.

When the team arrived at the depot, the engineer and his assistant already had the Mountain Goat exhaling large plumes of steam against the black sky. Everyone loaded their luggage into the boxcar and lined up to board the Pullman. Turl, the first on, saw that Henry and Joseph were already in their berths. He turned to the group and hushed them, then softly said, "The trainers are asleep. Get ready for bed and climb into your berths. We go against the cadets in Houston in . . ." He took out his pocket watch. "In thirteen hours."

The adrenaline from the game and social activities had ebbed, so as they lay down, the eleven felt the soreness they had earned during the day's bout. Soon ten of them were asleep, but Woody was restless. At the ball, Lillian had put him at complete ease. The feelings of inadequacy and awkwardness that accompanied his interactions with lovely girls had been absent for the almost two hours he was with her, and Woody thought she was the most beautiful girl he had ever met or would ever meet. Now, when sleep was imperative, he could not stop thinking of Lillian—her wit, kindness, pale blue, almost green eyes, and thick blond hair pulled back into a bun.

He sat up in bed and looked at his sprained ankle, throbbing and more swollen than it had been right after the game. He hoped he had not betrayed the team by dancing instead of putting his ankle up, wrapped in ice. Woody stood and took stationery and a pen out of his travel bag. Sitting at a table in the front of the sleeper car, he propped up his ankle and began a letter:

Dear Lillian,

For me the highlight of our football odyssey has been being in your company, and I know it will remain the highlight for years to come.

He imagined Lillian's face. She was smiling. Then he pictured himself playing the piano in his parents' house while Lillian stood at his side. Woody gazed at her and then looked down at the keyboard. Still playing, he returned to Lillian, who was now without clothes. She was shaped like Renaissance statues of Greek goddesses—Woody's only visual reference for female nudity. Supported by one hand, Lillian was leaning against the piano and, with the other hand, covering her pudendum with a fig leaf.

He dropped the pen and recoiled from the paper as if he had touched Lillian without her permission. His heart rate increased, and he felt clammy. Convinced he had defiled her and did not deserve to ever see her again, he returned to his berth. After fifteen minutes of agitation, he went back to the table and continued the letter:

However, since our wondrous evening together, my imagination has flown to indecent, fantastical landscapes where a lady would never acquiesce to travel. I am this blunt for two reasons: one, you need to know the depth of my depravity (in fact every female within my field of vision should know this), and, two, when you find no correspondence from me further than this one, it will not be due to my lack of regard for you, no doubt God's most outstanding creation. Instead it will be due to the necessity to keep my sin-stained soul from your mind and sight.

With humility and respect,
Woodward Partridge Barnwell

Chapter Six
Thursday, November 9th, 1899

At four in the morning, the Mountain Goat pulled into the train yard of Houston's Grand Central Depot. The engineer shut down the locomotive and rousted his assistant from sleep. The man was curled up on a short, lightly padded bench in the cab. The two men climbed down from the steam engine and walked to the depot's main building, where they refreshed themselves and sat down for a breakfast at the station's all-night diner.

Everyone in the Pullman car continued to sleep, except Patch, who woke up at five, his usual time to rise. He drank three cups of spring water and went to the platform, where he performed light calisthenics and stretches. While loosening up, he remembered that in Austin, Turl had forgotten to make him tote water for missing curfew on the eve of the team's departure. Pleased with himself and amused, he grinned. With his arms stretched out to the sides, Patch twisted at the waist and felt a sharp pain where his ribs had been hit the previous day. He lightly touched the painful spot and winced. Patch told himself that they just hurt because he had been sleeping on them all night.

Woody and Henry had stepped out of the Pullman and were standing on the rail car's steps.

Henry asked, "Mister Patch, how are your ribs?"

Patch untucked and lifted up his shirt. "They're just bruised, Henry."

"Mister Patch, cracked ribs show a bruise, too. And bruised ribs hurt but don't hurt when you twist or bend like you did."

Patch looked at Woody, who pointed to Henry and said, "A smart man listens to his trainer."

Patch went back to his twisting exercise, biting down on his tongue to keep from revealing his pain. He could tell by their expressions that he was not fooling them. Patch gave up his charade. "You said 'cracked.' That's better than broken."

"Sure enough, Mister Patch. Now let me touch them softly."

Patch held his shirt up again, and Henry lightly ran his fingers over the discolored area of ribs. "How much pain?" Henry asked.

"Not much, really."

"Now take five very deep breaths."

Patch did so, hoping his face did not betray any discomfort.

"How did that feel? The rib pain get in the way of you breathin' deep?"

"Just a tad when I sent the air down."

Henry frowned. "I'd say you have a slight crack in one rib, a couple bruised around it. But no rib bone has broken away. If it was a break, you couldn't take deep breaths like that without tearing up. Even a tough man like you couldn't. But you need time off the field or that rib will break and you could get pneumonia and maybe even your lung stabbed by a bone shard."

Patch looked back at Woody, who said, "Henry, you're going to keep icing them and rubbing your magic potion on them, right?"

"Yes, I'll change off between the two, like I've been doin'."

"For the games, you'll wrap up his rib cage?"

"No, sir, that would bind up his deep breathing and he might get the pneumonia that way. Think how bad it'd be after he gets out of breath and can't breathe deep—that won't work at all, no, too dangerous."

"What can you do? Patch has to play. We'll never all be together like this again."

"I'm sorry I don't have any other remedies. Ice, liniment, and rest are all I've got for Mister Patch."

"Henry, I've got to play today."

"Sirs, all I can do is tell Coach Lourie and Mister Turley about Patch's, I mean Mister Patch's condition—"

Woody said, "Henry, let's think about—"

"Henry, you think it is a cracked rib, correct?" Patch asked.

"Yes, sir."

Patch said, "But there is still a chance that they're all just bruised, right?"

Henry said, "Well, it could be, but—

"Ah, there's a chance!" Patch said.

"Mister Woody, Mister Patch, I've got to do everybody right in this situation, especially you, Mister Patch. Please excuse me, sirs, I need to rouse Joseph."

Everyone was up and eating breakfast at the depot diner by 7:00 a.m. Outside the depot, the coach, manager, captain, trainer, and assistant trainer all stood together. Henry was relaying his injury report: ". . . and Mister Woody's ankle is still puffed up, Mister Embree's throat is a little yellow and purple but otherwise fine. His voice sounds better, which means no real damage to his pipes. And Mister Kimbrough's wrist isn't too bad, but I'm goin' to keep treatin' it and lookin' after it." Henry paused.

Coach Lourie said, "What about Patch?"

Henry took a deep breath and said, "He has a cracked rib."

Turl said, "Cracked, not bruised?"

"Seems so, sir."

Turl said, "Finn's a good scrub—I think we should let Patch heal up for Auburn and Carolina. That'd give him three weeks."

Alfie didn't like this idea. For him, Patch was critical to Sewanee making football history by winning five games over six days. If Sewanee won all five, this trip and this team would become legendary, and such a feat would establish Sewanee as a perennial football power, the Yale gridironers of the South.

Coach Lourie said, "Hell, I played my final two games for Princeton with a cracked rib."

Turl said, "Henry, what do you think? Rest Patch?"

Henry looked down, then at Turl, and said, "He gets hit there, it's going to go ahead and snap."

Alfie said, "Hobie, why don't you let him play? If he's shy or shielding that side, you pull him and put in Finn. You know what a tough nut Patch is." Coach Lourie looked at Turl, who reluctantly nodded in agreement, and it was settled: Patch would start against Texas A&M.

During breakfast, the team coaxed Turl into recounting his touchdown kick return against Texas. Of the eleven on the field, only Turl had seen the football bounce off the crossbar. The others were engaged forty yards away with their backs to the goal line they were defending. Turl said, "It hit the crossbar at the exact right moment, and I was running toward it at the exact right speed, and the ball and I intersected in time and space. If I had been a yard slower or a yard faster, the ball would have hit the turf and shanked, leaving me to scramble for it, giving Texas more time to catch me. It was all physics, boys."

Patch said, "Or Athena's divine intervention."

Prayer Bear snorted. "What do you mean, Athena? You heathen."

Patch said, "Prayer Bear, God doesn't pay attention to which way a ball bounces."

Prayer Bear said, "But a pagan goddess who never existed is pulling tricks for us. Is that the story?"

Turl said, "Hey, can we keep matters closer to the ground and not get so lofty? Kickoff is in about three hours." Prayer Bear and Patch exchanged amiable grins and returned to their eggs and bacon. "I also want to, on behalf of the eleven, thank the scrubs for their devotion, Coach Lourie for his formidable strategy, our manager for his tireless orchestration, and our trainers for soothing our aches and pains." The team cheered and clapped.

Alfie shook Turl's hand and went into the kitchen, where Henry and Joseph were eating at a counter. "Fellows, I hope you heard that applause. Turl just praised you both and the rest of us for supporting the eleven."

Henry said, "We heard it. Thank you, Mister Alfie."

"You're welcome." Alfie looked at Joseph's breakfast. "Let's get finished up here, young Joseph. Take that biscuit with you—we got a ball game to get to."

"Yes indeed, Mister Alfie."

After breakfast, the team walked toward Herald Park, a nearby baseball stadium and fairgrounds where that day's game was to be played. On the way, they came upon the Cotton Palace, a large, elegant tavern. As the team walked in front of the Cotton Palace, a well-dressed man in his sixties flung open the entrance doors and greeted the team. He was short with a thick, powerful build. Flowing out from under his silk derby was a mane of wavy gray and white hair. He had large, wall-eyed green eyes. With a booming voice, he said, "Gentlemen of the great University of the South, I am John Jeddie Capps of Humboldt, Tennessee. I congratulate y'all on your triumph yesterday and invite you inside to meet other Tennesseans who live and work here in Houston and will be at Herald Park to root you on."

Alfie said, "Team manager Alfie Melville. It is a pleasure to meet you, Mister Capps, and we very much appreciate you and the others supporting our campaign so enthusiastically."

Capps shook Alfie's hand heartily. "Oh, we are behind you fellas, and we're making book on y'all." He patted his breast pocket. Motioning toward the Cotton Palace with his thumb over his shoulder, he said, "As you can imagine, we're servicing a large Aggie contingent inside there."

"What are you giving them, Mister Capps?"

"Odds were five to three, favoring A and M, but y'all whipping Texas moved us to even money."

Alfie said, "Well, you and your friends' money is in the bank, sir, in the bank. Please have all the Sewanee boosters come down to the field and visit with us after the game."

"Come on in and meet them now."

"I'm sorry, sir." Alfie shook his head. "At this moment, our men need to dress out and get ready for a wonderful showcase of their talents and fortitude—"

"We've got some Sewanee alumni inside. How 'bout just a quick hello to those whose hearts remain on the Mountain?"

Alfie said to the team, "All right, men, we're going in to thank the Sewanee folk. I'll do the talking so we're out in two minutes at the most."

The team filed in while Henry and Joseph waited on the sidewalk under a window awning. Inside, the Cotton Palace was crowded with boisterous men. Capps had Prayer Bear and Finn help him stand on a chair. "Mister Melville, please jump up on this chair next to mine." He gestured to the chair and Alfie hopped up on it. "Gentlemen, I say gentlemen of Houston! Please afford me your silence for a distinguished moment." The men quieted down just enough for Capps to make an introduction. "I bring to you the Sewanee football manager, Mister Alfie Melville, and the Sewanee Tigers!" The din rose again, accented by jubilant yells as the men jostled for a better look at the Sewanee team.

Alfie got the crowd to quiet down and said, "Much gratitude to all of you—boosters of the Maroon." The Aggie fans cheered loudly. "And boosters of the Purple, alike." Despite being outnumbered twelve to one, the Sewanee faithful amplified their voices almost as loudly as the Texas A&M fans had. "We look forward to a contest with the cadets which will be both arduously and honorably fought. See you all at Herald Park, gentlemen—"

Capps yelled, "I've got another fifty, even odds on Sewanee! Are there any Aggie sportsmen left in this tavern?" Capps thrust his fist full of bills to the sky.

A young dandy jumped up on the bar, took out a thick billfold from inside his jacket, and said, "I'll cover that, and I'll book for either side at a commission of ten." The scene quickly resembled a rambunctious auction, the gamblers jockeying to be within reach of the bookmaker. Outside, Henry pressed against a window to witness the commotion and check on his players. Inside, most of the Sewanee players' faces expressed surprise at the tumult ignited by the wager and its astounding amount. Amazement turned to calculation as several Tigers wondered aloud how they could also profit from that day's game. Alfie, Turl, and Coach Lourie hurriedly ushered the players outside to the sidewalk.

Finn said, "Alfie, if they get to turn a profit on us, so do we. We're not slaves. And they're just a bunch of guzzlers while we're the soldiers. Now, who deserves to collect some sheets? Us or them?"

Patch said, "Do you speak for everyone, Finn, or just the scrubs?"

Finn's face flushed.

"Patch," Coach Lourie said, "we're one team—the eleven and the scrubs united."

Patch said, "I apologize to you, Finn, and to the other scrubs. You all are indispensable. But let's not sully our mission and traditions." Finn's complexion remained hot. "I, for one, am not interested in mixing rapacity with athletics. The latter is for the love of sport and school."

Finn said, "What about fraternal love? Our pursuit of happiness?"

Dispassionately, Prayer Bear said, "'For the love of money is the root of all evil—which while some coveted after, they have erred from the faith, and pierced themselves through with many sorrows.' First Timothy six, ten."

The Sewanee captain, manager, and coach stepped away from the team to confer. Alfie said, "We all, except Woody and Prayer Bear, gamble at cards, on bicycle races, and at the horse track. Coach Lourie, you and I cashed in a bit on the men's win at Texas."

Turl said, "I have the same worry Patch has. Betting on one's own athletic contest could damage team spirit."

Coach Lourie said, "In the East, I saw the ill effects of athletes gambling on their team, but prohibiting it will only cause resentment. Let each man make up his own mind, and cap all bets at a dollar." The other two concurred.

Alfie announced the decision to the team and collected their wagers. He wrote down everyone's amounts in a pocket-size ledger book. All the players except Patch, Woody, Prayer Bear, and Turl placed bets. Henry stepped up last to bet two bits.

Joseph pulled on Henry's jacket, drawing his attention. "Henry, please bet this nickel for me."

"No, you earned that from Mister Victor. You keep it. Betting is for sport. Everybody knows you love Sewanee. You don't have to prove it with a bet."

"But you're putting in a bet."

"For sport."

"Why can't I do it for sport?"

Henry grinned and said, "Keep your nickel—you worked hard for it and you didn't even know it was coming. I'll put up your bet." Henry handed Alfie thirty cents.

Without telling him, Alfie added thirty additional cents to Henry's wager.

Alfie made the final entry in his book and said, "Coach Lourie, take them down to the field—I'll catch up. Uniforms and supplies have been delivered to the visitor's clubhouse. The A and M manager is Travis Bowie. He'll get y'all situated."

The team continued their walk to Herald Park. Along the way, Woody stopped at a mailbox to mail his letter to Lillian. After releasing the letter, he tried to recapture it, but it had dropped into the box. Suddenly queasy, he placed both hands on the mailbox for support.

Patch came up to him and said, "What's the matter, your ankle?"

Woody swallowed hard. "No, I'm fine."

"You sure?"

"I was mailing a letter to my parents and banged a knuckle on the box. It smarts a bit. How are your ribs?"

"Not bad at all. Your folks aren't coming to the game?"

"I believe they're in Mobile for my great-grandmother's ninetieth."

"That is a feat to celebrate. I hope I make it that long."

"More time for carousing, no doubt."

"So many to love. Why wouldn't I want to live as long as possible?"

Woody imagined himself and Lillian, in their seventies, walking through a garden. He remembered the letter he had just sent to her, and an image of him sitting alone on a bench in the garden appeared.

"What about you, Woodrow?"

"No. An average life span will be sufficient for me."

"Rushing off to heaven, are you?"

"Not rushing, but not dawdling either."

Alfie reentered the Cotton Palace, where the final bets were being placed. He recounted the cash in his pocket and checked it against his pocket ledger total. Both amounts were fifteen dollars. Alfie opened his billfold and took out a twenty-dollar bill. He added it to the Sewanee collective pot, covering Coach Lourie and his friend Jack's five-dollar bets plus the ten dollars Alfie was laying down for himself.

While jostling to reach the bar and the man taking bets, Alfie contemplated betting more on what he thought was as sure a bet as the one he'd made in Austin. He wished he had time to go back to the train to get some Sewanee money to wager. Alfie knew Billy Sims was right—Sewanee football needed capital, some of which was needed to fund the team's remaining travel.

Alfie decided to cut his bet in half and front the Sewanee team fund five dollars.

The fellow taking bets climbed down from the bar. Alfie approached him. The bookie said, "How much do you care to wager, Mister Melville? Please forgive me if I misremembered your name, sir."

"You got it right. And your name, please."

"Harold Cooper. All these gentlemen can vouch for me, especially your man from Tennessee over there, Mister Jeddie Capps."

"I've got thirty-five dollars on Sewanee. Even odds, can you cover that?"

"I sure can." Cooper had a beer crate in front of him teeming with cash. He pulled a pencil from behind his ear and turned to the back of a long ledger sheet. The backside of the sheet was littered with calculations. "With my fee added, you need to lay down thirty-nine to win thirty-five." Cooper did some more math. "Or, Mister Melville, you can wager thirty-five to win—"

"No, we'll risk thirty-nine for thirty-five." Alfie added four dollars to his stack of cash. "To be sure, you'll refund the bet and vig in addition to paying out the thirty-five when we win?"

"Only a preposition separates our understanding of each other."

"I'm sorry?"

"On my side of this bar it is *if* Sewanee wins, not *when*."

"Do we collect here? Or at Herald Park?"

Cooper handed Alfie his calling card and said, "I'll be here thirty minutes after your contest ends. Your money will be secure in the Cotton Palace strongbox." To the crowd he raised his voice and said, "Any additional football enthusiasts here care to hazard some coin on the Aggies or Tigers? Last chance, gentlemen."

***

At Herald Park, there were six hundred cadets and five hundred and fifty others cheering for the Aggies. A hundred additional spectators were there to root for Sewanee, and another hundred were solely fans of the game. The weather was muggy, and swarms of gnats periodically surrounded the players' heads.

The Aggies had arrived from nearby Bryan, Texas, at 8:00 a.m. Their eleven outsized Sewanee's but not as significantly as the Texas squad did. The first eight minutes of the game was a punting exhibition. Each coach felt he had the superior punter and that jockeying for field position was the right tactic. Sewanee's fullback, Kimbrough Lowndes, turned out to have a stronger leg than A&M's fullback, Chick Japhet. Also, the Tigers got under their own punts effectively, limiting the A&M return yardage. After trading kicks seven times, Sewanee had a first down on the Aggies' 30-yard line.

Coach Lourie knew that his players were fatigued from travel and the Texas game, so he wanted to score quickly now that Sewanee had established good field position. On the next play, he signaled for Turl to get Ham to run a timing play that could result in a big gain. They had run *Tackle Back Left Halfback Around Right End* in their first three games of the 1899 season with mixed results: fumbles against Georgia and Tennessee, but against Georgia Tech, a twenty-yard touchdown.

Sewanee's quarterback, fullback, right halfback, and right tackle quickly lined up far to the right, one yard behind the line of scrimmage. Turl was the sole player on the left side of the backfield. The Tiger center, Otay Carter, made sure his teammates were set and then executed a perfect quick snap to Turl. Simultaneously, just over a half ton of Sewanee bone and muscle rolled toward the Texas A&M left end and halfback. Turl watched as Ham, Brownlow, Woody, and Kimbrough leveled the two Aggies, leaving Turl a clear path around the end. Turl galloped in the open until he reached the A&M 25-yard line, where an Aggie back dove in front of him. In stride, Turl hurdled the defender and sprinted over the goal line. Uncharacteristically, Kimbrough missed the one-point kick after the touchdown. Sewanee five and Texas A&M zero.

At halftime, players on both teams had swelling, bruises, and scrapes. After their trainers gave them medical attention, all twenty-two starters returned to the field, ready to play.

Opening the second half, Kimbrough kicked the ball to Texas A&M. It was a line drive kick straight to a tall, broad end who caught and covered the ball with both hands and ran straight down the middle of the field. Running bent to the ground, he blasted through three Tigers before Woody jumped on his back and brought him down on the Sewanee 40-yard line. The Aggies' first second-half formation made it appear that they were going to punt again. Standing with Coach Lourie, Henry, and Joseph, Alfie said, "They still think they can out-punt us."

Coach Lourie said, "No, they don't. Japhet's going to plunge, he's not going to punt."

As soon as Coach Lourie made this prediction, the Aggie fullback caught the snap and shot toward the gap between the center and left guard. In front of Japhet, the Aggie quarterback lowered his shoulder into Ham, knocking him back. Japhet crashed through with two Aggies at his side and one behind him. Sewanee stalled the fullback after he gained four yards, so his escorts lifted him and pushed him forward for another five yards. The Aggies ran a variation of this play over the next eight downs, every time with Japhet as the ball carrier. On each run, they gained three to seven yards and eventually worked the ball down to the Sewanee 2-yard line. Japhet's jersey was torn and soaked in sweat. On the previous three downs, he had returned to the line of scrimmage with the uneasy gait of a tipsy reveler. It was first down and goal, Texas A&M.

Coach Lourie said, "They're going to have to shoot that horse after the game."

Henry nodded in agreement.

The Aggies ran Japhet two more times into the line. Instead of a mass carrying him forward, the Aggie backs blasted the hole ahead of him. The first attempt gained no yards, but the second try put the ball two feet from the goal line.

Henry turned his back to the field. It was his superstition that he should never see the Tiger defense scored upon—if he were to see the ball breach the Sewanee goal line, bad luck would befall his team.

It was third down. The Aggies approached the line of scrimmage. They had attacked the Sewanee left side the previous four plays. Turl was convinced that they would go at the Sewanee right this time. The captain called a shift. He and the other three backs stood in the slots between the right-side linemen.

The Aggie quarterback, Jo Joe Boyd, barked out a signal that sent Japhet from his fullback position to alongside the left halfback. When Jo Joe got the snap, he faked a toss to Japhet, who crashed the line pretending to have the ball while Jo Joe circled back toward the Sewanee left, where A&M was manhandling the defenders. Prayer Bear pulled from his right guard position and slid left. Through what appeared to be a wide hole, the Aggie quarterback turned upfield at the exact time Prayer Bear sliced into the gap. The collision between the two created a deep cracking sound heard on both sides of the field, and Jo Joe fell on his back with Prayer Bear on top of him. The quarterback's face was covered in blood.

Prayer Bear rolled off of him and ran toward the Aggie bench. "It's bad, it's bad, y'all, broken—!" The Sewanee guard staggered and fell facedown.

Henry ran onto the field. Joseph followed him toting a pail of water. Two Aggies carried the quarterback to their sidelines, directly in front of the grandstand. The crowd murmured at the sight of Jo Joe's bloody face.

Henry waved smelling salts under Prayer Bear's nostrils while Joseph gently splashed water on the guard's face. The Aggies' trainer, Kirk, was examining Jo Joe's nose. He looked up at the Aggie coach, Lieutenant Cook. "It's busted."

Cook said, "I know, we all know. We heard it. What are you going to do about it?"

"Lieutenant Cook, I can't set it," Kirk said.

"Why the hell not?"

"I've never done it before."

"Someone taught you how, didn't they?"

"Yeah, I've seen it done, but, sir, I could make it worse."

Cook stared at the trainer in disbelief. "Boy, you're just squeamish."

Alfie and Coach Lourie stood beside Henry. All three studied Prayer Bear, who was sitting up and drinking water from Joseph's ladle. The coach said, "Can you see straight, Embree?"

Prayer Bear said, "Almost. Give me a minute." The coach and Alfie looked at each other. "Whoa, I just turned upfield and bam, my forehead cracked his nose."

Coach Lourie bent close to Prayer Bear's forehead and said, "Big guy, you've got a goose egg rising up already."

Henry said, "And we're happy to see that egg 'cause the blood is fillin' up outside Mister Embree's skull instead of inside it."

Alfie gauged the activity around the Aggie quarterback. Jo Joe lay on a stretcher, and Kirk held a towel stained crimson over Jo Joe's upper lip and mouth. Alfie jogged up to the A&M coach. "How's your man doing, Lieutenant?"

"He needs his nose set, but our trainer doesn't have the stomach for it."

Alfie said, "Ours has done it several times. Do you want me to call him over here?"

"Yes, much obliged."

Alfie called out for Henry and waved for him to come to the Aggie sideline. "Henry, we need you to set this man's nose."

Cook motioned toward some Aggie scrubs and said, "Take Jo Joe into the clubhouse, men."

Alfie said, "Henry can fix him right here, Lieutenant."

Jerking a thumb toward the grandstand, Cook said, "You want them to see your boy inflict pain on a white man?"

Henry said, "Lieutenant, my name is Henry. I—"

Jo Joe said, "It hurts like hell! Fix it now, goddammit!"

"What is your player's name, sir?" Henry asked.

"I'm Jo Joe. Just do what you need to do."

Henry yelled, "Joseph, bring my medicine bag and a bottle of alcohol."

With both items Henry had shouted for, Joseph was already halfway across the field. Prayer Bear followed the young trainer to the A&M sideline.

Henry turned to Jo Joe and said, "Don't worry. Even your mother won't be able to tell a difference." Henry straddled Jo Joe and asked Kirk for a clean towel. "Mister Jo Joe, blow your nose as much as you can into this towel. It's gonna hurt."

"Give it to me." Jo Joe grabbed the towel, sat up, and blew his nose forcefully three times.

Henry had one of the cadets support the quarterback from behind. "The wall between your nostrils is your septum." Henry explained, holding Jo Joe's gaze. "I've got to feel inside to see how far and deep it's jumped out of its groove."

Jo Joe nodded.

The Sewanee trainer poured alcohol over his hands and rubbed them dry on a fresh towel. He slowly inserted an index finger into each of Jo Joe's nostrils. "It's pushed over to the right, and it's up out of the groove all the way back to where the little septum bones start."

Jo Joe said, "Just do it!"

Henry said, "On three, I'm goin' to lay it back in its groove." Jo Joe breathed deeply. "We gonna set this first try. You and me. Blink real quick-like when you're ready."

Jo Joe rapidly blinked several times. All were quiet, players and spectators. "One, two, three!"

There was a loud cracking sound, and Jo Joe screamed.

Henry gently cradled Jo Joe's face and examined his nose. "It looks right, Mister Jo Joe—how do you feel?"

"Like a workhorse stomped on my face."

Alfie said, "It was a bear."

Henry said to Kirk, "Ice his eyes but not the nose—lay a cold towel over the nose."

Jo Joe said, "All that'll have to wait." He started to get up.

The Aggie coach said, "Jo Joe, I'm calling it a day for you, son."

Jo Joe stood in front of Lieutenant Cook in parade rest. "Sir, I request an opportunity to remain on the field of play."

"Denied." The Aggie coach turned away and instructed a scrub to limber up and prepare to go in at quarterback.

Prayer Bear said to Alfie, "That cadet ain't going to give up this fight."

"Neither is that lieutenant."

"Nope."

"Where is that nose contraption your parents sent you and you refuse to wear?

Prayer Bear pointed to the Sewanee sideline. "In one of the duffles over there."

Joseph overheard Alfie and Prayer Bear. "Mister Embree, it's right here." He pulled the nose guard out of Henry's medical case. In a hushed tone and as he handed the piece of equipment to Prayer Bear, Joseph said, "I grabbed it when I saw all the blood. Had to be a nose break."

Still standing at attention, Jo Joe said, "Sir, this will be our most competitive game of the year."

Coach Cook said, "Son, I commend you for your zeal and pluck. However—I am sure Henry can confirm that just a mild blow to your nose could force you to pass out from the pain."

Henry said, "It's true, Mister Jo Joe."

Coach Cook said, "Too risky, Jo Joe, sorry."

"Sir, as team captain, I cannot abandon my men."

The Aggie coach gave Jo Joe a stern look.

Prayer Bear held up his nose guard for Coach Cook to see. The elongated hard rubber cavity covered the length of even a long nose. The rubber extended to a section that served to cover the mouth, and it had a bit on the inside that the player clenched down on to hold the nose guard in place. A strap went behind the head. Addressing Coach Cook, Prayer Bear said, "Do y'all have one of these, sir?"

Coach Cook looked at Kirk, who shook his head.

"It's a Morrill nose guard, coach," Prayer Bear said. "Makes you look like a platypus, but it does protect the nose. Jo Joe's welcome to mine."

The large young man tossed his nose guard to the Aggie trainer. Kirk caught it. He scampered over to Coach Cook and handed him the piece of equipment.

The Aggie coach examined the guard. He looked at Jo Joe. "Don't take this contraption off at any time. That's an order, cadet."

Jo Joe reentered the game protected by Prayer Bear's armor.

The Tigers were on their own 2-yard line. On his way back to the Sewanee sideline, Coach Lourie brushed shoulders with the Sewanee captain. Without looking at Turl, the coach said, "Stretch 'em wide, stretch 'em wide."

Turl put his arm around Ham and told the quarterback to work the Aggie eleven laterally—making them pursue runners to the far left and far right, softening their middle with fatigue and deception. The quarterback called his own number in a succession of left and right runs around the Sewanee ends. Each time Ham was tackled and yelled "Down," the eleven swiftly scrambled to line up at the new line of scrimmage, where Ham quickly called out the play and took the snap.

Progressively, Ham went wider and wider on each sweep around the ends. The Aggies adjusted by incrementally spreading out their defensive formation—sending their ends and halfbacks to set up farther down the line of scrimmage.

Sewanee ran nine straight quarterback runs around their ends, which resulted in four first downs. Ham called the tenth play—a sweep to the right. He caught the snap and took a counter-step to the left. Instead of then going to the right to follow his backfield blockers, he ran down the left line. He raced the Aggie right end toward the sideline. Two strides ahead of the Aggie, Ham turned up the field, left the end behind, and reached the Sewanee 35-yard line before Jo Joe wrapped his arms around Ham's thighs and took him down. Ham yelled, "Down." Wheezing, Ham asked, "Can you breathe with that thing on?"

"Caught you, didn't I?"

Ham laughed—half at the comment and half at Jo Joe's appearance with the bizarre contraption strapped to his face.

On the next play, the Tigers' fullback, Kimbrough, bucked for three yards. On second down with only two yards to go for a first, Sewanee seized another opportunity to wrestle field position from A&M. Ham pitched the ball back to Kimbrough, who cleanly booted it to the Aggie 27-yard line, where Jo Joe dug his heel into the turf and made a fair catch.

The Aggies tried to run around Patch's end on first and second down, but both times he caught the runner behind the line of scrimmage. So, from their 24-yard line, A&M punted the ball back to Sewanee. Kimbrough made a fair catch on the Sewanee 44-yard line and punted the ball back to the cadets, angling his kick toward the Aggie sideline. The ball landed on their 30-yard line, bounced, and rolled to the 15-yard line, where Jo Joe, sprinting over from the center of the field, scooped it up, took five steps, and was driven out of bounds by Franklin Brownlow.

Texas A&M bucked the line for four yards. On second down, Prayer Bear threw the opposing guard to the ground and wrapped his arms around the Aggie ball carrier, fullback Chick Japhet. The Sewanee guard held him at the line of scrimmage. Tigers quickly amassed behind Prayer Bear while Aggies did the same behind their fullback, and what resembled a rugby scrum ensued. The grappling, shoving, and tripping was frenetic. From the grandstand, it looked like a human hive, an animated mound slowly shifting back and forth. This went on for fifteen seconds until the scrum caved in on top of Japhet, who yelled, "Down." The referee and the umpire pulled bodies off the pile, then marked the ball at the original line of scrimmage, the Aggie 22-yard line. Texas A&M punted again.

The ball came in low and short toward Kimbrough, who was positioned on the 50-yard line. Kimbrough dashed straight ahead. He lunged forward and cradled the ball. At the Aggie 44-yard line, Kimbrough staggered but recovered. A Sewanee line of protection formed upfield. Japhet broke through it. Kimbrough angled sharply toward the Aggie sideline as Japhet approached. Patch raced to block for his teammate, and just as Japhet reached out to grab Kimbrough, Patch launched his 125-pound body at Japhet's shins, upending the Aggie fullback.

Jo Joe pushed through the Sewanee interference, but Woody smacked into the Aggie quarterback's side, raking Jo Joe's nose in the process. Jo Joe's borrowed nose guard flew into midair. He fell to the ground and rocked on his back, holding his face and head in agony.

As Kimbrough crossed the A&M 30-yard line, he ran straight toward an approaching Aggie. With the agility of a ballet dancer, Kimbrough spun around and dodged the tackler.

Approaching the 20-yard line, Kimbrough calmly held the ball between his two hands, pointed the ball's nose downward, and let it go. Just as it hit the turf, he drop-kicked the football. It flew through the goalposts and over the crossbar. In the grandstands, most of the Aggie faithful stood along with the Sewanee supporters to cheer the play and Kimbrough. It was the kind of spectacular on-the-run dropkick associated with the great northeastern and midwestern football contests that the crowd had read about in national magazines. Sewanee led ten to zero.

On the field, Jo Joe lay writhing in pain when the Aggie trainer and one of their scrubs arrived with a stretcher. Henry helped them get Jo Joe on the stretcher. He followed them as they carried Jo Joe to the Aggie sideline. The cadet's face was the color of white flour. He kept his eyes closed and whimpered. Kirk administered morphine to Jo Joe. When its effects manifested, Henry reset Jo Joe's nose. The Aggie quarterback didn't wail this time. Instead, tears leaked out of his eyes while Kirk gently dabbed his cheeks.

Over the final fifteen minutes, neither team penetrated past midfield. The only player on the field with fresh legs was Colton Jumper, the Aggie substitute quarterback. The other starting twenty-one players were thoroughly spent after exerting themselves under the sun and in stifling humidity. The remaining play was sloppy, but no one else was badly hurt, and the game ended at Sewanee ten, Texas A&M zero.

Alfie shook Coach Lourie's hand. "Mister Hobie Lourie, in two days, the Sewanee Tigers have shut out the two best gridiron teams the state of Texas has to offer."

"Indeed they have."

Woody sat on the visitor's bench with his leg propped up. His ankle was a pale yellow and more swollen than it was before the game. As Joseph iced Woody's ankle, the Galveston native saw his parents coming across the field along with four other people he could not make out. Woody's mother waved at her son, and he returned the gesture.

After wrapping a bandage around the ice on Woody's ankle, Joseph said, "Mister Woody, I can fix it if it's too tight."

"No, it's perfect."

"Then I'll go fetch you a crutch."

"Thank you, Joseph."

As Joseph left, Woody saw that one of the people with his parents was Lillian Lewis. A thrill ran through him.

The small group reached Woody. His mother kissed her son on the forehead. "Marvelous match, Woodward, kudos to you and the other boys."

"Thank you, Mother. Hello, Father, Missus Lewis, Captain Lewis, Edwin." Woody shook the captain's hand and Edwin's. Then he allowed himself to look at Lillian. "Good afternoon, Miss Lewis."

"Good afternoon, Mister Barnwell. Congratulations."

Woody said, "Thank you. Please excuse me for not getting up, everyone. I'm trying to get ahead of some swelling. Thank you all for attending our game." He turned to Edwin. "Glad to see you again, Edwin."

"Likewise. And you and your teammates, Woody, are excellent football players."

"Thank you. We love the game and our school."

Mrs. Barnwell said, "Woodward, you come over to the island with us and I'll draw you a salt bath and we'll—"

"Mother, we're getting back on our train this afternoon."

Mr. Barnwell said, "Della, Woodward wrote us the itinerary. The men have five games in six days—three more to go."

"I know, football, football. I am as fond of it as any mother. I simply would like to take care of my son a bit."

Woody glanced over at Lillian. She smiled at him, and he cautiously smiled back. He wondered how she had gotten to Houston so quickly, and whether she had traveled to see him. Then he thought of the confessional letter he had sent her just an hour prior to the game. He felt his heart rate increase, and his breathing became shallow.

Captain Lewis said, "I will tell you, Woodward, the Sewanee eleven would have thoroughly embarrassed the '79 Navy team I was part of."

Lillian said, "Daddy, you all were the first Navy team, ever. Sewanee has been at it for a while."

Captain Lewis said, "Understood, my sweet child. Just glad we didn't have to line up against Woodward and his teammates."

"Thank you, Captain Lewis," Woody said. "I'm sure West Pointers feared facing you and your mates."

Mrs. Lewis said, "Not that year, Woodward. Navy only played one game and it was against the Baltimore Athletic Club."

Lillian said, "And it was a tie." They all laughed except Woody, who smiled and felt self-conscious at the same time.

Woody looked at his parents. "Mother, Father, why aren't y'all in Mobile for Granny's birthday?

Mrs. Barnwell said, "We decided to go tomorrow so we could surprise you and visit with you and Patch."

Mr. Barnwell said, "And watch you all bring glory to Sewanee."

Captain Lewis struck his palm with his fist. "And by gum! You fellas play a spirited and intelligent form of the game. I'd wager it was a gridiron manner that the state of Texas hadn't seen before."

"Thank you, sir. A lot of the credit rightly goes to Coach Lourie and our captain, Titus Turley."

"Your father tells me that your coach quarterbacked Princeton last year."

Woody said, "Yes, sir."

"Where is home for him?" the captain asked.

Woody said, "Philadelphia, sir."

Captain Lewis said, "Some of the best sailors under my command were Yankees. And I believe it only fitting they share their passion for football with the youth of our reconstituted Southland." Everyone murmured in agreement.

Woody said, "Captain Lewis, you can meet both of our tacticians." He pointed toward the west end of the field. "Over there by the goalposts are Coach Lourie and Turl. And Turl's parents, they're from Brazoria, Texas."

Woody's father shook his son's hand. "All right, Woodward, we'll go introduce ourselves to your leaders and greet Mister and Missus Turley. Are you going to put full weight—"

"Our assistant trainer is coming back with a crutch, sir. When he gets here I'll round up Patch."

Mr. Barnwell said, "Very good, meet us in the taxi line and we can congratulate him there."

"Your roommate is the hardiest lightweight I've ever seen in action," Captain Lewis said.

Woody nodded. "Part billy goat, part cheetah."

Lillian touched her mother's arm. "Mother, I want to talk some more with

Woody. We barely had a chance to speak last night."

Mrs. Lewis said, "That's fine. You children enjoy one another's company, and be sure to remind each other of Galveston's magic, so your hearts will always be on your native island."

Woody stood on his good ankle. "I'm honored to spend more time with you, Miss Lewis, but perhaps the sun is too harsh for—"

Lillian extended her arms out from her side. "I find all aspects of today's weather pleasant."

As the parents and Edwin walked toward the goalposts, Joseph returned with a thick stick as tall as he was. Short of breath, he said, "Mister Woody, we left the real crutch on the train, and Henry is giving rubdowns in the clubhouse so he told me to find a sturdy stick in them woods over there."

"Let me see that, Joseph. Oh, this is Miss Lillian Lewis."

"Nice to meet you, ma'am."

"Very nice to meet you, Joseph. I saw you helping the team today. You seemed very serious and devoted."

"Yes, ma'am, thank you."

Woody leaned the staff against the bench and applied heavy pressure to its middle, but it didn't snap. "This will work just fine, Joseph."

"Oh, good, sir." Joseph picked up a water yoke that had two empty buckets connected to its ends. "I am going to take these down to the clubhouse and see how I can help Henry."

Woody said, "Good game today, Joseph. You were a big help."

"Thank you, Mister Woody. Congratulations to you and the rest of the eleven. Y'all were too tough and too smart for 'em."

Lillian said, "Safe travels, Joseph."

"Thank you, Miss Lewis, you too."

Joseph walked away with the water yoke across his shoulders.

Woody sat down on the bench and laid the stick across his lap. He twirled it like it was mounted on a lathe, intermittently stopping the rotation and inspecting a knot in the wood piece.

Lillian watched Woody fiddle with his crutch. She wondered what to say to ease his obvious timidity.

Woody stopped examining and turning the stick. He smiled. "I just want to be sure of its integrity."

"Of course. But maybe you should elevate your ankle."

"Yes, you're very right." Woody followed Lillian's advice.

There was more silence.

Lillian asked, "Would you prefer if I rejoined our parents?"

"No. Please. Stay here."

"I will, provided we converse."

"Of course. Why—how did—how was your travel?"

"Tiring."

"I'm sure it was. When did you decide to come to Houston?"

"After the ball last night, I cabled my parents that I had become a football enthusiast after seeing the 'highly dramatic' Texas-Sewanee game. My mother cabled back that my father and she were attending today's game with your parents and that she had already cabled Edwin asking him to escort me to the match."

"What time did you board—"

"Before dawn." Lillian was taken aback by Woody's formal demeanor. She began to wonder if he regretted the affectionate words he had spoken to her the previous night.

"That early?"

Lillian nodded. "Yes." She was tired of his superficial questions. He grinned at her. Lillian turned and looked across the field in the direction of the taxi line. She pivoted back and faced Woody. "It's not like I came all this way to see you again, so soon—don't worry yourself over that."

"I would not be so presumptuous. I am very glad to see you, regardless of what brought you here."

"I like football."

"I know you do."

"I mean, that is why I'm here. I wanted to see another spirited game as soon as possible."

"I will have to see you compete in tennis this spring."

Lillian was surprised and relieved. This was the warmth she had felt from him at the ball. Woody looked her directly in the eyes. She noticed he was blushing.

"Won't you be chained to a desk at Sewanee, attending to the rigors of a seminary student?"

"I'll escape. You saw me playing my sport, and I will travel to see you play yours." They both smiled and looked around the now-empty field.

"Will you be at Galveston for Christmas?"

"I will. I'll mail you my arrival date as soon as I . . ." Woody remembered dropping in the postbox his letter to Lillian, hours earlier. His face turned glum.

"What's the matter?"

"I must be deeply honest with you."

"You sound so serious."

"I have to be blunt because we live so far from each other, and because I . . . I sent a letter to you."

"You did? When?"

"This morning."

She experienced the same sensation that she felt when she aced a tennis serve. "Well then, I'll have something special to look forward to in Austin."

Woody clasped his hands behind his head. "Lillian. I have deep regard for you."

"Regard?"

"Yes. I mean, respect."

"Respect?"

Woody sighed. "I . . . I think you're wonderful."

"I think the same of you, Woody." From her purse, she took out the train stub from her trip. "Here is a token of my fondness for your company." She handed the stub to Woody.

"Five in the morning? You must be exhausted." He turned it over and silently read what she had written: *To Woody Barnwell, I will always remember our time together, and may you and your teammates have safe travels and continued victories. Lillian Lewis, 1899.*

"You must be exhausted." He held the ticket stub out to Lillian. "Will you hold this for me until I change? These britches have no pockets."

Lillian took the ticket stub from him and returned it to her purse.

"Thank you, Lillian. I will always treasure that ticket stub. Always."

"You are welcome, Woody."

"Lillian."

"Your serious face again."

"That letter I sent you. Please, burn it upon receipt."

"In the letter, you're unkind?"

"No, perhaps too kind. At least, too personal. Please, it was rash. I want to proceed with our relations in the most proper manner."

Lillian touched Woody's arm. "This will be a great, perhaps unfair temptation."

"I realize I am asking a lot of you. I will utter the most important aspect of my written words to you now in person. You put me at ease and you awaken me. Next to you, I am an inferior soul, yet next to you I feel hope for my own soul."

She looked around. Seeing that they were alone, Lillian stepped toward Woody and took his hand. They stood there quietly, holding hands. "I like football," she said, "but the truth is I only came to see you, and I am so happy I made this trip. I'll forever remember it."

Woody smiled.

"And you have my promise that I will not open your letter and I will burn it."

"Thank you, Lillian. Thank you for your grace."

From the other sideline, Patch saw Woody and Lillian holding hands. He stood there for a moment astounded. Then he slowly backed up and ducked around the corner of the grandstand, where he said to himself, "That's my boy, Woodward."

***

Alfie was back at the Cotton Palace to collect the largest sum of gambling proceeds he had ever been party to. Elated, he had jogged from the field to the bar.

At the Cotton Palace, he learned that the bookmakers, Jeddie Capps and Harold Cooper, had gotten profoundly drunk during the game. At halftime, they left Herald Park to return to the Cotton Palace but took a wrong turn and staggered around Houston's wharf. Three drifters spotted the two inebriated men, beat them, and robbed them of their cash and watches.

Fortunately, Capps and Cooper had signed an agreement to pay Bo "Salty" Dalton, the Cotton Palace's manager, a one-point fee for securing the wagered cash in the bar's safe. Unfortunately, the agreement stated that only Capps and Cooper could disburse the winnings. At the Cotton Palace, Alfie was part of an incensed group of men at the bar clamoring for their due. Salty, a massive man in frame and girth, paid little regard to the gamblers.

Alfie said, "I have a damn train to catch and a football team to manage. My men just waged war for the second day in a row in two locales separated by an overnight train ride. Give me their money, seventy-four dollars. Give it to me right now!"

A ward boss and gambler named Julius Cartwright said, "Give Sewanee their money, Salty. They worked for their winnings—a game of blood and sweat for them, a game of chance for the rest of us."

Salty pressed down on the bar with both hands. "I got my name on a contract with them two!"

The crowd of gamblers hissed at the bar's manager.

Cartwright said, "Salty, Mister Melville gets his team's winnings. We'll bring Capps and Cooper back here. Men, go home and get your pistols if you don't have 'em on your person. We're going hunting."

The men left, and Salty disappeared through a door behind the bar and returned with the Sewanee wagers plus winnings. Salty scribbled something on a piece of paper and said, "Sign here." From across the bar, he pushed toward Alfie a piece of paper that said, *In receipt of $74 on November 9th, 1899.* Alfie signed the improvised document and handed it back to Salty, who said, "All this chicken-shit trouble for a lousy point."

Alfie stuffed the cash into his jacket, pants, and vest pockets. "Thank you for your help, Mister Salty."

"Goddammit, boy, it's 'Mister Dalton.' You gotta spend a whole bunch a money in here before you can get familiar with me. Go catch your train, you runt, before I change my mind 'bout them frog skins."

Alfie nodded, tipped his hat, and left the Cotton Palace.

Ninety minutes later, Alfie was on the Pullman with his team. The Mountain Goat rolled toward New Orleans, where Sewanee would play Tulane. With his ledger book in hand, Alfie walked to the back of the train to start doling out cash. He had already paid Henry and Joseph, who lay in his berth polishing his new fifty-cent silver coin. Across the aisle from the trainers, Alfie held out two one-dollar coins to Ham. "Two dollars for you, Hamilton."

"Let it ride." Ham stood up and yelled to his teammates, "A bookie in New Orleans's gonna double my prize money! How 'bout y'all's?"

"Double me down, Alfie!" shouted Otay.

Brownlow called out, "Me, too!"

The Tigers cheered and whooped.

After offering the remainder of the players their spoils, Alfie sat down next to Coach Lourie, who asked, "Anyone cash in?"

"Nope." Alfie counted out twenty dollars, placing the bills in his friend's palm. "That takes care of you and your Princeton chum."

Coach Lourie handed the cash back to Alfie. "Bet it for us, please. How did you fare?"

"Ten."

"A fine payout. How about the Purple?"

Coach Lourie's question surprised Alfie. He had not told the coach that he was going to risk any of the team's funds.

"Come on, partner," Coach Lourie prompted.

"Ten for the team's travel account."

The coach tilted his head back and said, "Hell yes! Beat both ends of Texas and we're in the black rolling into New Orleans."

"Empire building one game at a time."

They shook hands.

Several rows behind Alfie and the coach, Finn sat brooding over Henry and Joseph's presence on the Pullman. He walked back to where Henry was seated. Finn grabbed the edge of Joseph's berth, leaned down toward Henry, and said, "Do you have my banjolin, boy?"

"Mister Finn, there's no boy sitting here right now, just a grown man."

"You insolent nigger."

Henry stood up and glowered at Finn. "Why would you use such hateful language, Mister Finn? I've never done nothing cross to you. Have you no fear of God?"

"There'll be a day when once again a nigger's sass will lead to the lash."

"Mister Finn, you want slavery again, or does every negro just need to bow down to you in all manner?"

"You all just need to know your place and all will be fine."

"Mister Finn, my place is with negroes like Nat Turner. So, I'd be careful if I—"

"Did you just threaten me, nigger?"

As the slur came out, Prayer Bear appeared and rammed his shoulder into Finn, wrapped his arms around him, drove him forward, and slammed him into the restroom door. Then Prayer Bear opened the door and shoved Finn into the restroom, following him in. He grabbed Finn with one hand and locked the door with his other.

"Damn! Telfair!"

"Shut your mouth, Finny!" Prayer Bear pushed Finn, who tripped over the commode and wound up wedged between the fixture and the wall. Prayer Bear picked Finn up by his pants and shirt and pressed him against the wall. "I warned you, Finny. I warned you to leave that man alone."

"He stole my banjolin, goddammit."

"No, he didn't, you rotten heathen. I put it in the boxcar."

Alfie, Coach Lourie, Turl, and six more players crowded together outside the door. Alfie knocked and asked, "What the hell is going on in there?" Alfie put his ear to the door.

Prayer Bear said, "I am not going to kill him. I promise I will not kill him." Then he swung Finn into the door.

Alfie jerked back and said, "Come on, Prayer Bear, open the door."

Prayer Bear said, "Only if I kill him."

Alfie said, "You promised you wouldn't kill him."

Finn yelled, "He's fucking mad. Get me out of here."

Prayer Bear covered Finn's mouth. "Shush, shush, Finny. Be a good Finny."

To no one in particular, Alfie asked, "How did Finn poke the Bear?" Then he pushed through the crowd. "Henry! Finn start something with you?"

The trainer sighed and rubbed his brow. "Mister Finn was talkin' 'bout whipping negroes, and I told him I wasn't going to sit for any of that, and out of nowhere come Mister Embree, and he tackled Mister Finn right into the restroom."

Finn's friend James Coffey said, "Now hold on, that's not the true story, Henry. You know you took Finn's banjolin and he just came back here to get it."

Prayer Bear shouted from the restroom, "Henry, of course, is telling the truth. I took Finny's little banjo and put it in the boxcar, 'cause he was making hateful music with it. Coffey, you go sit your ass down and shut up or I'll pull you into my den next."

Alfie said, "When you comin' out, Prayer Bear?"

"After I have enlightened Finny, here."

Alfie said, "That could take a while. What if one of us needs to go?"

"When I am convinced that Finny can comport himself as a Sewanee man ought, he and I will take our seats. Until then, everyone has Finny to blame for any biological consternations."

Except for Alfie and Turl, those outside the restroom returned to their seats. Prayer Bear and Finn sat on the floor with their backs against opposite walls.

"What did you do with Henry's schoolbooks?" Prayer Bear asked.

Finn said, "I don't know what you're talking about."

Prayer Bear raised his eyebrows. Finn huffed. He pointed to the small overhead cabinet, where he had stashed Henry's two textbooks. Prayer Bear retrieved them. He cracked open the door and held out the anatomy and chemistry books. "Alfie, Finny hid these from Henry."

He handed the books to the team manager, who took them to Henry. "Here are your medical books, Henry."

"Where did you find them, Mister Alfie? I've looked high and low for them."

"Finn won't be touching your property anymore." Alfie looked to the back of the car. "Yeah, I don't think you'll have any more trouble from Mister Grayson."

Alfie returned to stand with Turl outside the restroom. "Well, captain, we didn't foresee this happening."

"Finny didn't foresee a negro riding in a sleeper car with him."

"And he underestimated the protective wrath of a holy bear."

Inside the restroom, Prayer Bear squinted his eyes and looked at Finn. "You know, Finny, I really didn't know you at Woodberry. Thought you were a good kid, but your heart is dark. Isn't it?" Finn stared at the door. "I'm going to start praying for your heart, Finny. I suggest you do, too."

Finn kept his eyes set on the door. "I saw Joseph come in here at least once. Did you know they were using our toilet, Telfair? Did you?"

"Damn, Finny, you're a med student. Where do you imagine folks on a train are supposed to go when nature calls?"

"So, that doesn't bother you?"

Prayer Bear sighed and said, "We're not on the Mountain. These are special circumstances."

"*Plessy versus Ferguson.* Separate but equal, Telfair, separate!"

"Do you feel the demons coursing through you? The searing heat?"

"How do you call yourself a Southern man?"

"Now that's pretty easy, Finny, given I am from the South."

"Jonesborough, Tennessee."

"Come visit us sometime, Finny."

"The home of the South's first abolitionist newspaper."

"*The Emancipator.* The nation's first, actually."

"Who did your father fight for, Telfair?"

"As I am sure you already knew, my father fought for the United States of America."

"At twenty-five years of age," Finn said, "my grandfather, Colonel Atlas Spotswood, shot Union General Francis Waters clean through the neck. The Yankee reprisal on our estates and family members was thorough and harrowing."

Prayer Bear said, "Revenge is the fuel that perpetuates wars."

"Those blue devils burned our ancestral home to the ground. My grandmother lost her home and her husband! A Yankee artillery officer fired a cannon at my grandfather while he sat upon his beloved stallion, Vancivius. The ball blew them both into chunks of meat."

"The war was our Israel versus Judah—cousins slaying cousins. It was un-Godly, and now we must move on together as Christian brothers in a new South."

"Telfair Embree, son of Union Captain Ellis Embree, a man who led guerrilla missions throughout Virginia and North Carolina, a man who terrorized Southern women and children. A man who torched homes. A man whose band of blue bellies saw all in their path as fair spoils of war—material and carnal."

Prayer Bear pointed his finger at Finn. "If you ever slander one of my family members again, I will test the strength of your skull against a curb, or perhaps that porcelain sink."

Finn leapt to his feet and darted toward the door.

Prayer Bear tackled him and pinned him to the floor. "Your grandfather's horse was named Vancivius! Vancivius, the Vindicator—that's you, a lousy little tin-pot vindicator!"

Finn screamed.

Turl pounded on the restroom door. "Let him out, Embree, enough! Dammit, man, that's enough!"

Prayer Bear stood up, gripped Finn's collar, dragged him to the door, and tossed Finn out into the arms of Turl. "If he says one impolite word to Henry, Joseph, or me, he and I will dance in here again." The Sewanee guard slammed the door shut.

"Are you coming out of there?" Alfie asked him.

"Not yet. I've got some praying to do."

Turl called Peck and Coffey to help Finn back to his seat.

Finn pushed past his friends. Out of breath, he said, "I don't need any damn help."

Turl said to Henry, "Finn has a small cut on his neck." Henry grabbed his bag and followed Turl.

The captain stared at Finn and said, "Henry is going to doctor that cut so there's no infection. If you're surly in any manner, your last stop on this trip will be New Orleans."

While Henry cleaned and bandaged his wound and Turl watched him, Finn stayed silent and still.

The trainer finished his work. "That should take care of it, Mister Turl."

Henry returned to the back of the train and took his anatomy book out of his duffle bag. He sat down next to Joseph and placed the book on the armrests between them. Henry began reading the first chapter out loud. Joseph dragged his finger under the words he thought Henry was speaking. If Joseph lost his mark, Henry moved the young man's finger to the correct word.

***

After eating a light supper from the Pullman's dinette, the players began to retire to their berths. Patch lay composing a letter to Cecilia, providing her with a travelogue of the Tigers' tour de force so far.

Eventually, everyone except Woody was in bed. Reclining in his chair with his eyes closed, he was reliving his brief time with Lillian after the game. He pictured himself on the gridiron holding Lillian's hand. Soon a line from Hopkins's *God's Grandeur* narrated the scene: *There lives the dearest freshness deep down things.* These words floated in his consciousness for a time, but another scene replaced it. In his mind's eye, he saw the two of them swimming alone and nude, just past the surf off Galveston Island.

To block out the debasement of Lillian and their nascent relationship, Woody imagined himself at Sewanee's Saint Augustine's altar, but that was not enough to push the swimming imagery out of view. He began to pray, a continual whispered recitation of *Oh God, make clean our hearts within us. And take not thy Holy Spirit from us.* Woody nodded in time with the prayer and focused his inner sight on the Sewanee chapel's sanctuary.

After he stopped praying, he sat with an uneasy stomach. At some point, exhaustion became heavier than his anxiety and he fell asleep in his chair.

Chapter Seven
Friday, November 10th, 1899

Twelve hours after the Tigers boarded their sleeper car in Houston, the Mountain Goat delivered them to New Orleans. The Tulane Sailing Club met the team at the depot. The club's captain was Judah Levert, who was also Tulane's quarterback. He welcomed his school's afternoon opponents. "On behalf of all current Tulane men and our alumni, I welcome you all, the men from our Southland's most distinguished mountain campus. I welcome you gentlemen to the South's sea-level, balmy, and sensuous gateway to paradise, the Crescent City." The Sewanee and Tulane men applauded. "You have already conquered the best of Texas. Here we hope to further test Sewanee's well-girded eleven on the gridiron. Regardless of this afternoon's outcome, you all are our honored guests and we your appreciative shepherds."

The Tulane sailors presented each Sewanee man with a small basket of oranges, lemons, and bananas. As the new acquaintances shook hands and introduced themselves, the Sewanee players expressed their gratitude for the gifts.

Alfie stood on a bench and said, "Friends, I am Alfie Melville, Sewanee team manager, and native of New Orleans' cousin, Mobile. We are very glad to be your guests. Thank y'all for your noble generosity."

Judah responded, "Our pleasure. After you settle in at the Saint Charles meet us at Spain Street Landing for a quick sail across the river and lunch on Algiers Point."

Alfie smiled broadly and rubbed his palms together. "Jim-dandy!" Then he cocked his head. "But wait, you're not going to leave us there and register a Sewanee forfeit?"

Judah chortled. "No sir. We want a crack at y'all. We might get you a little liquored up, though!" This prompted laughter and jeers.

Porters loaded the Tigers' luggage, uniforms, and supplies on two drays, and the Sewanee entourage walked north for twenty minutes from Union Station to the lavish Saint Charles Hotel, at the bottom edge of the French Quarter. After stowing everything at the hotel, the team, coach, and manager gathered downstairs for breakfast in the Saint Charles dining room.

Henry and Joseph ate in the hotel kitchen. When they finished, they walked through the lobby, Henry carrying his suitcase and Joseph carrying his mentor's training bag. Alfie saw them from the dining room. He excused himself from the table and caught up with the trainers.

Alfie said, "Henry, Henry, hold on for a minute."

Henry said, "Yes, Mister Alfie?"

"You all are sure about where you're going?"

"Yes sir. Twenty-One Twenty-One Orleans Avenue, Miss Willie's Boarding House."

"Go straight up Saint Charles 'bout twenty minutes and then left on Orleans for another twenty minutes, and she's on the right. Orleans will take you out of the quarter and into the Tremé, the colored people's section."

"We'll be fine, Mister Alfie."

"Oh, and here." Alfie took out his billfold and counted out four dollars. "Give Miss Willie two dollars for the room and board. When you reach the Tremé, there should be plenty of dry goods stores for y'all—get Joseph a complete change of clothes, a little case, and . . ." He paused. "Be sure to get him a nightshirt and a toothbrush."

"I will. We appreciate your kindness."

Joseph said, "Thank you, Mister Alfie."

Alfie said, "Never mind, you've earned it. So we'll see you all at the Young Men's Gymnastics Club, Forty Four North Rampart, at one? Do I need to write down that address?"

"It's already written down and in my pocket. Please remind the men to carry over a full crate of my liniment with the other supplies."

Alfie took out his pocket-sized, leather-bound notebook and said, "Already written down right here." He slid the book back into his suit pocket and patted his jacket.

Henry and Joseph began their crosstown trek, and Alfie went to the hotel's Western Union desk. He wired a fraternity brother at Sewanee, asking him to get word to Joseph's father that Joseph was in fine shape and had contributed to the Tigers' two triumphs. Then he took out his notebook and found his detailed notes on the play-by-play action of the Texas and Texas A&M wins. He telegrammed Vice-Chancellor Wiggins and *The Purple* a dry possession-by-possession account of each game. However, at the close of these factual descriptions, he waxed poetic for the benefit of his brethren on campus:

```
IF HERE, THE MOUNTAIN WOULD BE SET
BETWEEN AN ELATED QUAKE ON SEWANEE NATURAL
BRIDGE AND A TRANQUIL DAWN AT TREMLETT SPRING
FOR OUR ATHLETES HAVE BEEN AS FIERCE AND
RELENTLESS AS IRON TIGERS DURING THEIR
CONTESTS AND AS GENTLE AS THE BROTHERS OF
SAINT JOHN BEFORE AND AFTER EACH MATCH. IN
SHORT, THE SEWANEE MISSION IS IN THE RELIABLE
HANDS OF ROBUST AND NOBLE MEN.
```

Alfie sent his telegram and walked into the hotel's bar, which was crowded with cotton traders and other wealthy men. He sat at the bar and ordered a draft beer. A bartender served Alfie the beer. Alfie said, "Are you Bernard?"

"No, sir." The bartender walked down to the other end of the bar where Bernard was speaking French with two patrons. "Pardon, Monsieurs Perine et LeBas."

Monsieur LeBas said, "Bien sur, Maurice."

Maurice smiled and said to Bernard, "The young gentleman in the derby hat has a special request."

Bernard introduced himself to Alfie, and the two shook hands.

Alfie said, "What are the odds, Bernard, on the Tulane-Sewanee match?"

"Sewanee giving up twenty-four points."

"Excuse me?"

"No odds, sir. Bookmakers insist on a spread for this afternoon's contest."

"What is that?"

"If you were to place a bet on Sewanee, their victory would have to be by twenty-five points or more for you to collect."

"What if they win by twenty-four?"

"A push, sir."

"I'd just get my wager back?"

"Correct, Mister Melville."

"What's the vig?"

"Zero for you, sir."

"Thank you." Alfie assumed booking twelve rooms at the Saint Charles covered the bookie fee. "I'd like to place seventy on Sewanee."

"I am sorry, sir, but I've been instructed to cap all bets at sixty."

"No exceptions?"

"I don't think so, sir, we're having a hard time laying off the Sewanee side of our book."

"Well, let's make it sixty on Sewanee, then."

Alfie decided not to bet his own money, so all the other wagers would fit under the sixty-dollar maximum. The Sewanee manager gave Bernard the cash. The house-bookie said, "Best of fortune, Mister Melville."

"Thank you."

Alfie joined Coach Lourie and the players in the lobby.

Patch said, "Where you been, Alpheus Melville?"

"Made a little investment."

Franklin Brownlow said, "Did you place our share?"

"Sure enough."

Finn said, "What odds?"

"Even odds."

"Even?" Finn asked.

"Yep, placed it all straight up." Alfie did not want to tell anyone about the twenty-four-point spread. He had decided the pressure to win was great enough after two road wins on the previous two days and shutting out all six teams they had faced during the season.

The Sewanee men walked to the designated spot on the bank of the Mississippi where they were to meet the Tulane Sailing Club. There the collegiate sailors and their Sewanee guests assembled to sail across the Mississippi to Algiers Point.

***

When Henry and Joseph entered the Tremé, both were astounded. Henry stopped at a corner and said, "Joseph, these stores and restaurants we're looking at . . ."

"Yes?"

"Colored people own them." The two stood there. Joseph scanned the commercial signage posted on both sides of Orleans Avenue and down North Miro Street.

Two blocks down they found Homer P. Dry Goods and went inside. An elderly man with light brown skin, long fingers, and blue eyes waited on Henry and Joseph. Thirty minutes later, Joseph walked out with a valise, new undergarments, a nightshirt, a toothbrush, windowpane knickerbocker trousers and matching vest, and a purple dress shirt.

After settling in at Miss Willie's Boarding House, Henry and Joseph walked toward the French Quarter to meet the team at the Young Men's Gymnastics Club.

As the two trainers walked down Orleans Street, they faintly heard percussive music. It became louder as they approached the French Quarter. The rhythm was frenetic, and the tones were low, mixed with popping accents. Upon hearing these foreign sounds, Henry and Joseph exchanged apprehensive glances. When the two trainers were six blocks from the French Quarter, they came upon a square where black men, women, and children were dancing or playing large wooden drums, which had cowhide heads. Henry and Joseph had stumbled upon Congo Square, where slaves were once bought and sold. A music and dance gathering occurred there on an almost daily basis.

Some revelers wore threadbare pants, shirts, and dresses, while others were well dressed in domestic servants' livery. Striking a tambourine and gesticulating wildly, a man in a tailcoat led the line of dancers. A lanky woman behind him lifted the hem of her faded blue dress and high-stepped in her bare feet. Neither Joseph nor Henry had ever seen music or dance like this. They both stood in Congo Square amazed but uneasy as well.

Joseph looked around to see if any white people were in the crowd watching. All he saw were black people—some with very dark skin and others with light brown complexions. The dancers seemed happy and angry at the same time. He wondered how long the drum beating would go on and why there was no fiddle or banjo, no singing.

Henry put his hand on Joseph's shoulder, causing him to flinch. "Come on, Joseph. We've got work to do."

***

Under a stand of ancient oaks on Algiers Point, the Tigers, their coach, their manager, and the Tulane sailors enjoyed a light picnic, eating Louisiana delicacies like crab and shrimp étouffée. Three Tulane sororities had taken the ferry over earlier and set up a luncheon for the boating party. The coeds served food and drink to the men. Turning to Woody, Patch said, "My, my. There are more beauties here than at the Texas German Ball."

After enjoying the food and lemonade, several of the Sewanee men took a walk with the young women from Tulane. At one point, there were thirteen newly acquainted couples strolling alongside the shore. The sororities' house mothers, unable to hear what was being discussed by the pairs, tried to at least keep their charges in sight.

From a distance of about thirty yards, Woody sat alone and observed Patch escort a petite young lady by the river. He watched his roommate take the sorority woman by the arm. Woody shook his head. "He's incorrigible."

A house mother walked briskly toward the couple and called out, "Florence, that is quite enough time with that young man!"

Patch let go of Florence's arm and said, "The approaching biddy has cut short our time. May I write you?"

"It's best not. And Miss Thompson is not a biddy. She's a caring soul who keeps us safe from impertinent men."

Florence walked away from Patch and joined her house mother. Woody laughed and wagged his finger at Patch, who saw his friend mock him. Patch laughed, too.

After an exchange of addresses between football players and their new female friends, the polite visit ended with the Tulane sailors taking the Sewanee men back to New Orleans.

Traveling to the Young Men's Gymnastics Club, the Tigers, with their gear and supplies, loaded on streetcars.

Finn and Peck sat together, eying the negroes seated on the streetcar. Holding a strap, Coffey stood next to his friends and said, "God almighty, niggers sitting while white folk stand."

Peck poked Coffey in the ribs. "They shouldn't even be here. You dolt."

Loud enough to be heard over the streetcar's clatter, Finn said, "Obviously, no one in this town gives a damn about the most important Supreme Court decision of our time."

When the team arrived at the Young Men's Gymnastics Club, Coach Lourie had the starters and scrubs run plays against each other in the gymnasium. In the club's training room, Turl stood naked in a round galvanized tub half full of warm sudsy water. Joseph had two large sponges in his hands and was bathing Turl, applying the sponges in a circular motion. Back at Sewanee, Henry had coached Joseph on the proper techniques for sponge-bathing an athlete. *Remember, Joseph, going 'round and 'round with the sponge brings the blood up for healing.*

Prayer Bear came into the training room, undressed, and stepped into a tub filled with warm sudsy water. Joseph dried off Turl, then started sponge-bathing Prayer Bear.

Turl climbed facedown onto the training table, and Henry began massaging his neck and shoulders with rubbing alcohol. Turl's muscles were as tight as iron, so Henry switched to his liniment. "I'm going to have to heat you up real hot, Mister Turley."

"I was hoping you would, Henry."

Henry kneaded Turl's muscles. "I got to work these knots out, Mister Turley. Tell me if I'm too rough."

"I can take it. Dig, pinch, whatever you need to do."

When Henry finished the massage, he said, "You're good and loose now, Mister Turley. Try to relax. Let yourself enjoy today's game."

"I'll try, Henry."

"My grandmother always said, 'Only thing worry buys is more worry.'"

"She was right about that."

"And the Tigers were right when they picked you as captain."

Turl smiled and lifted himself off the table. As soon as he did, Prayer Bear eased his big mass onto it.

Joseph started sponge-bathing the eleven's other halfback, Franklin Brownlow. The two trainers stayed in sync and treated all twenty-one players, one after another.

The Sewanee group left the gymnastics club and marched down North Rampart Street looking for streetcars to take them to the Crescent City Baseball Park, where they would play Tulane at 4:00 p.m. The players were dressed in their padded moleskin pants and cotton game jerseys. Each had his football boots tied together by the laces and dangling from his neck. The scrubs, Henry, and Joseph carried all of the training supplies and equipment. The entourage from the Mountain split up and loaded onto three separate streetcars.

Prayer Bear sat with Joseph, who was dressed in his brand-new clothes. Joseph had his sketchbook open and was shading an anatomically drawn heart he had rendered during the train ride from Houston. In the row in front of them, Henry sat next to a middle-aged black man with salt-and-pepper hair. In the man's lap was a large alligator-skin physician's satchel, softened by age and wear. At his feet, Henry had his leather trainer's bag—made of cowhide, smaller but the same shape as the gentleman's case. The streetcar travelled two short blocks and made a stop. As people got on and off, Henry slowly reached down for his bag and placed it on his lap.

The man next to him extended his right hand to Henry and said, "Doctor Robert Cromwell, sir. With whom do I have the pleasure to be sharing this bench?"

The streetcar lurched into motion. Henry grasped the man's hand. "Henry Jordan, trainer for the Sewanee football and baseball teams. You might know the school as the University of the South, sir."

"I know of it as both. In 1876, I was in the first graduating class of the Medical Department of Central Tennessee College."

"Where is that?"

"Nashville."

On the bench behind Henry and the doctor, Prayer Bear sat with his arms folded as he listened intently.

"Do you know our school, Mister Jordan?"

"No sir. It's still—"

"Still thriving, one hundred and eighty students. I am on the board of trustees."

"So, you come to Nashville?"

"I do, twice a year."

"My cousin Louis is the football and baseball trainer for Fisk."

"Is providing medical care a family tradition?"

"It is. My grandmother Rebecca tended to . . ." Henry looked down at his trainer's bag.

"To whom?"

"Well—we don't really have any doctors in our family."

"You mean you don't have any licensed doctors in your family. Is that correct?"

"Yes, sir. That's right. My grandmother was a healer for mountain folk, but she had no schooling."

Prayer Bear leaned forward and said, "Please excuse my rudeness, Doctor, but I must keep my friend's modesty in check. This man keeps me and my teammates alive and well. Henry Jordan has medical skills equal to many of our state-approved physicians. And an unrivaled caring demeanor."

Henry said, "Doctor Cromwell, this is Mister Telfair Embree—our eleven's right guard. From Jonesborough, Tennessee."

Dr. Cromwell said, "Jonesborough? Embree?"

Prayer Bear smiled. "Yes, sir, Elijah Embree was my great-grandfather."

"Making Elihu Embree your great-great-uncle."

"Indeed, and I cannot conceal my pride."

"Nor should you, sir. Mister Jordan, did you know the great Southern abolitionist Elihu Embree was this honorable young man's ancestor?"

Henry said, "I can only claim to know Mister Embree as a friend. I haven't heard much about his kin."

"Decades before the Civil War," Dr. Cromwell said, "Elihu Embree published the nation's first abolitionist newspaper."

Joseph dropped his pencil and said, "*The Emancipator!*"

Henry said, "The what?"

Joseph said, "*The Emancipator.* It's a newspaper. My daddy has a copy under glass. He's read it to me, a bunch of times."

A white man in his thirties, standing in the aisle and clinging to a leather strap hanging from the car's ceiling, glared at Prayer Bear. Staring back coolly, the prodigious football player waved the back of his hand twice at the man, signaling for him to move away. The man found a strap closer to the front of the car. Dr. Cromwell nodded at Prayer Bear in appreciation.

Dr. Cromwell looked down at the sketch in Joseph's lap and said, "Look at this!"

Henry said, "Joseph is my assistant and my neighbor's boy back in Sewanee."

"Young Master Joseph the artist," the doctor said.

Joseph smiled. "I haven't memorized the names of the different parts of the heart. Henry's still teaching me about all that."

Dr. Cromwell said, "Henry, you've studied anatomy?"

"I've read Claude Sinclair's *Human Anatomy* several times and sketched out his drawings."

Prayer Bear said, "Henry is studying chemistry as well and has concocted his own special liniment."

Henry smiled at Prayer Bear. "My grandmother deserves much of the credit—she taught me a lot." Henry asked Dr. Cromwell, "Are you going to see a patient right now?"

"No, I am reporting to the hospital. My stop is coming up."

Henry said, "It was very fine meeting you, Doctor Cromwell."

"It was a distinct pleasure meeting all three of you," Dr. Cromwell said. "Best of fortune this afternoon on the gridiron."

The three from Sewanee thanked the doctor. After a thoughtful silence, Dr. Cromwell said, "Henry, are you preparing for medical school?"

"I am, but I have no plan on how to find a place or how to pay for it."

Dr. Cromwell said, "I would very much like to begin a correspondence with you. Eventually, I could perhaps, if medicine continues to be of serious interest to you, sponsor your admission to the Department of Medicine at Central Tennessee College."

As his eyes grew wide, Henry drew a deep breath. "Doctor Cromwell, medical school has been on my mind almost every day and night since I lost my wife to typhus, three years ago."

"What was her name?"

"Emma, sir, Emma."

The doctor opened his satchel and took out a silver visiting card case from which he removed a card, handed it to Henry, and said, "Let's see what we can do to further your tribute to Emma Jordan."

The streetcar came to a stop. The doctor stood and shook the hands of his three new acquaintances, all of whom also stood.

After Dr. Cromwell stepped off the car, Prayer Bear put his hand on Henry's shoulder and said, "Don't lose that card, Henry. That's a pass to your Saint Peter's Gate on earth." Then the young man from Jonesborough let out a whoop, drawing stares from everyone on the streetcar. "Sorry y'all, just a little of my hillbilly slipped out. Guess I'm ready for your Tulane men." Prayer Bear whooped again.

Almost an hour later at Crescent City Baseball Park, the two teams were finishing their warm-ups. More than two thousand spectators occupied the grandstands and sidelines. This was Sewanee's seventh contest of the season but Tulane's first, and the Tulane faithful were enthusiastic. Tulane's olive-green and blue school colors dominated the crowd's palette, including young ladies in olive-green and blue vertically striped dresses and bright white hats. Swatches of Sewanee purple could be seen at various points around the field.

On the Sewanee sideline, Turl stood in the middle of the team huddle and said, "More gracious hosts we may never know again. Sportsmanship has imbued our day—it lifts our souls yet in no way tempers our competitive flames. To relent is as unsportsmanlike as foul play. Telfair, please lead us in praise and devotion."

Prayer Bear said, "Henry, may I borrow your Book of Common Prayer, please?" Henry reached in his jacket's breast pocket and handed the tiny volume to Prayer Bear. The guard found the scripture he wanted to share. "Oh almighty God, the Sovereign Commander of all the world. We bless and magnify thy great and glorious Name for this happy Victory, the whole glory whereof we do ascribe to thee, who art the only giver of victory. Amen."

In unison, all but Woody said, "Amen." He was distracted by his aching ankle and the grip of an obsessive thought: *God will never allow a sinner like me to spend my life with an angel like Lillian.*

Coach Lourie reminded the eleven that this was their third game and the sixth day they had ridden the rails since Monday. "So, if you're starting to fatigue, that's perfectly natural, but that is exactly how a smaller and less talented team can take advantage of a bigger and superior eleven. We're going to ease into this one and rely on Kimbrough's leg to deflate Tulane. Once we have them backed up, we will attack offensively."

Fullback Kimbrough Lowndes watched the opening kickoff soar toward him. He marked the turf with his heel on the Sewanee 30-yard line, the ball landed in his hands, and he punted it. On the Tulane 30-yard line, Tulane fullback André Broussard caught the ball and ran straight up the field for six yards before three Tigers gang-tackled him. Tulane tried to buck the Sewanee line twice but gained only two yards in total, so Broussard punted back to Kimbrough, who marked at the Sewanee 40-yard line and punted the ball over the heads of all the Tulane men. The ball landed and rolled to rest on the Tulane 20-yard line, where Broussard dove on the ball and cried out, "Down."

Tulane attacked the Sewanee line again. After no gain on first down, quarterback Judah Levert gave the ball to Broussard. Halfbacks Ollie Pipes and Tilden Peppers guarded Broussard's right and left while Levert led in front. The Tulane mass play shot at the gap between Woody and Patch. Woody tried to slide past his opposing tackle, but when he pushed off of his sprained ankle, pain shot through it and his opponent easily blocked him. This left Patch alone to fill the gap, but Patch was quickly flattened by Tulane's four-man wedge. The backs trampled over him, cleating his shoulders, thighs, and stomach, but they missed his ribs, which he shielded with his arms. Franklin Brownlow and Turl slammed into the Tulane juggernaut, slowing it down enough for other Sewanee players to jump on Broussard and bring him to the ground. It was an eight-yard gain and first down for the Olive and Blue.

On the next set of downs, Tulane's drive stalled at their own 35-yard line. Broussard punted to Kimbrough, who punted it directly back after marking for his fair catch. The soaring football sent Broussard jogging backward to the Tulane 15-yard line. He marked the turf and punted the ball back to Kimbrough, who galloped to midfield to snag the punt in stride and cut just in time to avoid a collision with Tulane's Ollie Pipes. Angling toward the sideline, Kimbrough carried the ball to the Tulane 35 before being shoved hard out of bounds. The crowd cheered in appreciation for Kimbrough's athletic punt return.

Turl looked over at the Sewanee sideline, where the scrubs were whooping loudly. Coach Lourie was expressionless and had his hands clasped behind his head, signaling Turl to abandon the field-position strategy and proceed with an offensive attack. Turl walked in front of quarterback Ham DuBose and gave him a quick nod. The referee, James Bayne, a prominent New Orleans lawyer, had followed the entire communication relay. Bayne blew his whistle, walked directly to Coach Lourie, blew his whistle again, and said, "Coach Lourie is expelled from this contest for instructing players from the sideline." The Sewanee coach acknowledged the referee's pronouncement with a grin.

Alfie said, "Now wait a minute, Mister Bayne—"

Coach Lourie stepped in front of Alfie and said, "Coach Melville, just stay out of Turl's way and everything will be fine." Alfie sighed and the two shook hands.

Coach Lourie went down the line and shook the hands of all of the

Sewanee scrubs. As the coach walked between the sideline and the crowd, some of the Tulane fans jeered him. Without giving any of his detractors any regard, he made his way to the clubhouse.

On the next play, Sewanee's Brownlow plunged for five yards. It was first down on the Tulane 30-yard line. Sewanee set up in formation, and Ham called out "44 trout line, 44 trout line." He and the three other Tiger backs shifted to the right side of the ball. Once he saw everyone was set, Ham said, "Hut, hut!" Sewanee center Otay Carter snapped the ball to what appeared to be no one, but Turl had pivoted and ran to his left. He caught the snapped ball, then curled back to the right. The Sewanee fullback, right halfback, and quarterback all swept right and led interference for Turl, sealing protection for him. He ran around the corner and into the end zone, untouched.

As the Tulane coach watched openmouthed from the sideline, Kimbrough kicked the point after the touchdown over the crossbar and through the uprights. Sewanee six, Tulane zero with fifteen minutes remaining in the first half.

The Tigers were hungry for more points, more dominance, but the Tulane squad had found a soft spot in the Sewanee line. For the next three plays, Tulane sent a mass of backs directly at Woody. The Sewanee right tackle did his best to stall the Tulane wedge, but he was mostly pushing off one leg, and Sewanee gave up forty yards in three downs.

Turl expected that Tulane would blast Woody for a fourth time, so he told the other three Sewanee backs to charge toward Woody at the snap. Judah Levert called his signals, took the snap, and pitched the ball to Broussard, who followed his fellow backs' wedge formation, pointed directly at Woody. Sewanee's Brownlow, Turl, Kimbrough, and Ham slammed the Tulane wedge at the line of scrimmage and broke it apart. Kimbrough's head collided with Broussard's. They both staggered but remained on their feet.

Levert locked arms with Broussard and pulled him forward. Woody plowed his shoulder into Broussard's side and drove him to the turf, but Levert didn't release his teammate's arm. The fullback dropped to his knees and yelled, "Down." The referee blew his whistle. Broussard let go of the football, stood up, and walked to the sideline, grimacing and cradling his arm.

Woody had a burning sensation behind his ankle just above his heel. He hobbled back to the Sewanee side of the line of scrimmage. Turl looked to the sidelines and signaled he was going to send Woody out of the game.

Alfie said, "Peck, get ready."

Turl walked over to Woody and said, "Buddy, you need to sit out the rest of this one."

"I'm not coming out."

Patch put his hand on his roommate's shoulder. "Just rest it up, pal. We'll finish off these runts."

Woody took a long look into the eyes of his friend. On the Sewanee sideline, Thompson Peck stood next to Alfie. Peck started to walk onto the field. Alfie grabbed his jersey and pulled the scrub back. "Wait 'til he comes off."

Woody said to Patch, "Bury them," and Turl and Patch helped the Sewanee tackle off the field. Peck shook Woody's hand, then ran onto the gridiron.

Inspired by Woody's courage over the past three games, the two Tigers went back on the field. They scored two more touchdowns, plus an extra point, before the first half expired, while holding Tulane to only one more first down. Turl scored the second touchdown, and Kimbrough scored the third. At the half, Sewanee led seventeen to zero.

In the clubhouse, Henry gave Woody a drop of laudanum. Ten minutes later, Woody felt slightly intoxicated. Joseph placed Woody's swollen ankle in a bucket of ice water. Patch stood behind Woody and braced him when he slumped or swayed.

As Joseph toweled off Woody's lower leg, Coach Lourie put his hand on Woody's shoulder. "Does it hurt right above your ankle bone?"

"It did, coach, but it's feeling better now."

Henry walked up and gently applied his homemade liniment to Woody's ankle and wrapped it.

During the second half, the Tigers continued to dominate the Tulane offense, but the smaller and less experienced Tulane eleven fought hard on defense, frustrating the increasingly worn-out Sewanee squad.

With twelve minutes left, Sewanee was finally able to buck the Tulane line several times and drive fifty yards over twelve plays. From the Tulane 15-yard line, Ham called out "66 stable boy, 66 stable boy, hut, hut" and Otay Carter snapped the ball to his quarterback, who handed it to Turl. Patch swept across the backfield to the left while Turl went right. As the two passed each other, Turl handed the ball to Patch, who raced around the left end for the final touchdown of the game. Kimbrough successfully kicked the point after the touchdown. The game ended: Sewanee twenty-three, Tulane zero.

Sewanee had failed to cover the twenty-four-point spread that Alfie had considered a safe bet. He had lost $120—his school's, the players', Coach Lourie's and his Princeton teammate's.

While the opponents congratulated each other, Alfie turned his back toward the field and vomited.

Prayer Bear ran over to Alfie. "What's the matter, Alfie boy?"

Henry came over and handed Alfie a towel. "Mister Alfie, you need something for your stomach?"

Alfie shook his head and grabbed the towel. After he wiped off his mouth, he said, "I'm fine."

Prayer Bear said, "Relax, Melville, we're undefeated, unscored on."

Alfie said, "Five to go." He retched but didn't heave. Henry furrowed his brow, and Alfie, seeing the trainer's response, repeated, "I said I'm fine. Go tend to the players, Henry."

Later, in the Saint Charles lobby after the game, the entire Tulane team sat ready to take the Tigers out for a night in New Orleans. One by one, the Tigers trickled downstairs after bathing and dressing up in their most natty attire. Patch and Woody were the last ones down. In their room, Patch had to button Woody's shirt and knot his tie because, thirty minutes earlier, Henry had administered some additional laudanum to Woody. Despite the pain creeping back, Woody had been reluctant to take another dose. But Henry had reassured him, "I'm not going to let you grow a habit to this stuff, Mister Woody, we just gotta stay ahead of the pain. If your Achilles is even slightly torn—well, that can bring a man to his edge."

Woody came downstairs on crutches. He and Patch joined their teammates and Tulane men in the hotel bar. Woody sat down next to André

Broussard, who was sitting at the bar with his arm in a sling and a drink in his free hand. Woody said, "Your elbow back in its place?"

André said, "Should be ready for Texas."

"Let me get a whiskey and we'll drink to that."

André lifted his glass and finished his drink. "I'm the host, what's your pleasure?"

"Jack."

"Bartender, two Jack Daniel's, please."

Patch joined the two young men, and the three finished off a fifth of Jack Daniel's, courtesy of André.

Judah Levert shouted over the crowd: "A toast!" Everyone quieted down and gave the Tulane quarterback their attention. "To the men of the Mountain and to the men of the Crescent City. May we all see each other again, may we all prosper, and may we all find contentment and joy throughout our lives."

Everyone lifted their glasses and yelled, "Cheers!"

Judah said, "And now, we go to feast on Antoine's divine delectables. On us. It is Tulane's honor to treat you men!"

The Tulane men took the Sewanee players, Alfie, and Coach Lourie to Antoine's, where each man was served a dozen oysters and then Pompano Montgolfier. To a man, this dish of crabmeat and shrimp drowned in white sauce delighted the Sewanee guests, as did the steam- puffed thin brown bag in which the extravagant seafood was served. Woody, Turl, and Patch sat at a table with Tulane players Judah, Ollie, and André.

Turl looked at André's right arm, which was in a sling. "André, how is your chicken wing feeling?"

"Really, fine, ever since the doc gave me some laudanum."

Woody took a gulp of white wine and said, "Patch and Sir Turley, I think when we return to the Mountain, we need to request an audience with Vice-Chancellor Wiggins to demand that Pompous Montpellier become standard Sewanee fare." The diners exchanged grins while Woody returned to attacking the seafood on his plate. Then he looked up, at no one in particular, wiped his mouth, and said, "Pompous Montpellier—that's not what it's called, ha!"

After dessert, the hosts gave their guests a choice of activities for the remainder of the evening. They could attend a play at the Bijou Theatre, where Euripides' *The Bacchae* was being performed. Or they could visit one of New Orleans' grandest and most cosmopolitan bars, Saloon Daroux.

Patch put his arm around Woody and said, "They tell me that play is riotous. What do you say we go to the theatre and then call it a night? We've got two more games to go before home."

"Are you daft? We are carousing in the Crescent City, tonight, Mister Mercer."

"I may be daft, but you are definitely intoxicated, my friend. Tomorrow morning's train ride is going to hit you like an iron mace."

"Caution and trepidation from you—I expect better. Wherever that fellow André wants to go, we'll follow."

André was standing behind Woody, overheard him, and said, "Saloon Daroux is both theatre and drink."

Woody said, "Then it is decided. Saloon Daroux!"

On the sidewalk in front of Antoine's, thirteen Tigers followed their theatre hosts toward Royal Street, while Alfie, Coach Lourie, and the remaining eight Sewanee players followed the Tulane starting backfield—Judah Levert, Ollie Pipes, Tilden Peppers, and André Broussard—to Bourbon Street.

It was a mild evening, and Saloon Daroux had all three sets of its double doors wide open. A block away from the bar, the entourage heard the blast of cornets, the thud of a bass, and the rattle of a piano punctuating the din of revelers.

On the sidewalk outside the bar, the Tulane and Sewanee men gathered and watched the dance party going on inside the saloon. Creoles of color danced with Creoles. Several of the Sewanee men had been to New Orleans as tourists with their families, but they had only heard of taboo bars. They had never stood at the threshold of such a raucous scene with wild, provocative dancing and no regard for Southern racial norms.

Some of the Saloon Daroux patrons were in loud colors, while others wore subdued attire—all were dressed up. There was a long bar with five bartenders, all young black men dressed in light blue shirts with pink puff ties and white sleeve garters. The shelves of glistening liquor bottles behind them took their light from several large chandeliers and cast prisms of greens and blues onto the crowd and the vaulted ceiling.

André and his new friend, Woody, were the last to reach the entrance. Leaning on his crutches, Woody said, "What the hell are y'all standing out here for?"

Imitating an old plantation colonel, Tilden Peppers said, "All right, boys, liquor in the front, poker in the rear. Let's get on in there, now."

From the sidewalk, Finn stared at the scene inside the bar. He looked like he was watching a house consumed by lurid flames. To no one in particular, he shook his head and said, "The pit of hell."

Addressing the four Tulane men, Alfie said, "Ah, fellows. I don't know if this will work for all of our guys."

"Does it work for you, Alfie?" Finn said. "*Plessy versus Ferguson,* Alfie." He pointed into the saloon. "Darkies and whites dancing together? Hellfire, Alfie!"

Woody said to Finn, "Why are you so mean, Grayson? We're in New Orleans, for heaven's sake. Let's just go in for some friendly drinking. It's not like we're stepping into a damn whorehouse."

At Woody's coarse language, the Sewanee men gave him startled looks. As one, they looked next at Patch, who said, "Morphine."

Finn said, "*Plessy* Supreme Court ruling, you know it, don't y'all?"

Woody said, "Oh, fuck yourself, Finn." Everyone's heads whipped around to look at Woody again.

Finn said, "What?"

Woody said, "Don't worry. I'm not going to throw you around in the bathroom."

Turl jumped in and said, "In fact, old Woody will buy you a whiskey if you'll come in here and simply behave like one of God's little children."

Woody said, "Make it two whiskeys. Bourbons, rather, of your choice, Mister Finn Grayson of Richmond, Virginia." Woody pressed on the handles of his crutches. "Come on, André, Sodom and Gomorrah here we come." The two entered the saloon.

Alfie turned to Judah and said, "They have billiards?"

Judah said, "Upstairs."

Alfie said, "Well, I'm in," and walked into Saloon Daroux. Tulane's Tilden Peppers and four Tigers followed Alfie into the crowded establishment. Alfie ascended the stairs to the billiards room, confident that he would recover the $120 he owed the others and the team fund.

Coach Lourie and the Tigers who remained outside looked silently at Finn, who scanned the group in disgust and said, "Hell no!"

Turl said, "Just fine. Finn, be sure to be back at the hotel by midnight. I'm goin' in with the rest. Coffey, Peck, y'all do what you want."

Coffey and Peck glanced at Finn and took another look inside Saloon Daroux. "We'll catch up with you later, Finn."

Finn said, "Shut up, Pecker," and sat down on the curb. Tulane's Judah Levert and Ollie Pipes laughed. Coffey and Peck entered the bar.

Turl turned to Patch and pulled him out of earshot of Finn. "Patch?"

"Yes, captain."

"Did you think I had forgotten about you carrying water for missing curfew the night before we left?"

Patch flashed the captain a sly smile. "Now, that's all water under the bridge, Turl."

"No, it's not, but instead of carrying water—your penance is to go with Finn and make sure he gets back to the hotel in one piece."

"What? Are you kidding? I'll just carry the water."

"He's your scrub. Just stay clear of the Tremé—he'll look at some black buck wrong and get his pea brain bashed in."

Patch looked away and then down at the sidewalk. "All right, then, I'll go find another bar with him."

"That's very collegial of you."

Patch shrugged. "Like you said, he's my scrub."

Judah stepped over and shook Turl's hand. "Don't worry. Ollie and I will take care of these boys." Signaling toward the sulking Finn, he continued, "And we'll show that one over there some pretty snow-white New Orleans girls."

Turl said, "Thank you, Judah. Your hospitality will be legendary even before your college days end."

Turl and Coach Lourie went into Saloon Daroux, and Patch sat on the curb next to Finn. "Hey, Finn—Judah and Ollie here want to take you and me around town."

"I'm going to the hotel."

"Come on, Finn, you and I don't pal around much. Let's make a night of it."

Finn rubbed his hands over his face. Then he hopped up and with a little bite in his baritone began singing "Dixie." Judah and Ollie joined in. Soon after, Patch added his voice as the four walked up Bourbon Street.

With their two tourists in tow, Tulane's Ollie and Judah walked briskly to the Old Absinthe House at the corner of Bienville and Bourbon Streets in the French Quarter. The establishment was long and narrow. Near the front was a small bar with six stools, all empty. Two to three patrons sat at each of nine tables, which extended toward the back of the room. A dark-skinned youth, named Tony, was playing an upright piano. He was nattily dressed in a brown three-piece suit and wore a saloon girl's feather headdress.

Patch said, "Dear God. This is delightful."

Finn said, "Can't we find a place with some room to breathe?"

"Forget it, Grayson," Patch said. "This is our destination."

Finn shook his head. "What's the draw? Why are all of these people here?"

Judah pointed to a wall that had French writing on it. "You read French, Finn?"

"German."

"Then let me translate for you. At this establishment in 1812, Andrew Jackson and the pirate Jean Lafitte came to terms on joining forces to defeat the Brits. This bar is a memorial."

Standing behind Finn, Ollie turned the Sewanee scrub around by the shoulders. "More importantly, this is where we dance with the Green Fairy."

Finn scrunched up his face. "What in the hell is that?"

Judah said, "Follow me, our new friends." Sitting on the bar was a six-spigot sterling silver absinthe fountain with an inscribed fleur-de-lis. Placing his hand on the basin, Judah said, "This vessel is packed with iced water. Jean, four absinthes, s'il vous plait." He turned back to Patch and Finn and explained, "All of the bartenders who work here are called 'Jean' in honor of Monsieur Lafitte."

The bartender presented a tray of four Pontarlier glasses, each with a deep emerald green liquid in its bottom third. Balanced on the rim of each glass was a tarnished, slotted, flat spoon in the form of the Eiffel Tower. In the center of the tray was a silver sugar-cube caddy with tongs and sugar cubes end to end.

Judah used the tongs and gently laid a sugar cube on each of the slotted spoons. "Absinthe is the Green Fairy, and she can be just a bit bitter, so we sweeten her up." While he and Ollie demonstrated the process, Judah continued, "Next, gentlemen, put your glasses under a spigot, open the spigot, and adjust your spoon so the water splashes on your cube."

They followed his instructions. Water slowly trickled over and dissolved the sugar cubes.

The four young men lifted their cloudy green glasses.

Ollie said, "Laissez les bon temps rouler!"

While Ollie and Judah were introducing Patch and Finn to the Green Fairy, Alfie was in the Saloon Daroux' billiards room upstairs from the bar. Of the ten men in the room, Alfie was the only one who was white. Alfie watched a man sink five balls in a row and then miss. The pool player's opponent was a long lean man who took his turn and ran the table.

From the spectators' loud response to the man's demonstration of skill, Alfie imagined that the man's feat was half skill and half luck and not typical. The man took a five off the table's head rail and asked, "Who else wants to try to take some of Snooks' cash?"

A jowly man sitting on a stool in the corner shook his head. No one took the offer.

"All right, table's y'all's. I am off to Crabby's." The man who called himself Snooks racked the balls, angled his cue to his right, shot, and scattered the billiard balls. Five of them dropped into five separate pockets.

Alfie said, "I'll shoot a game with you, Mister Snooks."

Everyone in the room looked at him.

Snooks said, "It's Mister Robinson, and you'll need to set down five dollars if you want to play me, sonny boy."

The man's nerve took Alfie aback, but he was sure he could put the arrogant black man in his place and take a lot of his money. At sixteen, Alfie was the best pool player in Mobile. Whenever he shot pool at the Lambda Psi house, he would spot his fraternity brothers two balls and still beat them.

Alfie took out his billfold. He slid out five dollar bills and set his cash on top of the head rail, forcing Snooks to walk from one end of the table to the other, where he matched Alfie's wager. Snooks said, "Rack 'em, boy. Eight-ball."

Reluctantly, Alfie racked the balls. In his entire twenty-one years, he had never heard a black man dare to tell him or any white person what to do. Preserving an opportunity to regain his team's money, Alfie didn't say anything or give even a slight look of disapproval.

The men in the room were silent, focused entirely on the impending match. Snooks shot the cue ball. It struck the one-ball with such force that the impact and chain reaction sounded like a dry, thick log snapping in the middle of the night. A red and a black ball each went into opposite side pockets. Snooks said, "Red." In four shots, he pocketed the remaining five red balls. For the eight-ball, he had a straight shot at a corner pocket, but he called the corner pocket at the opposite end. Without hesitation, Snooks took his shot. The eight-ball hit the foot cushion and rolled the length of the table into the called pocket.

Expressionless, Alfie held out a five-dollar bill. "Double or nothing."

Snooks took the five. "Rack 'em."

"Gladly."

Snooks ran the table again. Alfie doubled down two more times and never got a single turn to shoot. There was now forty dollars on the table. Out of the corner of his eye, Alfie noticed Coach Lourie standing at the top of the stairs that led to the billiards room. The coach nodded at the Sewanee football manager.

Snooks said, "I'm feeling a bit charitable, young man. You take this break."

As he racked the balls, Alfie said, "Very kind gesture, thank you."

He set up to break, and Snooks said, "Hold on. Where's your bet? I'm not feeling that generous."

Alfie took out his billfold, removed his remaining cash, and counted it. He had thirty dollars left. He stacked three tens on the pile of cash. "I'm good for the other ten, should you get lucky a fifth time in a row." Motionless, Snooks stared at Alfie.

Coach Lourie walked over to the pool table and placed a ten-dollar bill on the stack.

Alfie smiled, then launched the cue ball. Two red balls and a black ball dropped into pockets. "Red, naturally."

One by one, Alfie dispatched four more red balls, shaping each shot. He had a bank shot to sink his final red ball. He struck the cue ball and grazed the red ball, which hit a side cushion, then rolled slowly to the opposite side pocket and dropped in.

Alfie's heart began to race. His shot left him in a nearly impossible position for putting the eight-ball away. The cue ball and the eight-ball were aligned perpendicular to the foot cushion, with only half an inch separating the eight-ball from the foot cushion and from the cue ball. Alfie's best line was to the right corner pocket at the other end of the table. He pointed at that pocket.

Snooks said, "Lot of green, long masse."

Alfie remembered his uncle telling him to never forget to breathe when shooting pool. He swelled, then relaxed his chest. Alfie took his pool stick and threaded it between his left thumb and index finger. He angled the stick downward just off from the apex of the cue ball. He noticed his hands were remarkably still. He hit the cue ball. It spun backward while it slid forward and struck the eight-ball, which hit the foot cushion and rolled directly toward the called pocket. It slowly lost its momentum as it approached the pocket. Alfie knew it would drop and he would go downstairs with the same amount of money he had walked upstairs with. Snooks grinned as the eight-ball eased up to the pocket and stopped at its edge. Coach Lourie turned and walked downstairs.

Alfie had none of his own money left and was still $120 in the hole.

Downstairs Alfie joined Coach Lourie, who was sitting at the bar. "Hobie."

"Alfie."

"Thanks for spotting me. I'll get it back to you before we get home." Alfie sat down next to the coach.

"How're you going to do that?"

"Not sure yet, and I've got more troubles on top of that."

Coach Lourie saw that Alfie's right leg was bouncing up and down. "You want a drink?"

"Please."

"Bartender, double whiskey."

Alfie downed the drink. "You mind taking care of one more?"

The coach ordered another drink for himself and Alfie. "What are your troubles other than being flat broke? I can carry you for the rest of the trip."

Alfie took a sip. "You got one hundred and twenty dollars?"

"What?"

"That doesn't include the fresh ten I owe you."

Coach Lourie furrowed his brow. "One hundred and twenty dollars?" Alfie explained the spread bet. Coach Lourie had never heard of this betting technique, either. "You put yourself—no, all of us—in a fix, didn't you?"

"Yeah."

Alfie and Coach Lourie sat and slowly finished their drinks without speaking. Then Coach Lourie said, "Barkeep, I'd like to close out my tab."

Alfie asked, "You're all done?"

"We need to get these men to bed. They've got another train ride and football game tomorrow."

"I'll get Turl to help me round them up."

The bartender said, "Two bits, sir."

Coach Lourie laid a dollar on the bar. Without looking at Alfie, he slid off his stool and left.

***

At the Old Absinthe House, a portly man with jet-black hair was sitting at a table in the back of the room. Beside the man sat a blond woman wearing a gold wide-brimmed hat.

Finn leaned against a wall and stared at the man, who was sketching on a large tablet, without taking his eyes off the woman.

Standing next to Finn, Patch grinned as he surveyed the room and sipped his sixth glass of the Green Fairy. His gaze reached his teammate. He looked Finn up and down and nudged him. "Hey, your glass is empty. You wearing a dress tonight?" Patch laughed. Finn pointed at the artist and, in the air, tried to trace the large man's silhouette, but created a figure eight instead of an outline.

Patch squinted. "Magic? Wait." He nudged Finn again. "Is he drawing or scribbling?"

Dragging out the word, Finn said, "Drawing."

At the bar, Judah and Ollie stood in front of the absinthe fountain. "What are those two inebriates doing up there?" said Judah.

Ollie handed his empty glass to him. "I'll go see, and you pour four more."

The Tulane student weaved between the tables and reached his two guests. "Boys, we must not leave her waiting."

"Who?" Finn asked.

Patch grimaced. "The Green Fairy, you ninny."

Ollie put his arms around their shoulders and began to guide them toward the bar.

Finn pulled away from his host. "Wait a minute. Who's that fat man?"

"Papa Provenzano," Ollie said. He lowered his voice. "They say he was one of the dagoes who shot and killed New Orleans' police chief, back in '90."

"Dagoes?" Patch asked loudly.

Ollie put his finger to his mouth and shushed Patch. "Italians."

Finn nodded while smirking. "Dagoes, Patch, you know, dagoes. They were all over the Quarter today. Food stands, everywhere—Moretti's Fruit. Giordano's Fish. Damn papists."

Patch finished his drink and wiped his mouth. "He's drawing without looking at what he's drawing."

Ollie nodded. "He never looks even when he's finished. He draws peculiar portraits for people as they fly with the Green Fairy."

"Speaking of which," Patch said. "Time to return to her fountain, Finny boy."

The three rejoined Judah, who had prepared a tray of four absinthe potions. Standing next to the bar, the young men sipped their drinks.

The Tulane quarterback smiled. "Sweet euphoria."

Patch had his eyes closed. He nodded at Judah's comment.

Finn pointed toward the back of the room. "He finished!"

"Who? What?" asked Patch.

"The Papa. He gave her the drawing."

They all turned their attention to Provenzano's table. The lady looked at her portrait and kissed the artist on the cheek. Then she walked over to the piano and stood next to Tony. While he continued to play, she showed him Papa Provenzano's rendering of her. Tony grinned and nodded. She then kissed him.

Patch said, "Whoa! Back in Georgia, that boy'd hang from a tree."

Finn stood with his mouth agape and then said, "That black devil!"

He stomped toward the piano player, but Judah grabbed his arm and spun him around. "If you lay a hand on that negro, this crowd will send you back to Tennessee in a pine box."

Ollie added, "And we'll be personas non grata for bringing you here."

Finn scowled. "No white woman would do that without . . . He's doing something wicked back there."

"No ruckus, Grayson," Patch said.

Finn rushed to the back of the room. Patch and Ollie followed him.

Looming over Provenzano, Finn tried to speak, but nothing came out. On his sketch pad, Provenzano tapped his pencil to the rhythm of the tune Tony was playing. After a few moments, Finn turned and stared blankly at Patch.

Ollie said, "That boy has turned sheet white."

Finn's hands began to shake. Without looking up, Papa Provenzano pointed at the empty chair beside him. Expressionless, Finn slowly sat down, and the artist began a new sketch.

Patch sighed and ran his hand over his face. "I've got to get him out of here."

Ollie wagged his finger. "Can't do it. Very dangerous. The séance has begun." He pointed at a nearby empty table. "Let's sit down over there."

Finn sat motionless, while he stared at Provenzano's emerging portrait.

Ollie's glass was empty. He gently tilted it from side to side. "Another?"

Patch shook his head. "No thanks. My current altitude is fine. This is all thrilling enough."

"Don't be too concerned. Why, Papa hasn't shot a soul in almost a decade."

Patch raised his eyebrows at Ollie.

"Just a jest. You need another dose of the Green—"

"Good God!" Finn shrieked.

Tony stopped playing, and the Old Absinthe House fell silent. Everyone turned and watched Finn. He wadded up the drawing and bolted the length of the bar, zigzagging between tables. He grazed one and sent two Pontarlier glasses to the floor, where they shattered. Ollie and Patch chased Finn, who stumbled at the front door and smashed through it. He fell onto the sidewalk. A light fog draped the street.

Judah came out of the bar. "What the hell happened?"

Finn paced with his hands stuffed in his pant pockets. "Goddamn infernal trip! Here's what the hell happened." He pegged Judah in the chest with the crumpled sheet.

Judah picked it up and smoothed it out. "My, my." Papa Provenzano had created an eerily well-drawn likeness of Finn—except for the added feature of twisted horns growing out of Finn's head.

Finn stopped pacing, looked at Judah, and said, "Fucking dago."

Judah shredded the drawing and threw it in the gutter. "Sometimes the Green Fairy swoops down to hell for the thrill of it. Can't blame old Provenzano for it."

Patch walked over and put his hand on Finn's shoulder. "Come on, the Green Fairy is no match for Finn Grayson."

Ollie said, "You boys have the gumption to visit New Orleans' finest house of ill-repute?" Finn looked at Ollie and began to pace again.

Stepping in front of Finn, Patch said, "I'm game if you are."

Finn stopped and looked up at the moon. He started to say something, then paused.

Patch smiled. "What do you think?"

Finn snorted. "Well, shit, if I'm going to ride all over tarnation and not play a down of football, I'm at least going to wrestle with a naked girl."

The four walked to Storyville, New Orleans' tenderloin district, and arrived on Basin Street in front of Madame Lulu White's Chateau Mahogany.

Ollie said, "Here we are, gentlemen—the Crescent City's premier den of pleasurable delicacies." Patch smiled broadly and approached the front door. "Wait, tiger. First Mister Levert and I need to speak with Madame Lulu. Y'all wait here."

Patch and Finn stood with their backs to the Chateau Mahogany.

Patch looked up the street and saw a woman emerge from the fog. She was in a green gown and walking down the middle of Basin Street. Softly he said, "Cecilia?" The woman turned her head toward him. A white Greek chorus mask concealed her face. Patch's heart pounded and his spine tingled.

Finn glanced up and down the empty street. "Who are you talking to?"

Patch's eyes followed the woman. "What is she?"

Finn clicked his tongue. "Who?"

Patch looked at Finn. "You didn't see her?"

Finn raised his eyebrows. "No one out here, my friend, except we two. And our pocket horns." He chuckled and slapped Patch on the back.

"Green Fairy. She plays tricks."

"Damn right she does!"

They stared at each other for a moment. Then Finn gave Patch a suspicious look. "What did you say a minute ago? Cecilia?" Patch shrugged his shoulders and shook his head. "You know, pal. It'd be grand if you had Turl substitute me in for you."

"Would it? Pal."

"I just mean when we've put the game away. That's all."

Judah came out of the brothel's front door. "Y'all come in now and meet Madame Lulu and her ladies. Well, her girls, too."

They followed Judah into the house. After passing an ornate spiral staircase, they entered a large sitting room. "The octoroon parlor," Judah said. He introduced Patch and Finn to Madame White, who sat on a divan as she smoked a cigar.

She tilted her head back and blew smoke. "Welcome to our party, boys."

Gussie Davis's rich voice came out of the Victrola, the lighting was soft, and the Victorian furniture had gilded cabriole legs and equally curvaceous armrests. The ceiling was fifteen feet high, and two large bay windows were adorned with drawn green velvet drapes.

Patch surveyed the room, its furnishings, and its tantalizingly clothed girls and women. "Lascivious opulence," he murmured. Then he wondered if the scene was another one of the Green Fairy's deceits. The apparition on the street came to his mind. Patch envisioned Cecilia in place of the masked woman. He shook his head and, under his breath, said, "Nonsense. As thin a substance as the air." His imagination returned to Cecilia. She is in bed reading a book—*Over the Alps on a Bicycle.* Its cover is an illustration of a man and woman riding bicycles high on a winding mountain path, with a sheer dropoff. He pictured riding down a mountain pass on a tandem bicycle with Cecilia.

Madame Lulu's cigar smoke reached Patch's nose. The sweet smell brought his attention back to the room and dissolved the image of Cecilia.

The boys sat down together on a long sofa. Each was served a flute of champagne, which they quickly drained. As soon as a glass was emptied, a girl refilled it.

Patch's third glass of champagne revived the Green Fairy's benevolent side. He began to see everything in the room as slightly soft around the edges. The altered perception amused him. The same aura extended to the women and girls in the octoroon parlor. Several were sitting on sofas, with their arms draped over men—white men, all of them, young and old.

One girl, who Patch thought was several years younger than him, stood by the Victrola and drank champagne with a short, plump man in his thirties. Nearby, two ladies were dancing with each other. The young girl changed the cylinder whenever a song finished.

A tall, older woman was dressed in a sheer lime-colored gown held up by a thin strap over each shoulder. The straps were on the verge of sliding off her shoulders, but they held as she slowly twirled for a gray-haired man seated at eye level with her hips.

A young man with fire-red hair and beard sat at a tableau a jeu that had an inlaid ivory backgammon board. Sitting across from him was a lady who wore high-heeled boots and a canary-yellow chemise that barely covered the upper halves of her thighs. The two were playing a spirited match of backgammon and, under the table, were gently teasing each other with their feet.

At a circular couch divided by three armrests, three couples sat drinking and flirting. One couple included a tall thin man with a shock of shoulder-length silver hair. He sat caressing a woman's inner thigh. She wore thigh-high black needle-lace stockings with frond patterns traced with tiny pearl beads. A scalloped-lace shawl wrapped just below her shoulders. As the silver-haired man stroked her leg, he gently blew on the nape of her neck.

In a corner of the room was a girl Patch thought to be in her late teens or early twenties. All of the ladies had thick dark hair and olive to medium-brown skin tones, except this one, who had soft, curly, auburn hair and pale skin dotted with yellow and tan freckles. Drinking champagne and with her long, lean legs crossed, she sat slumped in a large baroque armchair. Red and white vertically striped stockings reached halfway up her thighs. A crocheted white half-sari cascaded over her breasts and almost met the top of her stockings.

Patch was about to stand and approach the young woman, but he relaxed into the sofa when he noticed Finn staring at her. Ollie elbowed Patch. "Your scrub is hypnotized."

"That he is," Patch replied. "What is that vision's name?"

"Cheri."

The auburn-haired girl looked at Finn and took a sip from her glass, smiled, and then slid over and made room for him to sit next to her. Finn stood and slowly crossed the room, never taking his eyes off Cheri's. He walked into her chair's armrest, grabbed the back of the chair to brace himself, and, standing over her, extended his palm to her.

Chapter Eight
Saturday, November 11th, 1899

The next morning, Finn awoke in a canopy bed next to Cheri. The two lay nude atop the sheets. Cheri was asleep facing the ceiling. Her auburn hair fanned out over the pillow. Finn surveyed her and decided she was the most exquisite creature he would ever hold—or even view. He moved to wake her with a kiss, then stopped, afraid he had missed the Mountain Goat's departure.

He bolted out of bed. Pain shot through his head, staggering him. "Goddammit!"

His outburst awoke Cheri, who wiped the sleep from her eyes and looked at Finn. She said, "Dancing with the Green Fairy is always expensive."

Ignoring her, Finn dressed quickly.

Cheri shifted so her left leg dangled over the side of the bed and her right was propped up. As she stared out the window, she said, "It is ten dollars for your dance with me. Leave it on my coiffeuse, s'il vous plait."

"Ten dollars?"

"Oui, monsieur."

"Forget it. I'm not paying that much."

Cheri pushed a buzzer attached to the near side of her nightstand.

"What is that?"

She rose, put on a robe, and walked over to a claw-foot bathtub in the center of the room. "I am sorry you are disappointed—you were so very pleased last night—but you can check the blue book. There is an added expense for my kind."

"What the hell is the blue book? A Sears and Roebuck for goddamn whores?"

A man with olive skin appeared at the door carrying a large pot of hot water. Six and a half feet tall and bald with a distractingly misshapen head, he wore knee-high leather boots and had a buck knife strapped to his leg. He looked Finn up and down and said, "Sois polis, touristique." His steps thundered as he crossed the planked floor to the bathtub, where he poured the water.

Addressing Cheri, Finn said, "So you're a Creole. There's a premium for Creole hookers?"

The attendant dropped the empty pot and patted his knife.

Cheri set her right foot on the edge of the bathtub, revealing her leg. She slid her hand up the inside of her thigh and said, "Should be twenty for an extra special girl like me. Je suis une Creole de couleur."

Finn said, "What? You're a—"

"You visited the Cynthean forest of a quadroon last night, monsieur."

Finn raised an open hand and moved toward Cheri. The attendant grabbed his arm, forced it behind his back, and steered him out of the room.

In the hallway, Finn squirmed. The attendant tightly gripped Finn's Adam's apple and said, "Dix." Finn dug into his trouser pocket and pulled out a gold ten-dollar coin, which he held out away from his side. The man reached, snatched the coin, and released Finn.

Finn said, "Mon ami?"

The attendant drew his knife and pointed it toward a closed door down the hall. Finn strode to the door and knocked once. He put his ear to the panel but heard no response, so he entered the room. Patch and a prostitute were passed out half dressed on a long royal-blue divan. Finn stormed toward his teammate and said, "Mercer, get up. Get up, Mercer!" Patch did not open his eyes. Finn put two fingers under Patch's nose and felt him breathe steadily. Finn stood upright and gazed out the room's sole window, which was over the divan. He looked down at Basin Street and then noticed the attendant leaning against the doorway frame.

Finn bent down and whispered in Patch's ear, "Mercer. We've got to go."

Patch didn't stir. Finn took a deep breath and quietly walked toward the door. As he slid past the man, he said, "Excusez-moi."

***

At the Saint Charles Hotel, eight teammates were searching the building for their team's right end, while another eight were looking for him throughout the French Quarter. Woody and Prayer Bear, badly hung over, were standing on a packed streetcar traveling to the Tulane campus to find Ollie and Judah. Propped up by his crutches, Woody had a steadily worsening sensation of a shovel blade prying open the front of his skull.

Back at the hotel, in its luggage room, Turl, Coach Lourie, and Alfie surrounded Finn, who sat slumped on a suitcase.

Turl put his face close to Finn's. "After the Absinthe House, where'd they take you?"

"I don't know. Have you ever drank that poison? Couldn't see the holes in a ladder half the time—goddamn, I'm lucky to be alive."

Coach stood with his arms folded. "Your teammate, Finn! Is he alive?"

"Of course he is. What're you saying. . . I left him for dead?"

Alfie began to pace. "When was the last time you spoke to Patch?"

Finn covered his eyes and rubbed them. "I didn't want to stay at the Green Fairy place, and he told me—"

Turl said, "Told you what?"

"It was our destiny."

The captain held Finn by the jaw. "What? Go get Embree, Alfie."

Finn pulled away from Turl's grip. "No! No Embree!"

"He and Woody are looking for Ollie and Judah," Alfie responded. "When did you last see your two guides, Finny?"

"At the Absinthe House, as I told you. Next thing I know it's sunny and I am walking down Rampart Street with a fucking ice pick splitting my skull." After a long pause, Finn asked, "Can I go bathe and pack?"

Turl took a step back from Finn, cocked his head, and asked, "You don't want to go look—"

"Yes, let me go look for him. I'll . . ."

Alfie said, "You better find him. Embree cussed you loudly in the lobby, called you a heathen Cain before he and Woody headed out."

Finn stared off into space.

Turl said, "Get!"

***

On the Tulane campus, Woody spotted the school's football team manager and waved at him. "Good morning."

The manager waved back and met Woody and Prayer Bear in the center of a courtyard. "I thought you gents would be on your way to Baton Rouge by now."

Prayer Bear said, "Train leaves in an hour."

Woody pushed down on his crutches' grips and stood up straight. "We're looking for your Judah and Ollie."

Smiling, the manager said, "Didn't y'all beat on those boys enough yesterday?"

Prayer Bear adjusted his eye patch and grinned. "Yes, we did."

Woody said, "We want to thank them for their exceedingly excellent hospitality."

Prayer Bear said, "And particularly we want to thank them for taking care of our star end and his backup last night."

For a few seconds, the manager looked blankly at Prayer Bear. Then he smiled. "Our pleasure. Ollie and Judah stay in that cottage." He pointed. "Third one up. Goodspeed to Baton Rouge, and we hope to host Sewanee prochaine année."

Prayer Bear said, "This is my and Mister Barnwell's last season, but I think all who remain will want to return next year. Please thank your whole team on our behalf for treating us so well."

The three young men shook hands. Woody hobbled on his crutches as fast as he could toward the cottage. Prayer Bear jogged ahead. The manager walked quickly in the opposite direction.

Prayer Bear reached the cottage he had been directed to and banged on the door. He smiled at the long, lean student who opened the door. "Hi there, friend. Ollie and Judah here?"

"They live in the gray cottage over there."

At Ollie and Judah's cottage, the Tulane manager busted into the back bedroom where the two friends were sleeping fully clothed with shoes on. They were piled on a large bed atop its bedspread. "Wake up, you mullets!" He shook them roughly. "That one-eyed giant and the beefy Sewanee tackle are outside hunting for you two."

By the time Prayer Bear entered the cottage and looked out the open bedroom window, the three Tulane men had dashed out of sight.

Fifty minutes later Woody and Prayer Bear were at the New Orleans Union Station with their teammates—all except Patch.

Woody and Alfie Melville stood on the platform alongside the Mountain Goat while everyone else sat in the Pullman. Woody's head and ankle throbbed.

With a hand on one of the Mountain Goat's wheels, Alfie stared at his pocket watch while Woody leaned on his crutches and stared at the gate he prayed Patch would walk through. Prayer Bear had put Finn in a full Nelson and had gotten him to admit that Patch and he had spent the night with two barmaids. Finn claimed he had tried, unsuccessfully, to pry Patch from the girl and pull him out of bed. After hearing this, Woody had told himself that his roommate was in no danger.

Now, with the Mountain Goat's departure imminent, Woody wondered if he should stay behind. Injured and unable to play, was his first obligation to be with his team or to wait for Patch? Increasingly anxious, several times he silently recited *Oh, God, make clean our hearts within us. And take not thy Holy Spirit from us.*

Alfie closed his watch and looked up at the Mountain Goat engineer. "Baton Rouge, sir!" He walked past Woody and said, "Let's get on board, Mister Barnwell—working on a legend, here."

***

Halfway to Baton Rouge, the team's Pullman car was quiet as the Mountain Goat passed cotton and sugarcane fields. There were no card games and no music. The passengers reclined, stared out the window, rested their eyes, or napped.

Woody had chosen to stay at the train station and wait for Patch.

Alfie sat alone. Back in Sewanee, he had promised the vice-chancellor that he would manage everything and that nothing but good would come from this trip. Now after a remarkable first five days, Alfie had abandoned the Bishop of Georgia's grandson in New Orleans and had no remaining travel funds. He also had left behind a prized seminary student who was on crutches.

Coach Lourie and Alfie's dream of developing a Southern football juggernaut had looked so promising just a day earlier. And now, for the first time on the trip, the coach had chosen not to sit next to Alfie.

They had become friends soon after Coach Lourie arrived on the Mountain in late spring to take over as football coach. In addition to enjoying each other's company, they were an enterprising partnership of mutual respect. Alfie and Coach Lourie had gone to the vice-chancellor three times before receiving permission and financial support for the trip west. Each time, they proclaimed that a dominant football program would bestow enduring national prestige on Sewanee. After the third interview, Alfie and Coach Lourie exited the vice-chancellor's study, and in the hallway the coach said, "Bring a crate of money back to the Mountain and he'll be Sewanee football's biggest booster."

"Oh, I will, and if you bring back five wins he'll make you the highest-paid coach in the South." A week later, Alfie and Coach Lourie received the blessing they had sought.

On the train to Baton Rouge, Alfie reached into his jacket's breast pocket and took out the vice-chancellor's letter of approval for the trip. He silently read the document he had hoped would be framed in a trophy room yet to be built and yet to be named after Alpheus Melville and Hobart Lourie.

Dear Mr. Melville,

My last meeting with you and Coach Lourie was both illuminating and reassuring. Subsequently, after prayer and consultation with colleagues,

I have decided to allow you to proceed with your well-conceived and well-planned nine-day Sewanee football excursion.

Alpheus, I have great admiration for your family, and you are proving as loyal to the New South as the Melville men whom I have been blessed to know for decades.

You and Coach Lourie have articulated a grand yet tenable vision of Sewanee as the first preeminent football institution in the South. The Yale for colleges south of the Mason-Dixon line.

I have every confidence that you will properly execute this tour, due to your breeding, sincerity, intelligence, and Faith.

Please make an appointment to revisit my office, so you can record the administration's reporting requirements and general expectations of you and the Sewanee team as you go abroad clad in Sewanee purple.

In Service of Our Lord, Country, and College,
Benjamin Lawton Wiggins, Vice-Chancellor, Sewanee, The University of the South

Alfie rested the letter on his lap.

Coach Lourie said from beside him, "You mind sliding over?"

Alfie, though startled, quickly obliged. "My window seat is always yours."

Coach Lourie sat down and watched black field hands scattered between rows of cotton. Then he looked over at the vice-chancellor's letter. The team manager, self-conscious, folded the letter and placed it back in his suit coat's breast pocket.

The coach turned his head toward the window. "Don't lose that letter."

Alfie looked at his friend and tried to appreciate Coach Lourie's optimism. Instead, he felt shame and desperation.

Someone was having a coughing fit in one of the berths behind them.

"I won't."

"It will be framed one day." The coughing stopped. "Have you come up with any ideas for your situation?"

"One I don't like."

As they sat in silence, the coughing began again. Alfie and Coach Lourie rose to see who was sick. It was Kimbrough. Henry was applying a balm to the fullback's chest. At the same time, Joseph cradled Kimbrough's wrist, sprained in the Texas game, and applied liniment to it.

Alfie and Coach Lourie slowly sat back down.

"Two more games, Kimbrough, two more," Alfie said.

"Don't worry. He's got too much grit to quit."

Alfie slowly nodded his head.

"So, tell me about this idea that you don't like."

With his palms, Alfie rubbed his eyes. "Something I've never done before."

"What is that?"

"Ask my father for money."

"That'd be hard for me, too."

After a brief silence, Alfie said, "Everything was clicking along."

"Well, there was Finn's assaults on Henry, and Embree's retribution." They both looked at Finn, who had his eyes closed and was sitting next to a sleeping and slack-jawed Peck. "And, of course, a missing right end."

Alfie jerked his thumb toward Finn and Peck. "Are those two prepared to play?"

"We'll know in a couple of hours." The coach pursed his lips. "Ah, we should be fine. They practice hard. They know the plays."

The Mountain Goat began curving to the right, which pushed Peck onto Finn's lap. Finn shoved his friend back over onto his seat. He closed his eyes again and returned to imagining himself at Patch's position, executing each of Sewanee's thirty-one offensive plays. The train's clickety-click beat set the rhythm of Finn's mental football practice. He was focused.

With Patch's football future uncertain, Finn saw the upcoming game against Louisiana State as an opportunity to take Patch's spot on the eleven for the remainder of the season. Finn's father had promised to attend the season finale against North Carolina. Finn dreaded the prospect of sitting on the bench with his father in the stands.

***

While the Mountain Goat burned wood and rolled along the Mississippi, Woody sat in the shed of the New Orleans Union Station. The trip, the games, his injury, and his night in New Orleans had exhausted him. Further fatiguing Woody were images of Patch beaten, dead in an alley, and floating in the Mississippi.

Unable to bear those horrible tableaux, Woody assured himself that God would take care of Patch. He prayed, asking God to protect his friend.

Soon, visions of Lillian interrupted his devotion. Woody pictured her smiling at him, both at the Texas German Ball and on the beach at Galveston. He saw flashes of her playing tennis. Walking to her classes. Dining at an elegant restaurant.

Then they were on the Houston field after the Texas A&M game had ended. Woody and Lillian were completely alone. The sky was a strata of slate blue and gray. Her shoulders were bare. He looked down and she was bare-chested.

A tap on his shoulder startled him. "Ah!" He whipped his head around and faced Patch.

"Easy, Woodrow."

"Where have you been?"

"Looking for you."

"Priceless, Patch. Tell me where you were. I've got a right to know—I stayed behind to wait on you."

"So, they left us."

"No, they left you, because you gave them no choice, unless they wanted to forfeit today's game."

"I bet Finn is licking his chops."

"Why are you so late?"

"What did Finn say?"

"That you were with a girl."

Patch grimaced and pressed his hands against the sides of his head. "Goddamn wailing cats."

"Lust and blasphemy, you're intent on infuriating our Heavenly Father. And, by the way, He has nothing to do with your wailing cats."

Patch looked to the sky. "Please forgive me, Lord, but you might want to smite that Green Fairy flying around this town."

"You know, despite guzzling last night and having to look for you this morning, we all made it to the train on time. You're the team prima donna, Patch."

Patch began to pace. He stopped with his back to Woody. "Thank you for waiting on me, Woody. You're the best friend I'll ever have."

"Don't try to charm me."

"When is the next train?"

"An hour."

"I'll pay for your ticket. How did they know I wasn't sliced up and bleeding in some alley?"

"Finn told us he tried to rouse you but you told him to go on."

"Everyone took him at his word?"

"It fits your reputation."

"Maybe we'll get there in time for the second half. I'll take great pleasure watching Coach take Finn out of the game."

"You don't understand, do you? Everyone is angry. You let us all down."

"I bet Finn was jolly."

"Forget about Finn and worry about Patch. You know—you and I are too inside ourselves. I'm buried in self-doubt and worry. You're all wrapped up in your prurient desires, serving yourself more than your teammates, fraternity brothers, or family."

"You think you're the only tortured soul?"

"What could possibly be torturing you, Patch?"

"How about being strapped to a life you have no interest in? Call it ungodly, base, or sinful, but I would be happier living a debauched life and brokering cotton here in New Orleans than becoming an Episcopal priest. Woody, I don't want to spend a single morning at the seminary. I'm not my father, my uncle, my grandfather, Prayer Bear, or you."

There was silence except for the sound of squeaky wheels. A porter was pushing a hand cart loaded with a wardrobe trunk.

Woody used his crutches to stand. "So, do you want a debauched life, or Cecilia Fontaine?"

Patch's whole body became tense. He scowled. "How long have you known?

"Since the beginning of fall."

"Who else—who else knows?"

"No one, as far as I know."

"Let me tell you—it has always been a tender but proper relationship between Miss Fontaine and me."

"I don't doubt that. She is an extremely fine person from an incomparable family."

"How did you find out?"

"I was cleaning up one morning, after a poker game in our room. You had left your jacket on the back of a chair. When I draped it over my arm, your money clip and a card fell out—"

"You read the card! Didn't you!"

"I did."

"Astounding."

"I returned the items to your jacket. Instead of going to class, I sat on my bed praying for God's guidance and forgiveness. I wanted to confess, but when you came in, I was too ashamed."

"So, you missed class?"

"Yes. Ironically, Moral Theology."

Patch watched the porter deliver a large crate to the shed. He noticed the wheels were not squeaking. "You've never missed a class, even at Saint Mathias." Woody sat back down, and Patch took one of his crutches and leaned on it. "How did you know it was Cecilia?"

"In the note, you mentioned the cello, tea, and Hiawassee House."

Patch sat down next to Woody and sighed. Then he held out his hand. Woody shook the proffered hand.

Patch said, "I actually feel relieved. At least I have someone to talk to about this. And I promise you—although our attraction to each other is strong, what Cecilia and I have is an affair of the heart, nothing further."

***

At the Baton Rouge Union Station's Western Union counter, Alfie read his telegram to his father out loud to Coach Lourie:

```
DADDY,

I HOPE THIS MESSAGE FINDS YOU AND MOTHER DOING
WELL. WE HAVE SWEPT TEXAS AND LAID WASTE TO
HALF OF LOUISIANA. HOWEVER, TEAM EXPENSES HAVE
EXCEEDED OUR TRAVEL FUNDS, DUE TO MY
MISMANAGEMENT AND ALSO UNANTICIPATED EXPENSES.
I WOULD LIKE TO EXPLAIN THIS TO THE VICE
CHANCELLOR IN PERSON. 230 DOLLARS WILL CARRY
US ON TO THE MOUNTAIN. PLEASE WIRE THIS AMOUNT
TO THIS WESTERN UNION OFFICE, AND I WILL
RETURN THE SUM THROUGH REDUCTIONS IN MY
MONTHLY ALLOWANCE.

LOVE AND GRATITUDE,
ALPHEUS
```

Coach Lourie paid for the telegram and said, "Will he send the money?"
"I don't know. Self-reliance is his motto."

Chapter Nine

Saturday, November 11th, 1899, Baton Rouge, Louisiana

The Louisiana State Tigers and the Sewanee Tigers warmed up on State Field on the Louisiana State campus. The crowd was the smallest the Tigers had seen on the trip, with eleven hundred coming through the gate.

Coach Lourie kneeled on the turf and ran his hand over the grass. He turned to Henry and said, "Feel this, Henry, it's like velvet."

Henry leaned over and swept his hand back and forth over the blades. "Our men are so used to that Sewanee sandlot, they could fall asleep when they get tackled."

Coach Lourie laughed and said, "They might, they're tired." He walked over to where the Sewanee team was stretching and doing calisthenics. "Turl, they ready to run through plays?"

Turl said, "Let's go, men. Line up." The eleven, with Finn and Peck in for Patch and Woody, walked through the team's offensive plays. After several simple mistakes, Turl gathered his team together.

Standing in the middle of the huddle, Turl said, "Do y'all hail from Sewanee Mountain or from the valley of sullen wenches? This is a historic march, men. We're down two of our eleven, but we have seniors Finn Grayson and Thompson Peck to fill the gaps. We start anew right here. No more debauchery of any type. The Mountain Goat has us rounding the bend—keep feeding her! We return to Sewanee better men, better Christians, and the pride of the South.

We've stumbled, yet we haven't fallen. Please lead us in prayer, Telfair."

They all bowed their heads except for Prayer Bear. He stared at Finn, who felt the gaze directed at him and lifted his head. Prayer Bear looked directly into Finn's eyes, then bowed his head. "'Lord, who shall rest upon thy holy hill? He who hath used no deceit in his tongue nor done evil to his neighbor.' Lord, as men of Your holy church, we ask that You reward our penance and our reverence, however unworthy we may be. It is in communion with our King that our prowess manifests. Our hearts must be open to Your Holy Presence for us to find victory on this field of play. 'The Lord shall give strength unto His people.'"

"Amen," the team said in unison.

At midfield, the referee and the umpire went over several rules with Turl and Louisiana State's captain and quarterback, Red Lemoine. The rest of the Sewanee team gathered on their sideline.

Finn sat down on the bench, shoulders tight and a crick in his neck. He looked over at Henry and thought about asking for help, but he couldn't bring himself to do it. Finn turned away and rubbed his neck and shoulders.

Henry walked over and stood next to Finn. "What's wrong with your shoulders, Mister Finn?"

Finn gave Henry a suspicious look. "Nothing. And I'm starting in this game, so forget about telling coach I'm hurt, because I'm not."

"Of course you're starting, Mister Finn, but you're going to have to drop them shoulders." Louder, Henry called out, "Joseph, please fetch some hot stuff." Joseph retrieved a bottle of liniment from behind the bench. "Please face the other way, Mister Finn." Slowly, Finn swung his legs over the bench. Henry rubbed his hands with his grandmother's liniment while Joseph untucked and rolled up Finn's jersey. Then Henry reached under the gathered jersey and massaged the player's neck and deltoids.

"Close your eyes, Mister Finn, and picture a big ole slather of butter melting on a hoecake."

Finn followed the trainer's instructions, reminded of the times he had sat in a nook in his grandmother's kitchen, eating a stack of buttered warm pancakes. Finn felt his shoulders relaxing. He was startled by the umpire bellowing for the teams to line up for the kickoff.

"Easy now, make your arms heavy and just let them hang to the ground. That's it, Mister Finn." Henry glided his hands from the nape of Finn's neck outward to the edges of his shoulders. "You're a good athlete, Mister Finn, and you know the plays. Just listen to your captain and you'll make all of Sewanee proud."

Finn tucked in his jersey as Henry said, "If you get tight—breathe low from your belly."

Finn turned and looked at Henry, then Joseph, back at Henry, and said, "I will." He ran onto the field and joined the rest of the eleven.

Louisiana State's Red Lemoine kicked off. Turl fielded the ball at the 25-yard line, immediately pivoted, and tossed the ball back to Kimbrough, who was trailing the Sewanee captain. In front of Kimbrough, Turl, Ham, and Brownlow formed a line. Kimbrough followed within two strides of the three-man formation, which veered toward the center of the field and soon engaged two Louisiana State players. Turl lowered his shoulder into the chest of the first charging Louisiana State Tiger and sent him flat on his back. Ham and Brownlow drove the other one to the right while Kimbrough followed Turl down the field. At the Sewanee 38-yard line, four tacklers swarmed Kimbrough and Turl, but the Sewanee captain led Kimbrough forward for six more yards before Louisiana State was able to wrestle the fullback to the ground.

On the turf, facedown, Turl felt like his first hit of the game cleansed him of the anxiety he was carrying. He hoped his team would forget about New Orleans after each of them smashed into an opponent.

The next play, Ham pitched the ball to Franklin Brownlow, who gained three yards around the left and then, on a direct snap, gained four following Kimbrough and Ham behind Peck.

Turl immediately noticed that Louisiana State's linemen were sluggish getting out of their four-point stances. He took Ham aside. "Only call bucks and dives—off-center, off-guard, off-tackle—nothing around the end until I tell you otherwise."

"Are you sure? They seem slow."

"They move like apes. We'll hit them before they come out of their stances."

On the eighth play, Kimbrough followed a spearhead of Sewanee blockers who blasted a hole through the Louisiana State line and backfield. Kimbrough carried the ball for thirty yards, scored the first touchdown, and then kicked a one-point goal.

Ten minutes later, Turl plunged the line, held the ball to his chest with both hands and forearms, drove his legs like the Mountain Goat's side rods, and ran through three Louisiana State players. One of their halfbacks had a clear shot to take down Turl, but when the defender dove to wrap up Turl's legs, the Sewanee halfback's right knee met the tackler's mouth, knocking out a front tooth. Turl sprinted another ten yards for a fifteen-yard touchdown, and Kimbrough kicked the goal.

Kimbrough scored Sewanee's final touchdown of the first half—a five-yard dive between Peck and Prayer Bear on the right side. Kimbrough missed the point after, hooking the ball to the left. At the half, Sewanee led Louisiana State seventeen to zero.

Within the first twelve minutes of the second half, Sewanee sent two Louisiana State players out of the game with injuries—one with a bruised sternum and the other with a dislocated jaw. Also during that stretch, Brownlow scored Sewanee's first second-half touchdown—a forty-yard serpentine run. Kimbrough made the after-touchdown kick and, eight minutes later, scored his third touchdown of the day and his fourth point-after-touchdown goal. Midway through the second half, Kimbrough had accounted for nineteen of his team's twenty-nine points, despite hacking throughout the game and playing with a sprained wrist.

With eight minutes left in the contest, Louisiana State made their fifth first down of the game. On the next play, their quarterback fumbled the ball over to Sewanee on the Louisiana State 10-yard line.

Turl huddled with Brownlow, Ham, Prayer Bear, Peck, and Finn. "Ham, call *Tackle-Back Straight Plunge*, except run it with our right guard instead of our right tackle."

Prayer Bear rubbed his hands together. "Ah, finally, my paws around the pigskin."

"That's right, big man," Turl said.

Ham put his hand on Prayer Bear's shoulder. "You line up in the backfield just to my right. Peck, slide over to Prayer Bear's guard spot. Brownlow, you take Peck's spot on the line at tackle."

"Why?" Finn asked. "Since it's a *Tackle-Back Straight Plunge Right*, shouldn't the right-side tackle run the ball?"

Peck cocked his head. "Yeah, it's my run."

Turl pointed at Peck. "If this play bothers you—or you, Finn—we've got scrubs on the bench who would love to finish this game."

Finn looked away and smirked, while Peck cast his eyes downward.

Ham said, "Everyone know what to do?" They all nodded. "Let's pound another one in."

The referee stuck his head in the huddle and said, "Line up, Sewanee, or you're getting a delay-of-game penalty."

The Sewanee team hustled to their positions. Louisiana State's Red Lemoine turned to his defensive backfield. "Clog east—clog east!" He shook his head. "No. Clog west—clog west!" The four Louisiana State backs moved forward and stood in the gaps on the left side of their line.

With the defense stacked to his right, Ham paused and thought of changing the play. Under his breath he said, "Nope, Prayer Bear's turn." The quarterback barked the signals, "Two grits, two eggs, 26–26!" Sewanee's center, Otay Carter, sent the ball under his legs to Ham, who shoveled it to Prayer Bear. With Kimbrough at his left hip and Turl at his right, Prayer Bear followed Ham through the line. The three Tigers running interference plowed into their opponents, none of whom were able to grab Prayer Bear until he reached the 4-yard line. There, a defender wrapped his arms around Prayer Bear's waist and another jumped on his back. The Sewanee guard dragged one and carried the other over the goal line. Elated, Prayer Bear hugged Ham and lifted him off the ground.

Kimbrough missed the one-point kick. With five minutes left in the game, Coach Lourie sent all eight scrubs onto the field to finish the match.

When the umpire fired a gun into the air to signal the end of the contest, the score was Sewanee thirty-four and Louisiana State zero. Sewanee was undefeated and had shut out four opponents in four days. It was their eighth shutout of the season, and they had played eight games.

The Sewanee faithful cheered:

Tigers! Tigers! Leave 'em in the lurch!
Down with the heathens!
Up with the church!
Yea, Sewanee's right!

All exhausted and some bloody, the Sewanee Tigers gathered in front of their supporters and shouted back:

Rah rah ree, who are we?
Sewanee, double e!
Rough, tough, we are the stuff.
We play football, never get enough!

In the Sewanee locker room after the game, the players sponge-bathed themselves, standing in small galvanized tubs. The starters' bodies were covered in old and new bruises, and several had cuts on their faces and heads. Henry and Joseph attended to their players quickly and carefully.

While Turl bathed himself, Joseph stood on a stool and cleaned a cut on Turl's head. Using a cotton ball wet with antiseptic, he patted the wound, then spread plaster on the cut.

Henry and Joseph worked in tandem until they took care of all the players with open wounds. Then, while the players dried off and dressed, Joseph cut bandage strips, which Henry carefully wrapped around the heads of the Sewanee players with head wounds.

Alfie and Coach Lourie had been assessing the extent of damage to their players' bodies. The two stepped outside the locker room and stood next to a barrel of Tremlett Spring water. They each scooped a cup full and drank it.

Coach Lourie said, "Glad you had the good sense to build in a day off before Ole Miss."

"Yep."

They helped each other roll the barrel onto a hand truck and pushed it toward the campus depot, where the Mountain Goat waited.

Chapter Ten

Saturday, November 11th, 1899

ored with waiting for the rest of the team at the Baton Rouge Union Station, Patch was hopping around the passenger area on Woody's crutches. Woody, resting his eyes, lay stretched out on a bench.

Patch planted the crutches and launched himself as far as he could. He did this several times. On his last attempt, he lost his balance and staggered. A rolled-up newspaper fell from his back pocket. While leaning down to retrieve the paper, Patch turned his head and saw his teammates standing in a group and staring at him. "Howdy, men. How did it go?"

No one responded. Woody opened his eyes, sat up, and saw the team. He looked at Patch. "Give me those."

Patch handed the crutches to his roommate. "No one gonna tell us how y'all played? Y'all look so glum—don't tell me you lost to those tiger lilies." Everyone remained quiet. "Well, I can tell y'all what the premier newspaper in New Orleans has to say about the Sewanee Tigers." He opened the *New Orleans Picayune* and turned pages until he found the article on the Sewanee-Tulane game. Patch read aloud, "'The team from Tennessee has a pretty game, a potent defense and attack, and a line often compared to a brick wall.' It goes on to mention a few of the team's stars, including 'a bantamweight end with springs in his feet.'"

Patch neatly folded the newspaper and laid it on the bench. He scanned the faces of Coach Lourie and Turl. Then, averting his eyes, he said, "It's all there in fine print if anyone wants to read about a historic team in the making—historic, that is, if y'all shut out Louise Anna State."

Kimbrough coughed, then there was more silence, which was broken when Peck had a coughing fit. When Peck's spasm stopped, Patch continued, "All right, I betrayed my team and my team abandoned me—I'd say it's a wash, y'all agree?"

No one spoke until Alfie said, "Climb aboard, men." The players, Henry, and Joseph left the passenger area, heading for the platform. Alfie, Coach Lourie, Turl, Patch, and Woody stayed behind. "Patch," Alfie said, "Coach Lourie and I made the decision to pull out of New Orleans, no one else. The team searched for you, and at the station we waited. We would have forfeited if we hadn't left."

"You picked a barmaid over your teammates," Turl said.

Patch was glad that Finn had told Turl and the others that Patch and he had been with barmaids. The previous night was not the first time Patch had employed a lady of pleasure, but Woody had no knowledge that he had ever been with a prostitute. Over the past twelve hours, Patch had disappointed his friend more than ever before. For him, there was less shame in perpetuating the lie than confessing the truth to Woody.

"Finn tell y'all he couldn't find me?"

Coach Lourie said, "It doesn't matter what Finn or anyone else said. Your job was to be with your team when we left, and you weren't."

"Who plays against Mississippi? Finn?" Patch demanded.

Turl's face flushed. "Do you have any humility, Mercer?"

"All right. Again, I'm sorry."

Alfie said, "'Again?' When did you say it the first time?"

Patch rubbed the stubble on his chin. "I guess I only implied it."

Turl and Coach Lourie, Woody, and Patch boarded the Pullman while Alfie went to the station's Western Union window.

On the train, Patch sat across from Woody, watching him silently pray. Woody's lips were moving almost imperceptibly. The sounds of coughing emanated from the back and front of the train and caught Patch's attention. When his grandfather recounted his Civil War stories, there were always descriptions of sick soldiers on marches, in camps, and in battle. He thought of a framed photograph of his grandfather in his Confederate officer's uniform. The portrait sat on Patch's desk at home in Savannah.

Patch was ashamed of himself. His teammates did battle just hours earlier. They were exhausted, and some sick, and he had abandoned them, sleeping late with a hooker. He thought of the frequent times he had stayed with Iris in Monteagle while knowing he would be late to practice. Remembering the arrogance he had displayed at the train station deepened his regret and filled him with embarrassment. He bowed his head and tried to begin a prayer for forgiveness, but his mind went blank.

Alfie boarded the train and walked down the aisle. Patch raised his head as Alfie passed. The team manager looked straight ahead. Patch noticed he was bearing a slight smile and wondered what had lightened Alfie's mood.

Woody opened his eyes and gazed out the window. Patch said, "Are you sure it's all right for me to sit here?"

"Of course."

"Are you and I on good terms again?"

Woody leaned forward and put his hand on his roommate's shoulder. "I am deeply thankful to God that you're safe and unharmed."

"Thank you. And I thank God, too."

"Do you?"

"I do."

"I'm also asking God to quell my present anger toward you."

"I'll do the same." Patch reclined and rested his eyes.

At the front of the train, Alfie sat down next to Coach Lourie, who said, "Is everything good?"

Alfie patted his left breast. "Amply good. I am a blessed man."

The Mountain Goat rolled its Pullman and boxcar out of the fourth train station in four days. Three hours later, another three Sewanee players had added their rasp to the chorus of coughing. Henry and Joseph stayed busy soothing chests with balm and cooling throats with spring water.

Patch said to Woody, "It's starting to sound like a consumption ward in here."

"I hope we stop soon and let some fresh air into this car. How are those wailing cats in your head?"

"A few are still wailing, but most are down to a hiss. What about you? Last night, you went from a drinky lad to a thorough swizzler in a flash."

"Booze and laudanum, an idiotic transgression. I am still feeling the effects of my sins—persistent head pain and guilt."

"Sins? Come on, Woodrow—you're an Episcopalian, not a Methodist."

"Try to find an Episcopal priest who promotes drunkenness."

"Don't worry. I'm sure God still considers you a sober drinker."

The two sat quietly for a moment as several of their teammates coughed sporadically. "Yesterday afternoon, I was wallowing in self-pity," Woody said.

"Because of your ankle—missing games?"

"It's torturous to sit out."

"I know the feeling."

"Your absence from the eleven was self-inflicted."

Patch leaned his head back on the chair's headrest. He closed his eyes and sighed. Under his breath he said, "Self-inflicted." An image of his grandfather soothing a feverish soldier came to his mind.

Patch stood and walked to the front of the sleeper car and faced its passengers. He waited for a gap in the coughing. "All of you, I beg you to please give me a minute of your attention." More coughing ensued, so he raised his voice and said, "Henry, can you hear me back there?"

"Yes, Mister Patch."

Patch said, "I humbly apologize to everyone on this train for my utterly selfish and reckless conduct in New Orleans. And for my pathetic and cocky behavior at the station." He cleared his throat. "Too many times I've taken y'all for granted. No more." He looked down, then took a step forward and stopped. Patch faced his audience. "And I congratulate each of you for dominating Louisiana State."

Prayer Bear said, "I thought it was Louise Anna State." There was some laughter and a few jeers.

Patch said, "I apologize for that jealous comment, as well. Regardless of the extent of my punishment, I will forever be thankful to have been one of the 1899 eleven. Thank you for listening." Some of the Tigers' faces softened, but as Patch walked down the aisle to return to his seat, only a few eyes met his. He nodded at these teammates and hoped they had forgiven him. Finn didn't look at Patch, and Patch didn't look at him.

Alfie exchanged glances with Coach Lourie. He took a pack of playing cards out of his suit coat pocket and shuffled them. "Gin rummy?" Coach Lourie nodded. "Patch seems contrite."

"Time will tell."

"Wait. You deal when I get back." Alfie reached for his billfold. "I'm going to put a stack of this cash in the safe."

"And the rest?"

"Dole it out."

At the back of the Pullman, Alfie secured a hundred dollars in the safe. He turned and called out, "All right, Tigers. I've got your ill-gotten but well-deserved gains to hand out. Spend it wisely, 'cause there'll be no more wagering on our games this season."

Brownlow asked, "Does that include you and coach?"

Yelling over the laughter, Alfie said, "It surely does, Mister Brownlow! It surely does."

***

At midnight, two-thirds of the way to Memphis, the Mountain Goat pulled into a train station in Bobo, Mississippi. In an all-night diner inside the station, a cook heated up dinner rolls, fried chicken, and green beans and fed the hungry young men from Sewanee. Alfie hurried through his meal along with Turl, Coach Lourie, and Prayer Bear. The four had arranged to meet on the train platform to decide what to do with Patch for the Ole Miss game. Alfie went outside and nodded at Henry and Joseph, who were on a bench eating their dinners. He walked to the edge of the platform, where Coach Lourie and the two players soon joined him.

Turl sighed. "If I had enforced the consequence for his folly the night before we left, he might have gotten to the damn hotel on time."

Coach Lourie asked, "What happened the night we left?"

"The little rake was down in Monteagle with his girl, Iris." Turl said. "He failed to make curfew. I told him he'd carry water before the Texas game, but I didn't make him do it."

Prayer Bear said, "Might have humbled him a bit, but his libertine impulses would have prevailed."

Coach Lourie said, "Here it is. Even with all hell beaten out of us, we can take Ole Miss, but I don't know about another shutout."

Turl said, "It's the win we want—"

Alfie spoke up. "Wins and shutouts all the way through, gentlemen, that's the path to immortality. So the question is, can we shut out Ole Miss without Patch?"

Prayer Bear said, "That's not the question at all. The question is, will we continue as a brotherhood if Patch gets special treatment? Any scrub who did what Patch did would be kicked off the team. We're talking about a one-game suspension for Patch. As to why only one game, he's an amazing end."

Alfie muttered, "And his grandpa is the Bishop of Georgia."

Turl furrowed his brow. "I'm the captain of this team—it's up to me to put us back together. We've got nine men with coughing fits, four with head injuries, Woody out, bad feelings going around as much as the bug infecting our players' lungs."

Prayer Bear said, "I could sleep for a week, and I know that's true even for the scrubs."

Turl said, "Patch sits out the Ole Miss game and carries water. If his spirit is affirming and he doesn't do any girling, he starts against Auburn." They all looked at each other. "Anyone have a differing point of view?"

Alfie pursed his lips, looked down, and slowly shook his head.

"Coach?"

"Nope. Your decision."

Prayer Bear said, "It's the right thing to do, Turl."

Chapter Eleven

Sunday, November 12th, 1899, Memphis, Tennessee

At 6:00 a.m., the Mountain Goat arrived at the Memphis Union Station. Turl went from berth to berth and roused the players who were asleep, and the haggard and battered passengers stumbled from the train. From the front of the Pullman, Turl addressed the team. "So far, we've been victorious yet also beaten. We need to restore our fraternal spirit, and we need to thank God for our triumphs, for each other, and for our Mountain. In preparation for Ole Miss, we will only leave the hotel to attend church—the remainder of our time will be spent together at the hotel. There will be no drinking or gambling. And there will certainly be no girling. Does anyone not understand our plans for today and tonight?" He paused, then said, "Let's restore ourselves on this day of Sabbath."

The team checked into the Peabody Hotel, ate breakfast, and went to their rooms, where most lay down and rested or slept. The sick roomed with the sick. Henry and Joseph had remained in the Pullman car, where they would spend the night.

With his sprained ankle resting on a stack of pillows, Woody lay on his bed in the room he shared with Patch. Woody ruminated over what had happened in New Orleans, ashamed of how inebriated he had been and his careless abandonment of his errant best friend in the South's Sodom and Gomorrah. He looked over at Patch, who was soaking in a bathtub.

Woody silently prayed, *O God, make clean our hearts within us. And take not thy Holy Spirit from us.*

Patch said, "Our Sanhedrin sat me down after breakfast and informed me that I will not suit up for tomorrow's game. Instead, I will carry water."

"How does that sit with you?"

"The punishment is a relief."

"In what manner?"

"Could've been worse. I'm seeing what I did in a harsher light."

"What has that light exposed?"

Patch ducked underwater and resurfaced. "How selfish and reckless I have been."

"Now you get a fresh start, a tabula rasa."

"Indeed, and I will make amends—I'll be an even better water boy than Joseph."

***

By 11:00 a.m., the Sewanee football players, their coach, and Alfie had all bathed and were in the Peabody lobby. From the hotel, the group walked ten minutes to Calvary Episcopal Church for an eleven-thirty mass. Conversations between the players were short and seldom.

After church, they returned to the Peabody for lunch. Then some went back to their rooms while others remained in the lobby and did schoolwork or played cards. Dinner was at six, and everyone was back in their rooms by seven-thirty.

A little later, Henry and Joseph arrived at the Peabody. A bellman escorted them to the players' rooms. Henry changed bandages while Joseph applied a balm to all of the players' chests, even those who weren't coughing. When they finished administering to the entire team, they were taken to Coach Lourie and Alfie's room, where Henry gave an assessment of the players' health.

Walking back to the Pullman, Joseph asked Henry, "Do all black folks have to sleep on trains when they stay over in Memphis?"

"No, there are a few black hotels on the other side of town. Mister Alfie was going to put us up in one, but I told him I wanted us closer to the team. I've never seen young men this gimped up."

"Why did that man at the hotel ask if you were the Sewanee rub-man?"

"The bellhop?"

"Is that what he's called?"

Henry nodded. "Some people call a trainer a rub-man."

"Oh, 'cause of rubdowns."

"Right. That's right."

"Everyone at Sewanee calls you a trainer."

"They're showing respect."

Henry and Joseph arrived at Union Station's rail yard, where the Mountain Goat was connected to the sleeper car and boxcar. They stepped over a series of railroad tracks and climbed into the Pullman. Joseph gazed at the empty rows of seats. He wondered if the team members felt bad every time he and Henry couldn't stay at a hotel or had to eat in a restaurant kitchen.

Joseph washed his face and scrubbed his teeth with baking soda. Then he got into his berth.

Henry scooped a cup of Tremlett Spring water for himself and one for Joseph. "Here's some water." He started to hand the cup of water to Joseph and then pulled it back. "Next time you want to be my assistant trainer on a Sewanee trip, you're gonna ask your daddy and then ask me, right?"

"Yes, sir. I promise."

"It sure has been good to have you along."

"It's been good to be along."

Chapter Twelve

Monday, November 13th, 1899, Memphis, Tennessee

Injured in a variety of ways and nine with a persistent cough, the Sewanee Tigers were about to face the University of Mississippi at Billings Park for an 11:00 a.m. kickoff. It was a gusty day. In the stands, men held their hats on their heads and women had their hats' ribbons tied under their chins. Almost three thousand were in attendance. Most were there to cheer for the Ole Miss Rebels. Yet news of the Tigers' victories across Texas and Louisiana drew almost five hundred Sewanee alumni, students, and other supporters to the game. Oxford, Mississippi, was only a three-hour train ride from Memphis, so passenger cars were packed that morning with Ole Miss students, many from Memphis or nearby.

Nonpartisans were present to witness a dramatic contest and a test of Sewanee's endurance, scoring streak, and shutout streak. From their season opener through the Louisiana State game, the Sewanee Tigers had scored 223 points and had shut out all eight opponents.

News of these young men from a small school on a Tennessee mountain had reached beyond the South via newspaper articles about the Sewanee Tigers' unprecedented cross-country schedule and flawless record. Scattered throughout the Northeast and Midwest were aficionados who had begun to take note of Virginia, North Carolina, Auburn, and Vanderbilt football. And now they were curious about the Sewanee team. A team led by the previous year's renowned Princeton quarterback. A team on a daring journey to five gridirons in six days—a feat never before executed by any football team.

During warmups, Patch hustled buckets of Tremlett Spring water to the Sewanee sideline. Henry finished applying new plaster to the gash on Turl's head. The cut from the Texas game hadn't closed completely and periodically bled. In addition to Turl, three other members of the Sewanee eleven wore bandages wrapped around their heads—Kimbrough, Brownlow, and Otay Carter, who also had a swollen thumb.

Coach Lourie watched Mississippi's eleven run through plays. Alfie walked up to him. "I guess there are no barbers in Oxford," Alfie said as he lifted his bowler hat off his head and ran his hand through his hair.

Lourie quickly scanned the Rebels' heads. Most had shaggy hair that fell an inch or so below their ears. "Some northeastern teams had players with bushy heads." Lourie returned his attention to the plays. "Theory is it provides extra cushion against head blows. We never bought it at Princeton."

"Maybe we should buy it. They don't have any wrapped heads."

"Their cuts have healed, but their brains have been rattled as much as our eleven's."

Alfie nodded. "Good." He walked toward the Rebels' sideline, so he could meet their manager. On the way, he passed the Mississippi coach. "Morning to you, coach."

"Good morning." The two continued on their paths.

The Ole Miss coach walked up to Coach Lourie and extended his hand. "Hobie Lourie, Princeton quarterback '98." They shook hands and there was a pause. "I'm sorry. W. H. Lyon, member of last year's Yale eleven."

"Oh. You seemed familiar but I couldn't place—"

"That's probably because I spent so much time facedown in the dirt when we played Princeton last year."

"No shame in that match. We went undefeated but only scored five against you fellas. Hardest game of the season for us."

"And you scored that one goal—a dropkick."

"I did. Tough game. A lot of clouds of dirt. How did you become the Mississippi coach?"

"A Yale alum who lives in Oxford recommended me. How did you find your way to Sewanee?"

Coach Lourie pointed to the Rebel sideline and said, "That man in the bowler over there? He's our team manager."

"A Sewanee student?"

"Yep, a senior. He champions the game, been reading the *New York Times* sports page since he was a kid. Last year he liked what he read about Princeton and me, so he talked the vice-chancellor into hiring me."

"Enterprising."

"Yeah."

"And bold. Everyone I spoke to was sure Sewanee would lose two or three games between Austin and here."

"I'm sure your eleven will test us." Coach Lourie turned to face the wind. "Glad we're not playing baseball today."

"Beats rain, though." The two shook hands and wished each other a good match.

As the Mississippi coach walked toward his team, he stopped and watched the Sewanee eleven practice. He was especially interested in the Tigers' right end and fullback.

Carrying a water yoke across his shoulders and balancing two full buckets, Patch crossed in front of the coach, who said, "Excuse me." He pointed toward the Sewanee team. "Is that right end's name Patch Mercer?"

"No, I'm Patch Mercer. That's Finn Grayson."

"You sitting this one out?"

"Yep."

"Why's that?"

"Bad ribs."

"Oh. Well, speedy recovery."

"Thank you."

Coach Lyon watched Patch hustle to the sideline and wondered why Lourie had an injured star lugging water. Regardless, Lyon was pleased. The previous week he had telegraphed the Texas A&M coach for a scouting report on Sewanee. The A&M coach wrote back: *Their fullback, Kimbrough Lowndes, is the best football player. The best athlete is unquestionably Patch Mercer, the right end—he's a speedy, pint-sized devil, and pound for pound he's their strongest.*

The Rebels' coach smiled and rubbed his hands together.

The teams lined up along their sidelines. Turl and the Mississippi captain gathered with the referee and umpire at midfield. The referee said, "Mister Turley, Sewanee is the visiting team, so you call heads or tails."

"Heads."

The crowd quieted while the referee flipped a silver dollar toward a blue sky streaked with long thin clouds. The coin landed on tails, and the Mississippi captain elected to receive the kickoff and defend the goal that put the wind at his team's back.

The Sewanee team formed a circle behind their bench. The players put their arms around each other's shoulders. Turl said, "When you're hurt and tired and just want to get under a blanket on a soft bed—that's when champions rise and fight."

Prayer Bear said, "Bow your heads, Tigers. In silence, let's all ask our Lord for the strength we need to bring glory to His Church." Everyone bowed their heads and remained quiet until Prayer Bear said, "Amen!" The team responded, "Amen!"

The two elevens took their positions on the field and faced each other for the opening kickoff. Kimbrough made a divot in the turf, used it to prop up the ball, and took five steps back. He waited for the wind to calm, but the referee motioned for him to proceed. Kimbrough's kick fluttered through the air like a knuckleball. The Mississippi return man leaped to make a catch, but he misjudged his jump and the ball flew over his head. Ham and a Mississippi player chased the football, dove for it at the same time, and knocked heads.

Soon the ball was buried under a mound of players at the Mississippi 20-yard line. A scrap ensued under the pile. The referee and the umpire pulled players off the pile and revealed Brownlow wrestling with an Ole Miss Rebel who clearly had possession of the ball.

The referee raised his right hand. "Mississippi ball!"

On the game's first play from the line of scrimmage, Mississippi bucked between Finn, starting for Patch at right end, and Peck, Woody's substitute at right tackle. The Rebels gained five yards. On the next play, they exploited the same gap and gained eight yards. Mississippi continued to move the line of scrimmage forward, running at Finn and Peck one out of every three plays.

Within twelve minutes, Ole Miss had reached the Sewanee 43-yard line. In the season's eight games, only Texas had crossed the Sewanee 30-yard line.

Coach Lourie said to Alfie, "We look like late-round punchers."

"Maybe four games in four days was the limit."

"To hell with that."

Turl motioned the Tigers to make a huddle. "Y'all better find your hearts fast or we're all going to have ten pounds of shame strapped to our backs for the second half."

Prayer Bear said, "Hellfire, men—we're Sewanee!"

On the next play, Mississippi's left tackle and end drove Peck and Finn, respectively, to the outside and the fullback plunged behind his blockers, but Turl and Kimbrough anticipated the attack on the two substitutes, met the fullback at the line of scrimmage, and pushed him back four yards. The fullback dug in and resisted the two Tigers until Prayer Bear and Otay shoved their teammates from behind and toppled them and the Rebel. Ole Miss lost seven yards on the play.

They bucked the other side of the Sewanee line and, in a scrum, pushed forward five yards. It was third down at the Sewanee 45-yard line. Instead of punting, the Rebels' quarterback swept left behind his interference, gaining four yards but leaving them three yards short of a first down. The ball went over to Sewanee.

Turl said to Ham, "Mix it up—confuse them."

On the next five downs, Ham called bucks and plunges to both sides of the ball, and the Tigers ground out nine yards.

Turl grabbed Ham's arm. "Deception. We can't last smashing the line every play."

Sewanee lined up on the fifty-yard line. Ham called out, "88 puddin', 88 puddin'. Hut!" Finn pulled from his end position and cut across the Tiger backfield and Ham pitched him the ball. Running around the Ole Miss end, Finn reached the Mississippi backfield, where a Rebel stripped the football out of his hands. Mississippi recovered the loose ball.

On first down, the Rebel right halfback dropped a pitch. Peck scooped it up and was immediately downed.

Attempting to confuse the Rebels, Ham ran a delayed pitch, which resulted in a two-yard loss. He called a fake pitch and Ole Miss sacked him for a three-yard loss. The Tigers faced a third down with ten yards to go.

Turl yelled, "Punt! Get under it, men!"

Kimbrough kicked the ball rugby style, sending it wobbling, swerving through the air. The Rebel return man braced to catch the ball, but it floated right, landed, and bounced toward the Mississippi goal line. He chased the ball and dove on it at the Ole Miss 16-yard line. Ham downed him.

After two long, intense scrums, Ole Miss was left with two yards to go on third down, so they punted from their 19-yard line. Kimbrough caught the ball and took it up the middle of the wide-open field as his teammates blocked all the Rebels except one halfback. Just before they met at the Mississippi 30-yard line, Kimbrough faked left but went right and past the Ole Miss player. The halfback sprinted after Kimbrough and tackled him from behind on the Mississippi 20-yard line. Kimbrough slowly stood up and bent over with his hands on his knees.

"Don't think I've ever seen him caught from behind like that," Alfie said to Coach Lourie.

Turl stood with his back to the Rebels and mouthed to Ham *call my number.*

The teams got into position. Ham called out, "24 Maggie Majors, 24 Maggie. Hut, hut!" He caught the snap and immediately turned and sent a long toss to Turl. Kimbrough ran left as a decoy. The Sewanee captain followed Ham and Brownlow around the right flank. Mississippi's fullback broke through the protection and lowered his shoulder to hit Turl, but the Tiger stiff-armed him, shoving him to the ground. Turl reached the 15-yard line. From the corner of his eye, he saw a Rebel catching up with him, so he pivoted left and drove his forearm into the defender's rib cage, causing the man to stagger. Turl raced past Ham and Brownlow, who had turned to face the Mississippi pursuit. Untouched, the captain dashed into the end zone.

The Sewanee eleven scrambled into formation for the point-after-touchdown attempt. Kimbrough kicked and pulled the ball to the left, but a gust of wind pushed it to the right, and it floated just inside the left goalpost.

Patch smiled and said, "Athena."

Time expired. Sewanee six, Mississippi zero.

In their locker room, some of the Sewanee eleven stretched out on benches while others sat on the floor with their backs against a wall. Kimbrough was lying on a training table, dozing on and off. Henry and Joseph hustled around changing bandages, starting with the head wounds. Also in need of attention was Ham, whose ear, still bruised from the Texas game, had been reinjured during the first play.

Coach Lourie addressed the team. "With fifty seconds left in the half, the Sewanee eleven continued their scoring and shutout streak. You've scored in all seventeen consecutive halves of the season and allowed no points." The scrubs clapped.

Sitting on a bench next to Woody, Patch scanned the room. "Go Sewanee," he said softly. Woody smiled and nodded his head.

After a twenty-minute halftime break, the teams retook the field. Mississippi kicked off, facing the wind. It was a short kick, twenty yards. Kimbrough caught the ball on a bounce and dug his heel into the turf. He shanked his punt. The football traveled only nine yards, putting Mississippi on the 50-yard line.

Coach Lourie rubbed his forehead and looked at Henry. "He's finally exhausted."

"Yes, sir, he is."

Turl approached Kimbrough.

The fullback shook his head. "I'm fine."

"You've been our ox for nine halves in six days. You're losing your legs. I'll field the punts."

"Just a shank, Turl. My first of the year."

The captain pointed his index finger to his own chest, indicating that he would return the punts for the rest of the game.

Turl lined up next to Ham. "When we get the ball back, don't call Kimbrough's number—he's got to have his legs for kicking." Ham nodded, and Turl ran back to his safety position.

Mississippi punted. Turl fielded the kick and returned it to the Sewanee

44-yard line, where a Rebel punched the ball out of the captain's hands. Mississippi recovered the loose football.

Ole Miss's quarterback quick-kicked the ball, angling toward the Sewanee sideline. The football rolled out at the Sewanee 10-yard line.

The Tigers gained four first downs and moved the line of scrimmage up to their own 38-yard line, where Mississippi forced a third down with four yards to go. Kimbrough punted the football twenty-five yards. After a five-yard return, Ole Miss had possession on their 42-yard line.

While shaking his head, Alfie turned to Coach Lourie. "Do you have a signal to change punters?"

"Nope."

Alfie began chewing on a thumbnail.

Pushing and pulling their fullback through the Sewanee defense, the Rebels advanced the ball four yards. On the next play, the Tigers controlled the scrum and, after thirty seconds of scrapping and clawing, downed the Ole Miss runner for a four-yard loss. The Rebels punted. The ball dropped into Turl's hands, and he ran twenty yards down an open field before a Rebel hit him low and flipped him into the air. He landed on his back.

Ham and Prayer Bear went to help him up.

"Give me a minute," he said.

Prayer Bear asked, "You hurt?"

"My head is ringing, that's all. Give me a hand." Turl's two teammates helped him stand up. "I'm steady. Let's go." Walking unevenly, he took his position.

From the 50-yard line, Ham called out, "10–32 red, 10–32 red," faked a pitch to Turl, and tossed the ball to Brownlow. At the moment the Tiger caught it, a Mississippi end slammed into his side and caused him to fumble. Ole Miss recovered the football.

On the next play, the Rebel fullback broke through Sewanee's left side. Kimbrough squared his shoulders and hammered him chest to chest. The ball runner's arms went limp, and the ball dropped to the turf. The Ole Miss quarterback recovered his teammate's fumble.

Coach Lourie said, "Was that the fifth fumble? What a sloppy match."

Standing next to Coach Lourie, Patch yelled out to his teammates, "Here we go, Sewanee!"

Mississippi had the football on the Sewanee 40-yard line. Their coach was pacing back and forth along the sideline. After a quick huddle, the Ole Miss players, except the quarterback and left guard, lined up on the line, right of the Rebel center.

Turl yelled, "Shift, shift!" The Sewanee squad quickly realigned on their left side of the ball, but Prayer Bear stayed in his right guard position.

The Rebel quarterback shouted "Hut, hut," and the center snapped him the ball. He stood holding it, freezing the Sewanee backfield. Ole Miss's right end pulled and crossed in front of the quarterback, who handed him the ball. Passing the Ole Miss left guard, who was driving Prayer Bear backward, the end cut and dashed upfield. Fourteen yards later, Brownlow dove at the runner's feet, tripping and downing him. Back near the line of scrimmage, Prayer Bear stomped in a circle and roared.

Joseph said, "Mister Embree is an angry bear now."

Mississippi quickly lined up in a regular formation. Their quarterback took the snap and faked a pitch to his fullback. He hesitated, looking for a hole to his left.

With a lowered shoulder, Prayer Bear hit his opposing guard and jerked him to the turf by the Rebel's jersey. After he caught the quarterback and slung him down at the line of scrimmage, Prayer Bear beat his own chest.

Two and a half minutes remained in the game. Alfie jerked his hat off his head and turned to Coach Lourie. "They can't tie us, Hobie. Might as well be a loss!" Coach Lourie rested his hands on his thighs.

The Ole Miss captain shouted, "Buckle down, Rebs!"

It was second down, and the Rebel quarterback pitched to his left halfback, who followed his interference around the right side. Sewanee busted apart the back's protection and stopped him at the line of scrimmage. Ole Miss ran the same play to the left side and gained five yards and a first down.

On the Sewanee 21-yard line with ninety seconds remaining in the game, Mississippi had three downs to scamper behind the line of scrimmage and run out the clock, which would make them the first team to hold the 1899

Sewanee Tigers to zero points in a single half. Or they could continue to pursue a touchdown and an extra point to tie the famed Tigers. Either narrative would spread across the South in the next day's newspapers.

Henry didn't turn his back to the field. He and Joseph, with Alfie beside them, faced the game and their team's impending first blemish of the season. The crowd was the loudest it had been all day, with Sewanee fans yelling for a miracle and the Mississippi supporters yelling for their Oxford boys.

The teams lined up at the line of scrimmage. Ole Miss's left end was set deep in the backfield, leaving Finn without opposition.

"33 boardwalk, 33 boardwalk, hike!" The center snapped the ball directly to the fullback.

Finn read the play, charged into the Mississippi backfield, dove, and deflected the fullback's perfect spiral, intended for the Rebel end. The football bounced and rolled toward the Sewanee goal line. Kimbrough scooped it up and carried it seventy yards for a touchdown. In the end zone, he rolled onto his back. His chest was heaving.

Prayer Bear draped his arm over Finn's shoulders. "There you go, Finny, there you go!"

On the sideline, Alfie looked at Henry. "You almost have a heart attack, Henry?"

"'Bout five of them."

Eighteen seconds remained in the game. Ham knelt and held the football upright on the ground under the pressure of his index finger. Kimbrough approached the ball and struck it cleanly. The ball flew over the goalpost. Patch put his arms over Alfie's and Coach Lourie's shoulders and said, "Ole Finn!"

Coach Lourie said, "And Ole Kimbrough—how he galloped seventy yards, I'll never know."

The clock expired and Sewanee won, twelve to zero. For the season, they had nine victories, scored in eighteen consecutive halves, and outscored their opponents 235 to 0.

Prayer Bear stood on the field away from his teammates. "To the Mountain, Lord, please."

Chapter Thirteen

Tuesday, November 14th, 1899, Shelbyville, Tennessee

At midnight, with Memphis nine hours behind, the Mountain Goat slowly pulled out of the Shelbyville, Tennessee, depot. Under a starless night sky, the locomotive had 60 miles left of its 2,500-mile trip. Most of the team members were asleep. Hats, coats, handkerchiefs, ties, shoes, dopp kits, textbooks, and other sundry items were scattered throughout the Pullman car.

Woody was rereading a letter to Lillian:

Dear Lillian,

After nine days on rails and five gridirons, we are finally within a few hours of our beloved Mountain. Oh, how good it would be if you were there to meet me at the depot. Please forgive me if my fantasy is too presumptuous or effuse.

We, the Sewanee Tigers, have finished our tour de force and remain unbeaten and unscored upon. Unfortunately, my ankle injury sidelined me for the Louisiana State and Mississippi contests, the latter of which we played today. I am confident that I will be fine for the final three games of this glorious season. I will never forget this team and our time together. I am proud of everyone in this sleeper car from which I pen this letter to you. No doubt the Almighty has infused us with the vigorous spirit of brotherhood.

How are you, Lillian? How are your fine parents? Of course, I so much look forward to spending time with you and your family at Galveston over Christmas break.

Well, I hope you're playing a lot of tennis down there in balmy Austin. How are your studies coming along?

You and yours are in my prayers, and I will write again next week.

In great admiration and sincerity,
Woody Barnwell

Patch asked, "Is that to Miss Lillian?" He folded Cecilia's note and slipped it into his breast pocket.

"Yes, it is. Whom is that tattered little note from? A conquest or Miss Cecilia?"

"Woody, I had a revelation standing on the sideline in Memphis."

Smiling, Woody said, "You're going to the seminary next year."

"No. I was pulling for our team."

"Of course you were."

"No, I wasn't sure how I'd react to being kept out of the action. I was very pleased that my mind sat upon higher ground."

"That is God's guidance."

"Maybe. If so, he also had me thinking about how childish all my girling has become. It's to the point that I cheated myself out of joy."

"The joy of being on the gridiron and helping your battle-worn brothers."

"Yes." Patch clasped his hands. "I might be through chasing after loose women—even the well-bred. I am pondering the notion of one member of the fairer sex in my life at a time."

"This is, if not a miracle, a blessing, an awakening and opportunity. I know you will be released from a great burden if you choose this path."

"Thank you, Woodward, your patience and concern sustains me. And please let yourself enjoy my *thank you*."

Woody nodded his head. "Where does this leave you with Miss Cecilia?"

"Time will tell. Time will tell." Patch rose from his seat. "I'm going to clean up and then sleep for the rest of this trip."

"Me too. Sleep, glorious sleep."

Patch helped Woody extend and connect their bench seats to form Woody's bed. With his nightshirt over his shoulder, Patch walked toward the back of the sleeper car. When he returned from the restroom, Woody was tucked in under his covers.

"Refreshed?" Woody asked.

"And renewed. Where's your pillow?"

"Not sure."

Patch sprang and pulled himself up onto his berth. Then he tossed his pillow down to Woody. "Sweet dreams, Mister Barnwell."

"You, too, Mister Mercer."

Patch rolled up his suit coat and placed it under his head.

Finn passed him, nodded, and said, "Patch."

"Hey, Finn, you played a good game today. You really came through."

"Thank you. We could've used you."

"You did good."

Finn continued to the back of the sleeper car. In the restroom, he noticed a folded piece of paper on the floor. He picked it up and unfolded it. "Who in the hell are Esplanade and Charlton?" He turned the note over. With his finger, he followed the sketched path, which began at Sewanee's Hardee Field, meandered through the forest, and ended behind Tremlett Spring. The terminus was marked by a star.

Finn put the note in his pants pocket.

Thirty minutes from Sewanee, most of the Pullman's residents were asleep. Alfie Melville and Coach Lourie were enjoying the quiet. On the table in front of them, they occasionally took turns splitting a deck of cards, competing for the high card.

Alfie looked out the window and noticed that the night was so black he could barely discern the contours of the hills or mountains. Then what looked like a sliver of the sun crept into his view. Pitched high in the window frame, an undulating white light with an orange center slowly grew.

Alfie said to Coach Lourie, "Look."

The coach saw the lurid light and said, "Good God."

Alfie stood and stepped into the aisle. He scanned the car to see who else was awake. Turl was looking out his window. Alfie caught the attention of the captain, and Turl joined Alfie and Coach Lourie.

Alfie said, "Why the hell is the engineer driving us into a forest fire?"

Turl walked away, opened the vestibule door, and walked out onto the platform. Alfie and Coach Lourie followed him. Cupping his hands, Turl shouted, "Hey up there!" No one appeared, so he shouted louder several times. Finally, the engineer's assistant appeared. "Are we heading into a fire?"

"Boss says it's Saint Elmo's fire, whatever that is."

Alfie turned to Turl and Coach Lourie and said, "We need to wake everyone."

At that moment, the vestibule door flew open, and Prayer Bear joined them on the platform.

Prayer Bear said, "Sewanee's on fire! Pray with me, boys. 'God is our hope and strength, a very present help in trouble. Therefore will we not fear, though the earth be moved, and though the hills be carried into the midst of the sea.' Amen."

"Amen," Turl and Coach Lourie said together.

Alfie said, "Engineer thinks it might be Saint Elmo's fire."

Prayer Bear pointed toward the light. "It's possible it's not a fire. Upon our triumphant return, the Holy Ghost might be manifest and hovering above our beloved school."

Alfie said, "Or the devil has set Sewanee on fire."

They watched the glow spread as the Mountain Goat strained up the mountain. A mile outside Sewanee, the orange core writhed, and the white light separated into a galaxy of stars. Ham opened the vestibule door and shouted, "Luminaria and a bonfire, at one o'clock in the morning!"

Alfie and the others reentered the Pullman to find everyone awake. The wheezing, the aching, and the badly injured were lined up in the aisle with their arms around each other. They chanted:

Everywhere we go
People want to know
Who we are
So we tell them
We are the Tigers,
The mighty, mighty Tigers

They repeated these lines three times. Henry and Joseph watched the jubilation and clapped to the rhythm of the cheer. Then Prayer Bear roared *Born on a mountain top* and everyone joined him:

Raised by a tiger
I'm no dandy fop
I'm a Sewanee fighter
Sewanee, Sewanee we run farther
Sewanee, Sewanee we drink harder

Slowly the Mountain Goat approached the Sewanee depot and came to a stop. Turl weaved his way down the aisle to Henry and Joseph. "We'll all unload this train in the morning," he said. "And you two better be on the depot platform with us."

Everyone disembarked. The Tiger supporters roared like a university of three thousand students instead of three hundred. Alfie climbed onto the Mountain Goat and said to the engineers, "You fellas come join us. No trip without y'all." With their coal-ash faces and clothes, the engineer and his assistant obliged and stood behind the team.

The players' bandaged bodies and labored movements contrasted with their grateful smiles and eyes. In front of the Tigers were the faces of hundreds of supporters lit brightly by individual candles, Japanese lanterns, and a two-story bonfire.

The Sewanee orchestra played Souza's "King Cotton." The scene was like a carnival, with many of the students in fanciful costumes. The medical students wore halved skulls as masks strapped around their heads. They also wore white sheets as ghostly gowns with holes for their eyes. Women, young and old, donned gaudy bonnets recently accessorized for this homecoming. Men from The Cut launched fireworks that left glowing trails over the gathering.

Vice-Chancellor Wiggins climbed onto the platform and asked the band director to conduct the band to play softly. With the music low, the vice-chancellor shook the hands of each player and everyone else being honored—except the engineer and his assistant, whom the vice-chancellor acknowledged with a smile and a thank you. He then signaled for Coach Lourie and Alfie to follow him to the edge of the platform, where he honored them with a formal bow. Alfie and Coach Lourie returned the gesture.

The vice-chancellor addressed the crowd: "As temperate yet fierce men, your heroes, with divine guidance, showed the world what it means to be a Sewanee man—a superior to the common college man. When engaged in the battles of life, each of you need only to remember the '99 Tigers, their struggles and glory."

The throng roared. Alfie cupped his hand to his ear and smiled widely. The students gathered in the field cheered:

Tigers! Tigers! Leave 'em in the lurch!
Down with the heathens!
Up with the church!
Yea, Sewanee's right!

They shouted the school's hallmark cheer four times, progressively louder each round.

Alfie held his hands above his head. "From Sewanee!" He paused. Soon most of the crowd gave him their attention. "From Sewanee to Austin to Houston to New Orleans to Baton Rouge to Memphis and now back to the Mountain." The crowd chanted *Tigers, Tigers* repeatedly with a beat between each phrase.

Alfie gestured for silence. "Before reaching here, the Mountain Goat"—chants of *Goat, Goat!* interrupted him. He waited for the supporters to subside. "Our herculean chariot made its last stop in the hills of Shelbyville. We were on the cusp of the Cumberlands' chilly November air. And now here we are with all of the Mountain. We are sanctified." A resounding *amen* followed. Alfie said, "On behalf of everyone on this platform, we thank you all for welcoming us in such a grand manner. You could be in your warm beds, but you are here after midnight, ecstatically and generously hailing your crusaders with your hearts, a warm salve for their wounds."

The crowd shouted *Henry, Joseph, Henry, Joseph!* Turl walked over to the trainer and his assistant, raised their arms like a referee lifts the arm of a victorious boxer, and brought them to the front of the platform. The crowd chanted louder.

Then the gymnastics team carefully carried up to the platform three long tables, all covered with white tablecloths. They set the tables end to end, then vaulted off the platform and disappeared into the depot shed. They returned with chairs and a smaller table, which they placed behind the long row of tables. After they set the long tables' chairs, all facing the crowd, they placed four chairs around the smaller table. Then Chloe Pelham, head cook for the Sewanee dining hall, ascended the platform stairs with six other cafeteria servants behind her.

The seven servants gathered in the edges of the tablecloths and lifted them, revealing a banquet meal stretching the length of the three joined tables. After folding the tablecloths, they sat the Sewanee players, coach, and manager. Miss Chloe gestured for Henry, Joseph, the engineer, and his assistant to take their seats at the smaller table.

Father Brodie came onto the platform and asked everyone to bow their heads. He gave thanks to God for the food and drink they were about to enjoy and for the safe and triumphant return of the Sewanee Tigers.

While the players ate and drank whiskey, half of the crowd lined up in front of the fire pits where men from The Cut had been roasting whole hogs and cooking beans in large kettles. When this nighttime breakfast was over, the students sang the Sewanee alma mater.

A male servant drove a long flat wagon onto the field and stopped next to the platform. The wagon was drawn by six work horses. The players, coach, and manager loaded onto the wagon. Henry and Joseph descended from the platform. Alfie and Coach Lourie lifted Henry up onto the wagon and were about to do the same for Joseph, but from behind Joseph, his mother gripped his shoulder and said, "Don't you dare anger your father more than you have."

The horses began moving at the crack of the driver's whip. Henry jumped off the wagon and said, "I'll walk him over to Silas, Rose."

Scanning the crowd, Patch saw Cecilia for the first time that night. She waved at him, and he waved back. He had a flashing thought to jump off the wagon and go to her and tell the world to go to hell. He knew doing that would shame her to the point that she would have to move from the Mountain.

Cecilia mouthed, "Tomorrow night." Patch smiled.

Students, with steins full of beer or whiskey, surrounded the wagon. A short, skinny freshman jumped in front of the horses, raised his arms, and yelled, "Halt!" The horses stopped. The crowd quieted.

A student shouted, "Dewey, get out of the way. You stupid initiate!"

Dewey cupped his hands around his mouth. "Brothers of Lambda Psi! Help me unhitch these brutes and take these warriors to campus!"

Twelve of Dewey's fraternity brothers, including the one who had just admonished him, freed the horses. Gripping the harness straps, they dug in and strained but couldn't budge the wagon.

Half drunk, Alfie, the Lambda Psi president, stood up. "All Sewanee men are brothers!" He dove off the wagon and into the arms of classmates. Someone handed him his bowler, which had fallen off his head. He flung it into the crowd. "We are the Tigers, the mighty, mighty Tigers!" The supporters joined in the chant. Alfie shoved his way through the crowd and leaned his bony shoulder into the rear of the wagon.

This prompted students to drop their steins and push from behind and alongside the wagon while others helped the Lambda Psi brothers pull. All in varying degrees of drunkenness, revelers took or followed their heroes up University Avenue.

Left behind was a field covered in trash, including pig rib bones, flasks, hats, and extinguished Japanese lanterns. Throughout the dinner portion of the celebration, the servants—almost all of whom lived in The Cut—had begun the long cleanup process by picking up discarded dirty tin plates and stacking them into several four- to six-foot towers.

When the crowd was gone, three horse-drawn wagons pulled onto the field and came to a stop. The women servants picked up the party's remains and loaded them onto two trash wagons, while the men cooled the fire pits and wrapped canvas blankets around the pig carcasses, each of which still had some meat left on their bones. These were loaded onto the third wagon.

Joseph stood near a fire pit that his father was extinguishing with buckets of water and shovel loads of dirt. The tall muscular man worked briskly. When he finished his task, Silas noticed Joseph and said, "Go help your ma and the others."

It took over an hour for the campus servants to finish the cleanup. At the end, Joseph approached Silas. His father was talking to a man from The Cut, so Joseph stood back and waited for the men to finish their discussion. While standing there, Joseph's eyes closed and he started to sway, but he caught himself and kept his balance. A few minutes later, it happened again.

"See y'all up at The Cut, Isaac," Silas told the man.

"We'll pick them pig bones clean."

"Yes sir." Silas patted his neighbor on the shoulder and turned toward Joseph.

Joseph took a step forward. "Daddy. I'm sorry I snuck away."

Silas squatted next to a bucket of water and rinsed his hands. He looked back at Joseph, whose eyes were closed. As his son teetered toward the ground, Silas lunged and grabbed him. He carried him to the pig wagon, where Rose sat on the bench. With his son leaning his head on him and his wife on the other side of Joseph, Silas drove his family to The Cut.

Chapter Fourteen
Tuesday, November 14th, 1899

At six in the morning, the vice-chancellor awoke, canceled all classes for the day, and went back to bed. Young servants were dispatched to the residence halls to bang on doors and loudly announce that classes were canceled. Most of the student body awoke to headaches, some to nausea, and some to both. Upon hearing the news, students rolled over and continued to sleep.

Joseph knocked on Patch and Woody's door. Already dressed and on his way to class, Woody opened the door.

"Mister Woody. Mister Wiggins has canceled all classes for today."

"Well, that's unfortunate."

Patch sat up in his bed and cradled his head with both his hands. "Actually, Joseph, that is wonderful and merciful news." He gently lay back down, still holding his head, and slept for another two hours. When he awoke, he went outside and repeatedly dunked his head into a barrel of cold rainwater. After somewhat dulling his alcohol-induced headache, Patch went back upstairs, bathed, and shaved. Then he walked to the Hiawassee House, where Cecilia and a few of her boarders were having muffins and tea. To everyone, Patch said, "Good morning."

One of the boarders said, "It's almost one o'clock."

"Well, it's morning for me. Miss Cecilia, will there be music here at the Hiawassee House this evening?"

"Not tonight, Patch. It is my turn to spend the night at Miss Thompson's."

"How is she?'

"Very frail and nervous."

"Please give her my regards and assure her Woody and I are praying for her."

"I will do so."

Patch left. Cecilia said, "Oh, how rude of me. I didn't congratulate that young man on his and his team's victories."

A boarder said, "Don't worry. We hoisted him and the others a thousand times, almost until dawn."

Cecilia said, "I will be right back." She went out on her porch where Patch was tying his shoes. "Four o'clock?"

"Yes."

"You have your map?"

Patch pointed to his head.

"Wear shoes more rugged than those."

"You, too."

***

At twilight that evening, with three mules in tow, Turl, Ham, Peck, Finn, and Otay stood at the trailhead that would take them to Tremlett Spring. After the previous night's victory celebration, the Tigers all committed to camping together next to Tremlett Spring on the following night, but when it was time to go to the stable and pack mules for the trip, only those five players showed up.

Turl sat down and leaned his back against a tree. "Let's give 'em another five minutes."

Finn snickered. "None of those dang lazybones are—"

"Can't blame fellows for wanting to lay them bones on soft beds," Otay said.

From another direction, Patch was walking to the same trailhead. He saw the mule train. Otay said, "Hold on, y'all. There's Patch."

Patch had forgotten about the proposed camping trip. "Damn it to hell." Then he waved at them.

Finn turned to Turl. "What's he doing up here with no mule? No gear? Just that little sack?"

Turl said, "Hush."

Patch caught up with his teammates and said, "Where's everyone else?"

Otay said, "They're curled up like girls under their quilts."

"What've you got in that sack?" Finn asked Patch.

Patch gave Finn a hard look. "My flute and a headlamp."

Turl raised his eyebrows. "Going down the mountain to woo your Monteagle sweetheart. Aren't you?"

Patch asked, "Where's the campsite tonight?"

Ham pointed toward the woods and said, "The shelter's a stone's throw north of Tremlett." The quarterback patted a cowboy bedroll strapped to a mule. "We've got five of these. Join us and we'll draw straws on who gets a bed."

Patch scanned the group. "Sounds equitable."

Turl said, "We've got bacon, trout, and black-eyed peas—"

"Liquor?"

Peck pulled up a fistful of onion grass. "Yeah boy, we've got Jack and a jug of moonshine." He fed the grass to a mule.

"Deck of cards, too," Finn said. "If you have some money to spend."

Patch looked at the jug hooked onto one of the mules' rig. "I might hike up and find y'all tonight. If I'm not there by nine, eat my portion of food and drink my share of libations."

Otay said, "Hope to see you, Patch. If not, have a fine time down in Monteagle." The large young man winked. Patch mocked him with an exaggerated wink and a fake guffaw. Otay laughed.

The campers started up the trail to Tremlett Spring, and Patch walked toward the railroad tracks that led to Monteagle. Between the rails, he jogged a quarter mile down the mountain. Then he sat on a boulder.

When he thought the campers had reached the spring, he walked back to the Tremlett trail and hiked up to the spur that led to Cecilia's cabin. Patch dug his headlamp out of his rucksack and strapped it on. Without lighting the lamp, he continued hiking. Twenty minutes later, it was turning dark, and Patch was at the spur's terminus. He lit his headlamp and turned to his right.

After navigating through a stand of pine trees for about forty yards, Patch came to a small clearing with a cabin on the far side of the field. Smoke floated out of the cabin's stovepipe. Patch looked back at the woods he had just marched through and wondered how far away his teammates' campsite was. Retracing the route he had just taken and his many hikes to Tremlett Spring, he had the sense that they were camped about a quarter of a mile due east. Patch wasn't comfortable with the proximity.

Cecilia was standing at a wood-burning stove and stirring a pot of turtle soup when Patch knocked on the cabin door.

"Who is it?"

"Charlton."

Cecilia flattened out her dress, slid the bolt over, and opened the door. They both stood silently for a moment.

"Good to finally have you here, sir. Please come in."

Patch entered the cabin. "Thank you, Esplanade." He sniffed the air. "What is on the stove? The aroma is inviting."

"Tonight, we have Louisiana's best turtle soup. Creole grandmothers consider it medicine."

"What ails you? Or me?"

"An arduous adventure compromises even Patch Mercer. And there are those bumps on your head, and it is rumored that a Texas brute cracked your ribs."

"Bruised. Never mind. It is delightful to see you, Esplanade."

"Thank you, Charlton. I missed you."

"Read your note several times. Thought of you often." Patch scanned the cabin. "Did Silas build this?"

"He did."

"A true craftsman."

"He carried the materials here in the dark. Took him from June to October to finish. Dug a well, too. Rose is the only other soul aware of our hideaway's existence."

"Ours?"

"A refuge for both of us to enjoy. Now let's eat dinner."

Patch examined a small table in a corner that was set with a white linen tablecloth, china, and polished silverware. There were bowls of rice, red beans, cooked greens, and a bottle of red wine and two silver cups. "This is all extraordinary, Cecilia, but we have to go back to Sewanee."

Cecilia turned and stirred the turtle soup. "I don't understand."

"I've got five teammates camping out tonight at Tremlett Spring."

"In daylight, the spring is thirty minutes from here, traipsing mostly through woods. Hard to imagine they would stumble upon us. It's pitch dark."

Patch stared out the cabin's one window. "Yes, it's unlikely they'll discover us, yet if they were to . . . it would be devastating. I can't risk your reputation."

Cecilia walked over to Patch. "You take risks every time you step on the gridiron. Nothing in life is worthwhile without taking risks. And this is my risk to take."

With his head down, Patch began to pace, then turned and faced Cecilia. "All right. But when we finish, we have to leave."

"We'll see. Now, please take your seat, Mister Mercer."

Patch and Cecilia sat down and bowed their heads. Patch said grace.

Cecilia served Patch portions of rice, beans, and cooked greens. From a pot, she ladled turtle soup for both of them. As they ate and drank, Patch was enchanted by every word she spoke and every gesture she made.

Cecilia blew on her soup and stirred it gently. "Was it puzzling to find your way here?"

"No. Your map was precise. I had to wait for the Tremlett Spring gang to hike ahead, which made me late."

"The turtle soup's flavors were at their peak just as you arrived."

"It is superior to any soup I've ever tasted. I imagine all the inns and taverns in New Orleans would prize your culinary talents."

They ate in silence for a few minutes.

"Have you ever traveled abroad, Patch?"

"No. In fact, our visit to the University of Texas a week ago is the farthest I've ever traveled from Savannah."

"Well. Perhaps one day, we'll find ourselves in Paris together."

"Paris. I'd like that."

"My aunt and uncle escorted me there for my sixteenth birthday. We spent the summer with our French cousins, ate exquisite meals, and toured the Louvre on two separate days for hours each visit."

"I've read it is vast and wonderful."

"A temple housing countless works of grandeur."

"Grandeur? Then you're the most apt guide through that temple."

Patch thought of a large portrait of a young lady that hung in his grandfather's study. Growing up in Savannah, he frequently viewed it and always thought she had to be the most beautiful woman who ever existed. Now in front of him was this kind, confident, and intelligent woman. The young lady in the painting was plain in comparison to Cecilia.

When they finished dinner, Cecilia gathered up the dishes. "Patch. I'm short of water. Please fetch some for me. The pump is out back."

"Cecilia, we must go."

"Do you expect me to leave dirty dishes? I'll return here to a mob of vermin."

"I'll get the water and help you clean. Then escort you down to Sewanee. There's plenty of oil remaining in my lamp. I'll hold your hand until we reach campus. Once there, we'll have to walk in different directions."

Cecilia gave Patch a coy glance. "No trouble from me, Charlton."

Patch sighed and walked outside. He pumped two buckets full of water. As he released the handle, he thought he heard voices and listened hard. All he could hear was an owl.

Inside the cabin, he poured the water into a basin for Cecilia, who said, "Now, go rest your warrior bones."

"No. I'll help."

Cecilia soaked and scrubbed, while Patch dried. When they finished, Patch sat down and took Cecilia's hand. "Esplanade. Thank you for such a sumptuous meal."

"I hope you enjoyed the company, as well."

"So much so, I crave a stroll down the mountain with my dinner companion."

She released his hand. "We've waited since summer for time alone. We should not let a few drunken louts, half a mile of thick woods away, send us home." She retrieved her cello and bow from the rear of the cabin. "And whether you leave or not, I will remain here tonight. This cabin is my refuge from my matron responsibilities. I'm going to stay."

Cecilia sat down and began tuning her cello.

***

At the campsite, the five Tigers, wrapped in heavy blankets, sat around a fire. Ham said, "That moonshine has stewed me."

Turl said, "I'd say we're all pretty well pickled at this point. Nature is calling me, gentlemen."

Finn said, "Me too."

Turl and Finn stepped behind the shelters to relieve themselves.

"Turl, let's see, ah, my father, you know, one of the stars of the '78 Princeton eleven, he'll be at the Carolina game."

"Well, that's sure fine. Your mother, too?"

"Yeah."

"We'll have to put on a show for them."

"Yes. Umm, my question is, will I be part of that show?"

"Finn. That's more up to Coach Lourie than me."

"Y'all decided about Patch?"

"We plan for him to be part of the eleven for the final three games."

"I thought so. I tell ya, Turl, if you could put in a good word for me— maybe remind . . . Yeah, remind him how I made a difference against Mississippi. And really, I played well in Baton Rouge, too. Don't you think, Turl?"

"You did, but Patch did his penance, so he's back on the eleven. We get a big lead against Cumberland, I'm sure coach will put the scrubs in—"

"I don't give a damn about Cumberland!" There was silence except for tree branches creaking in the breeze. "Shit. I'm sorry, Turl. The Carolina game just means everything to me. My last game and the first time my daddy will see me—hopefully see me—in a college game."

"I understand. Just hope we whip Carolina by five or six scores in the first half so you and other scrubs will get in."

"I guess that's my best shot."

The two rejoined the campfire. Finn took a sip of moonshine. On a log next to Peck, he sat slumped over. Peck put his hand on Finn's shoulder. "What's with you?"

Finn handed him the moonshine jug and said, "Nothing, Pecker. Just drink this."

Peck took a swig.

Otay stood and stretched. "Where's that Patch?"

Glumly, Finn said, "No doubt, he's making the beast with two backs."

Ham reached toward the fire to warm his hands. "That sounds like envy."

"I get my share."

Otay guffawed and the others hooted Finn.

"Listen here. I might not be as busy as Mercer, but . . . Wait a minute."

"But what?" Ham asked.

Finn dug into his pocket. "Hold on." He pulled out the note he had found in the sleeper car's restroom. "Yes sir. Hold on." The fire crackled as he read the note to himself. "Anyone know an Esplanade or Charlton?" He glanced at the map.

Ham stood and reached for the note. "What do you have there? Give it to me." Finn passed the note to Ham, who read both sides and gave it to Turl. "Where'd you get that?"

"Found it in the bathroom on the train. See where that map leads to?"

Turl turned the paper over and followed the map's path.

"Not far from here, is it?" Finn said. "And I've got a dollar that says Patch is Charlton."

Turl handed the note to Otay. "And who is Esplanade, Mister Holmes?"

Finn said, "I don't know, but she has an elegant hand and prose."

Otay crumpled the note and threw it at Finn, who caught it. "You're hoping for a scandal. Aren't you?" Turl nodded in agreement.

"No! I just think it would be fun to follow the map's path. An adventure. If Charlton is our star end, well, it'll be hilarious to barge in on him and his Esplanade."

Wearing his blanket like a cape, Otay walked toward the campsite's shed to get his bed. "Have at it, Finn. I'm going to drag my cowboy bed next to this fire and rest up for tomorrow's hangover."

Finn replied, "I'm off on an expedition and hopeful prank. Who's with me?"

Ham pointed toward Otay. "I'm following our mighty center."

With a stick, Turl stoked the fire. "I'm legless. I'm not going anywhere."

Finn gestured for Peck to come along. "It's you and me, Peck. Get your headlamp and let's go."

"I'm too drunk to crawl around the woods."

"You scared?" Finn scoffed.

Peck pushed up from the log and threw off the blanket he had draped over his shoulders. "Your little map better be right. Dammit."

Turl laid two logs on the fire. "You two looped toads better not tromp around the woods too long. We're no use to you."

"Just a little night raid, nothing compared to what our Confederate heroes did," Finn responded.

Ham picked up the moonshine jug and held it out for Finn. "Y'all might want this in case you run into any hideaway Cherokees."

Everyone laughed but Finn, who waved off the jug. After putting on long coats and affixing their headlamps, Finn and Peck left the campsite and quickly disappeared down the Tremlett Spring trail.

Thirty minutes later, they were at the edge of the woods that led to the cabin.

"Where now, Finn?"

Finn checked the map. "We turn to our right. Proportional to the directions so far, we shouldn't be too far away."

"Too far away! What does that mean? My hands are cold. My feet, too."

"Don't be soft. Do you think Jeb's men whined about their cold hands up in Fredericksburg?"

"I imagine they did. And, anyway, they were fighting for the Cause, hardly a comparison to our silly little foray."

"Silly! Don't you get it? If it's Patch secluded with a girl of standing, my father will see me play against North Carolina."

"A scandal. We're freezing for a possible scandal followed by a possible suspension and—"

"Sitting on the bench in front of my father would be mortifying." Finn breathed deeply.

Peck scanned the woods to their right. "Let's hurry then."

With leaves crunching under their boots, the two scrubs marched through the stand of trees, but they zigzagged and failed to reach the clearing.

Peck said, "We're lost, Finn. You said it wasn't far."

Finn held his index finger to his lips. Softly, he said, "Music."

***

Inside the cabin, Cecilia was playing "The Hall of the Mountain King" with Patch accompanying her on flute. They finished the piece, and, both smiling, they stood and bowed to each other.

"What time is it, Patch?"

He checked his watch. "Almost twelve."

"My. We've been playing for over an hour."

"The whole evening has been . . . has been every bit worth the long wait and then some. I'm glad I stayed."

"I am, too. Very glad."

Patch heard a clank at the window behind him. He turned and saw the flame of a headlamp against the windowpane.

Someone shouted, "I knew it. I got him now!"

Patch threw open the cabin door and shot outside. Two figures ran toward the woods. Their spotlights bobbed on the trees in front of them. Patch caught the hindmost. He tackled and straddled the prowler. "Finn!" He yanked Finn's headlamp off and tossed it. The flame extinguished in flight. He shook Finn by his coat lapels. "How did you know I was here?"

"We're just out exploring."

"Liar!" Patch pressed his forearm into Finn's neck. Finn began to choke, so Patch released the pressure and punched Finn's right eye. The scrub whimpered and covered his face. Patch pinned Finn's arms and head-butted the same eye. "Tell me, or I'm going to pound your eye into a sack of pulp."

"Get off me, you bastard, and I'll tell you."

Patch got up and bent over Finn, who dug in his pocket and drew out a crumpled piece of paper. Patch snatched it and, with the aid of the stars, could tell it was Cecilia's map and note. Again, he grabbed Finn's lapels and lifted the scrub's limp body. "Where did you get this?"

Holding his eye and wheezing, Finn said, "The train."

"What?"

"The train, bathroom floor."

"Who was out here with you—Peck? You go find him and tell him I'll beat both of you within an inch of your slimy lives if anyone hears about my visit up here."

Finn crawled around searching for his headlamp. Patch found it and picked it up, then he stepped on Finn's hand and dropped the lamp. Finn yelped and grabbed it.

Patch watched Finn scurry away and light his lamp at the edge of the woods. Patch knew the beating he had just given Finn would not keep his scrub from telling the other campers whom he saw together in a cabin. Then, each of the five would confide in someone who would confide in someone until the entire campus was talking about him and Cecilia.

Patch picked up and hurled a rock in Finn's direction. He listened to it crash through the trees, and then there was silence.

Chapter Fifteen
Wednesday, November 15th, 1899

By noon Wednesday, word had spread throughout campus and the town that Miss Cecilia was leaving Sewanee. The explanation for her departure was that her uncle in St. Louis had suddenly died and left Cecilia's invalid aunt without anyone to care for her.

Around midafternoon, this narrative was in competition with rumors that Patch and Miss Cecilia had an assignation deep in the woods in a cabin. Finn was skulking around campus with a large bruise around his eye. He told his classmates that he had fallen and hit his eye on a rock, but news that Patch had given Finn the black eye spread throughout the day.

That evening, Silas Hill, with Henry riding alongside him, pulled a two-horse wagon in front of the Hiawassee House. The two men loaded a wardrobe steamer trunk onto the wagon, followed by another trunk, two crates, and two bags of luggage.

Dressed in academic gowns, Ham, Woody, and Patch stood uphill from the Hiawassee House. Patch forced himself to watch until Cecilia made her final exit from the place where she had taken great care of her boarders and hosted warm and entertaining tea parties.

Ham said, "No more music recitals at the Hiawassee House. She plays the cello like an angel straight from heaven."

Woody added, "She is an angel straight from heaven."

Cecilia came out of the house, and Silas helped her onto the wagon seat.

Patch looked around and saw several students gawking at Cecilia. He reset his eyes on her and watched the wagon pull away and move down the street.

Ham said, "Well, Patch, you've turned Miss Cecilia into Sewanee's Hester Prynne."

Chapter Sixteen
Monday, November 20th, 1899

Alfie and Coach Lourie stood at the center of Sewanee's Hardee Field, a sandlot with clumps of grass. Alfie watched the Cumberland University football team gather around the gridiron's north goalpost. The team and their pep club had just arrived after a four-hour train ride from Lebanon, Tennessee.

Alfie scooped up pea gravel with one hand and began tossing pebbles with the other hand. "The Phoenix. That's a strange nickname."

Coach Lourie nodded toward Sewanee's opponents. "They're punier than we'd heard."

"Yeah, well, I bet their hearts aren't as puny as ours."

"Damn Patch—betrayed 'em again."

"Yep." Alfie turned away from the visitors and threw the remaining rocks. He watched them scatter down the field. "Everything was smoothed over after Ole Miss."

"And then there's Finn."

"Viper." Alfie picked up more gravel and let the pebbles fall between his fingers.

"I've heard Patch was sincere this time."

Coach Lourie shook his head. "All the sincerity in the world didn't matter. He's lucky he didn't get sent off in disgrace the way she was."

"His father might have called him home, but Patch wasn't going to be expelled. Wiggins and the alums have become feverish for a legendary season."

They watched the Cumberland team run ten-yard sprints.

Coach Lourie pointed toward Cumberland's fullback. "That little redhead is quick."

"We're so sulky, they'll probably poke a few holes for him."

"Gaps won't have to be too wide for that fire head to scamper through."

Alfie slid his hands together to dust them off. "Let's go see if our captain has steered his sailors out of the doldrums."

They walked to the fieldhouse, where they found the Tigers dressed for the game. Alfie stood in the doorway and observed the team. He thought back to a week ago when the team's spirit was palpable. Now, no one spoke. Their bodies and faces were visibly drained. Alfie was convinced the Tiger's shutout streak was in peril. He was afraid the despondent Tigers were about to tarnish their legacy.

Alfie turned to Coach Lourie and quietly said, "Thank the Lord we don't play Auburn or Carolina today."

"Thank the Lord we play Cumberland."

Along with emotional challenges, no starter or scrub had fully recovered from the cross-country expedition. Woody was off his crutches, but his ankle wasn't strong enough for him to play. Kimbrough's wrist strain was painful when he flexed his hand up or down. Prayer Bear was experiencing muscle spasms in his calves. The remaining members of the Sewanee eleven all had one or more battle scars, including jammed fingers, bruises, blisters, stiff necks, slight sprains, and cauliflower ears. Brownlow still had a lingering cough from his bout with the bronchial virus that had infected nine Tigers.

With a jar of liniment in his hands, Henry approached Prayer Bear. "Are they bothering you right now, Mister Embree?"

"This left one is, Henry."

The trainer massaged liniment into the guard's calf. On the other side of the room, Brownlow held up his jersey while Joseph rubbed ointment on his chest.

Sitting between Woody and Kimbrough, Patch stared at the floor.

With ten minutes left before kickoff, Patch stood and addressed his teammates. "I, ah, I have—"

Otay smacked his hands together. "Hey! We don't want to hear any of your fimble-famble, Mercer."

"That's right," Finn murmured.

Ham jumped to his feet and shook his fist at Finn. "Shut your bone box, you weasel, or I'll give you a matching black eye."

Finn, who had been battered in practice over the past week, subsided.

Patch scanned the room. The only teammate who met his gaze was Prayer Bear, who raised his eyebrows. Patch said, "I have nothing to say that's worth a damn." He turned away from the team and pulled off his jersey.

Kimbrough grabbed Patch's arm and pointed at his bare ribs. "I see you're still a little bruised here." Patch nodded slowly. "You leave us in the lurch, and I'll cave in this side of your tiny birdcage."

"Amen! And I will have at the other side," Prayer Bear said.

While looking at Patch, Turl flashed the palm of his hand in Prayer Bear's direction. "Put your jersey back on, Patch."

"Turl, I'm poison. We—"

"Now."

Patch followed his captain's order.

Turl turned toward Prayer Bear. "Embree, lead us in a short prayer."

"Dear Lord. Your children from Lebanon go by the name of the Phoenix. In your honor, we will turn this idolatrous bird back into ashes. Amen."

The Tigers responded, "Amen," and filed out of the fieldhouse.

On one side of Hardee Field was a grassy bank topped with hickory trees and tall pines. Below the tree line, Sewanee supporters filled the hillside. The Phoenix fans and neutral spectators stood behind the rope that lined the other side of the field.

With a loud whistle, the Sewanee Tigers kicked off and began their tenth game of the season. From the start, the home team dominated. In addition to being overpowered physically, the Cumberland team lacked football acumen and at times seemed confused.

On the first play from the line of scrimmage, Ham followed Turl through a wide hole between Prayer Bear and Peck, who was starting in place of the injured Woody. Ham took the ball seventy-five yards down the field for

Sewanee's first score. Kimbrough kicked the extra point.

Cumberland kicked off. The ball only carried twenty yards and fell into Patch's hands. He ran straight down the middle of the field. A Phoenix lunged at his right side. Patch could have accelerated past the tackler but instead forearmed him in the sternum and sent him to the ground. In front of Patch was Cumberland's quarterback. Patch didn't cut or veer away. A few yards before the two collided, the quarterback dove at Patch's knees. Patch attempted to hurdle the defender but caught his trailing foot on the quarterback's shoulder. Patch flipped into the air, hit the ground on his back, and fumbled.

Cumberland's red-headed fullback, Dickie Dyer, scooped up the ball and rushed toward the Sewanee end zone. The Phoenix crowd cheered, but so did the Sewanee side, seeing Patch leap to his feet, like a Russian folk dancer, and chase the fullback.

Just after the Sewanee ten-yard line, Patch launched himself at his prey's feet. He caught a heel to the chin but managed to wrap his arms around the Cumberland player's legs, tripping him three yards shy of the goal line. Patch's ears rang and his jawbone throbbed. He felt inside his mouth, checking for loose teeth. His teeth were fine, but his tongue was bleeding slightly.

None of Patch's teammates were jubilant when they reached the end zone, but a few nodded in his direction, and Prayer Bear shook his hand. Turl walked up to Patch. "Great recovery. Next time don't fumble."

On first down and second down, the Phoenix quarterback pitched the ball to Dickie Dyer. Each time the Sewanee rush overpowered their opponents, but the agile star runner danced around the backfield evading tacklers, giving the crowd a show. With both attempts, he was eventually caught behind the line of scrimmage.

Coach Lourie said to Alfie, "Poor guy. It's him against the world."

Alfie looked in Dyer's direction. "To hell with him."

Coach Lourie smiled and shook his head.

Cumberland had lost seven yards and had the ball on the Sewanee ten-yard line. On third down, they pitched the ball to Dyer again. He attempted a dropkick, which went wide of the left post. The Tigers took over possession. In only six plays they marched in for their second touchdown, which Patch scored on a twenty-five-yard end around. Praise for his score lacked the usual exuberance, but he did receive a few handshakes. Kimbrough successfully kicked the extra point.

During the remainder of the first half, the Tigers scored another six touchdowns, and Cumberland never crossed into Sewanee territory and made only two first downs. At halftime, Cumberland had zero points and Sewanee had forty-seven. The Tigers had knocked three members of the Phoenix eleven out of the game, and the other eight were exhausted and bruised. Otay Carter had knocked heads with the Phoenix center and had given him a goose egg on his noggin. Otay was fine, as were the other Sewanee starters.

The Tigers followed their captain to the fieldhouse for the ten-minute break. Holding a ladle, Joseph stood in front of the fieldhouse by a barrel of Tremlett Spring water. Turl turned around and addressed his teammates. "Each of y'all drink some water. Scrubs too."

Coach Lourie and Alfie caught up with the team. They stood off to the side talking. Turl walked over to them. Prayer Bear noticed the conference and joined it.

Turl said, "No reason to risk losing any of the eleven. We need to put all the scrubs in."

"I haven't done the research," Alfie said, "but I've never heard of a hundred-point shutout here in the South. What about you, Hobie? You know of any teams up north who've posted a shutout by a hundred or more?"

"No, I haven't. But it doesn't matter if we score one hundred or forty-nine points or anything in between! Crushing five big schools in six days and finishing out without a loss will be why people remember this team a century from now. Not because we buried Cumberland under the field."

"A hundred years and beyond," Turl added.

Prayer Bear put his hand on Alfie's shoulder. From low in his throat, he said, "Hmm. I'll tell you what, Alfie, if I twist an ankle out there or suffer some other injury, you're gonna put on a scrub's uniform and take my place."

Alfie slid away from Prayer Bear's hand. "You're the one who told the Almighty that we were going to reduce them to ashes."

Turl pointed at Alfie. "Damn it! We have turned them to ashes."

Alfie took his hat off and rubbed his eyes.

Coach Lourie looked at Alfie. "We rest ten, then we get Woody back, and our eleven's ready for Auburn and North Carolina."

Alfie put his hat back on and nodded. "Sorry, y'all. I'm overstepping my bounds. And," Alfie paused, "being foolish."

At the start of the second half, all ten scrubs were on the field. Coffey kicked off, and Cumberland punted directly back to Sewanee. The Tigers were downed at midfield. Within three plays, Sewanee had the ball on the Cumberland fifteen-yard line.

Coffey was playing quarterback. On the fourth play of the drive, he faked a pitch to the right halfback, Tom Smith, who was in for Turl. Finn pulled left from his right end position, and Coffey handed him the ball and followed him. Dickie Dyer slid down the line, tracking Finn, but all ten of his teammates took the fake and attacked the Sewanee right, going after Smith. As Finn rounded the corner, Dickie Dyer was ready to launch into him when Coffey blindsided Dickie, headbutting the side of his head. The hit created a loud thud. On his back, the Phoenix star was passed out. Finn waltzed into the end zone.

The referee pointed at Coffey. "Unsportsmanlike conduct. You are expelled. No Sewanee touchdown. Cumberland's ball."

While the Cumberland trainer scrambled to find his medical bag, Henry reached Dickie and placed smelling salts under his nose.

Coffey walked up to the referee. "What'd I do?"

"You could have knocked him down without hammering him with your forehead. Now go." The referee pointed toward the Sewanee sideline.

As Coffey walked off the field, a Cumberland student yelled, "You'll get yours after the game!"

Lugging a bucket of water, and short of breath, Joseph asked Henry, "Do you want me to dump it on him?" The trainer took the bucket and threw the water into Dickie's face, reviving him.

Dickie tried to stand but couldn't. He teetered while kneeling. Four of his teammates carried their fullback off the field. A Cumberland scrub took his place.

On the sideline, standing next to Coach Lourie, Alfie threw his hands up. "Now we play a man down."

"Don't worry about it. Ten of ours will handle eleven of theirs." The coach waved Peck to the sideline. "You play quarterback."

"I've never even practiced it."

"Neither have the other nine," Coach Lourie replied.

Despite playing short one player and with a novice quarterback, the Tigers continued to pummel the battered Phoenixes.

When the game ended at dusk, Alfie tossed his hat into the air. He went to catch it, but Coach Lourie lightly pushed him aside and snagged the hat. "There's your shutout, partner!"

The Tigers had scored twelve touchdowns on runs ranging from six to eighty yards. The final score was Sewanee seventy-one and Cumberland zero.

After ten games, five of which were road games played in six days, the Sewanee Tigers' shutout season continued, with a point total of 306.

Chapter Seventeen

Thursday, November 30th, 1899, Montgomery, Alabama

In 1899, Auburn had played only four games before playing Sewanee. They had dominated their first three games, including a sixty-four to zero win over Georgia Tech. At the end of their fourth contest, the Orange and Blue had tied Georgia. They now faced the undefeated, unscored-on Sewanee Tigers.

Auburn played their home games in Montgomery instead of at Auburn, which was in the middle of Alabama farmland. The team had a much bigger draw in Montgomery, the hometown of many Auburn students, past and present. The Sewanee-Auburn game was on Thanksgiving Day, providing additional incentive for Auburn students and alumni to come home for a long weekend. Montgomery Union Station was swollen with arriving travelers all day and all night before the game and the morning of. An excursion train from Atlanta brought hundreds of fans wearing orange and blue, plus a goat dressed in the same colors.

An hour before the 3:00 p.m. kickoff, two thousand fans had arrived for the game. Many of the Sewanee supporters, including sixty-five students from the Sewanee campus, wore purple sweaters. In the grandstand, streaks of purple contrasted with the prominent Auburn orange and blue. People lined up three deep along the roped-off sidelines.

At 2:30 p.m., the Sewanee players sat on benches in their assigned locker room. Woody's enthusiasm was high. His ankle injury had forced him to watch the past three games from the sidelines, but today he would play.

While Henry wrapped his ankle with zonas tape, Woody studied Patch, who sat across from him and was staring out a window. "Patch," Woody said, "you acted as a gentleman. One day, if God ordains it, you and Cecilia will find each other." Patch looked at Woody. "Let God guide you and restore you. Presently, you have a football game to win. You love football. You love to win."

***

The temperature was forty-eight degrees, and the sky was blue with only a few clouds. Sewanee sprinted onto the field to play their eleventh game of the season. They gathered in the north end zone, where Turl led his team through a brisk set of calisthenics. Afterward, the Tigers' eleven walked through plays opposite the scrubs. Then the Sewanee squad jogged over to their assigned sideline.

On the opposite side of the field, adjacent to the grandstands, Auburn's benches sat empty. At exactly 3:00 p.m., the Auburn team appeared on the south end of the field. Wearing sweaters with horizontal orange and blue stripes, the team formed a single-file line and ran up the Sewanee sideline. Each Auburn player looked straight ahead as he passed the visiting team.

Remaining in formation, Auburn cut across the field at the goal line, turned right, and walked in procession along their sideline. The Auburn fans in the grandstand stood and applauded while those on the field reached across the rope and patted the players' backs and, in unison, called out the eleven's names. When the team gathered at midfield, the Auburn fans chanted *fight, Auburn, fight!* When the refrain faded away, the much smaller Sewanee crowd began a cheer, but the home team quickly drowned them out, shouting *sis, sis, boom, orange and blue!*

Turl said, "Ham, you're going to have to yell out your signals louder than usual."

"I know. I've heard they never shut up."

Sewanee won the toss and elected to receive the opening kickoff. The Auburn kick landed in the hands of Brownlow on the Sewanee 25-yard line. He ran six yards before an Auburn tackler downed him. The two teams lined up for the first play from the line of scrimmage. The Sewanee linemen were in their four-point stances. Woody turned to Patch and said, "Are you ready?"

"Do or die."

Otay snapped the ball to Ham, who tried to buck the center of Auburn's line but ran into two Auburn halfbacks, who knocked him back into Turl. With Ham and Turl off-balance, two Auburn linemen shoved them to the ground. Other Auburn players quickly piled on, but the referee did not call a foul for their unsportsmanlike conduct.

The Tigers slowly set up to run their second-down play. Turl skirted the left end and picked up five yards and a first down before being dragged to the turf.

The teams lined up, and Ham shouted, "Cornfield 48, cornfield 48." Prayer Bear stood up from his four-point stance and cupped his ear. In response, Ham ran down the left side of his line, then the right, yelling, "Cornfield 48, cornfield 48."

Ham took the snap and pitched the ball straight to Kimbrough. Turl grabbed Kimbrough's pants and shirt from behind, lifted him, and pressed him against Prayer Bear's back. Prayer Bear led the drive through the Auburn defense for seven yards and another Sewanee first down. Auburn piled on, and again, there was no penalty called.

Alfie said to Coach Lourie, "My God. What are we in for?"

On first and second down, Auburn stopped Sewanee at the line of scrimmage, so the Tigers punted. Kimbrough sailed the ball forty-five yards. An Auburn back fielded the punt, and Turl immediately tackled him.

Thousands of Auburn supporters blasted out their pleasure at seeing their team line up for their first offensive play. From their 18-yard line, Auburn put the ball in play and ran en masse around their left end for twelve yards. They swept right for another six yards. Auburn continued to attack Sewanee's wide left and right, only occasionally trying to buck the Sewanee line.

After earning their fifth first down, Auburn had the ball on the Sewanee 38-yard line. Preston Hugo, Auburn's quarterback, took the snap and followed his backs, who locked arms as they approached the line of scrimmage. Woody tried to ram through the human chain. It flexed but didn't break. Auburn gained nine yards before Patch wrapped up Hugo's legs from behind and took him down.

With his backs locking arms and running interference, Hugo ran four more sweeps and worked the ball down to the Sewanee 4-yard line.

Fifteen minutes into the game, Auburn's fullback plunged over his right tackle and crossed the Sewanee goal line. For the first time in the Sewanee 1899 season—twenty halves of football—an opposing team had crossed the Sewanee goal line.

Auburn missed the point after touchdown. The score was five to zero.

Kimbrough kicked off for Sewanee, booting the ball forty yards. Auburn returned the kick to their 22-yard line.

On first down, Auburn's Hugo ran the ball off tackle for three yards before Prayer Bear shoved him into Turl, who tackled him. Hugo softly said "Down" and moved out of the way of the football. Auburn's left halfback picked it up and sprinted toward the Sewanee goal line. Sewanee's eleven sprinted after the Auburn man. Patch caught him and tackled him at midfield. The Auburn halfback shouted, "Down."

The referee picked up the ball and jogged it back to the umpire, Joe Joslin, who placed it on the Auburn twelve. "Unsportsmanlike conduct. Auburn loses ten yards."

Coach Lourie said, "That son of a bitch."

Alfie said, "Who?"

"Coach John Heisman."

"I've always heard he was a real gentleman."

"He often leaves that trait at the gate."

"What'd he hope to gain with that stunt?"

"He's trying to waste away our legs. Remember, Heisman hasn't traveled his team, except the Georgia game. They're fresh as daisies."

"Wily Yankee."

Over the next six minutes, the Orange and Blue continued to run around the Sewanee ends and gain first downs. Eventually they reached the Sewanee 45-yard line. From there, they ran a sweep for eight yards. After the football had been downed, the Auburn center picked it up and lumbered up the field.

Five yards past the line of scrimmage, Brownlow jumped on the lineman's back, but it took Woody and Otay to complete the tackle. Several Tigers piled on the Auburn center. The referee and umpire peeled Sewanee men off the stack. Auburn players ran to the action and started pushing Sewanee footballers and yanking on their jerseys. Sewanee responded with the same. Meanwhile, the umpire marched the ball back to the Auburn 45.

Coach Heisman ran halfway onto the field and screamed, "Piling on, Sam, piling on." The referee, Sam Smith, responded, "Can't be piling on, John, it was a dead ball."

Auburn students pushed down the stakes that held up the crowd rope, ran onto the field, and joined the ruckus. Hugo began grabbing fellow classmates and slinging them toward the sideline. "Off the field! It's a football field, dammit!"

The rest of the Auburn eleven left the shoving match and joined Hugo's effort to clear the field. With their scrubs' assistance, the eleven corralled the trespassing Auburn students. One slipped past the Auburn players and began to taunt Sewanee. "You miserable milksops—"

"Get, Dilworth, you spoon, get!" Hugo grabbed the student by his coat and swung him around, then pushed him toward the sideline.

John Heisman, standing on the Auburn bench, admonished the disrupters. "Stake that rope and stay on the other side of it or I'll have the constables run all of you out of here!"

The students complied, and the umpire called for play to resume.

Turl glanced at Coach Lourie, who had his hands behind his head. Turl read the signal: make a defensive change to stop the Auburn sweeps.

To keep the referee and umpire from becoming suspicious, Turl counted to four before calling his team into a huddle. "Brownlow, you and I are sealing off outside the left end. Ham, you and Kimbrough go wide of the right one."

Brownlow asked, "Every play?"

"Of course not. We'll mix it up."

On Auburn's second down at the home team's 45-yard line, the Auburn center snapped the football to Hugo. The Sewanee backs ran out to their assigned ends, leaving a wide gap between Prayer Bear and Otay. Conditioned to anticipate an Auburn sweep, Otay was sliding down the left side, and Prayer Bear took the same tack to the right. Turl had forgotten to let them know which one would stay in case of a buck play.

Hugo faked the pitch, pressed the ball to his chest with two hands, and ran through the hole and into the empty Sewanee backfield. The crowd's cheering increased as Hugo flew down the field, becoming deafening as he crossed the goal line and saluted the crowd after his fifty-yard touchdown run.

On Auburn's point-after-touchdown attempt, Prayer Bear broke through the Auburn line, dove, and blocked the kick. The home crowd sighed. Auburn ten, Sewanee zero.

Kimbrough kicked off, aiming the ball to the right and away from the Auburn halfback, who was positioned in the center of the field to receive the kickoff. The ball hit on the fifteen and rolled over the goal line. The Auburn halfback sprinted to scoop up the free ball. Turl and Ham got under the kick well and trapped the Auburn back in the end zone. He attempted to cross the goal line and enter the field of play, but first Turl, then Ham, grabbed him and pushed him to the ground.

The umpire ran into the end zone. "The ball is down behind the goal line and goes over to Sewanee!"

The Auburn fans booed. Students from the Auburn sideline went under the rope and rushed toward the Auburn goal line. The Auburn scrubs intercepted them as Coach Heisman screamed at the students, "Off the field, you mullet heads!" All eleven Auburn scrubs successfully wrangled the protesting Auburn men and pressed them back toward the sideline and under the rope. The Montgomery chief constable and eight of his men, all carrying batons, dispersed along the rope behind the Auburn sideline.

Fearful of further and more aggressive Auburn disruptions, the referee conversed with the umpire. Then the referee reversed his call and said, "The ball remains in Auburn's possession and on the one-yard line."

Coach Lourie yelled, "Hey, Sam, hey! We're playing under protest, got that, Sam?"

Alfie waved his pocket-sized rule book in one hand while shaking his fist with the other. "Have you read this book, you clowns?"

Coach Lourie pushed Alfie's arms down. "We've got enough trouble with them."

Auburn set their formation on their 1-yard line. Hugo took the snap and rolled to his left. Patch skirted around the Auburn left end. Just before the quarterback pitched the ball to his fullback, Patch wrapped his arms around Hugo and caused him to fumble. Woody jumped on the loose football—touchdown Sewanee.

Kimbrough missed the point-after-touchdown kick. With six minutes remaining in the first half, the score was Auburn ten, Sewanee five.

Auburn kicked off. Patch fielded the kick and pitched it back to Kimbrough, who punted over the heads of the charging Auburn eleven. The kick was high and long, awing even the Auburn crowd, who joined the Sewanee faithful in a collective *ahhh*. With Patch, Turl, and Kimbrough flying toward him, an Auburn end marked the turf, reached above his head, and caught the ball. Turl and Kimbrough saw him make the mark and passed him, but Patch didn't see the player's signal for a fair catch and dropped his shoulder into the punt returner's waist. The end held onto the football as he went to the ground.

Another row broke out between the teams. This time the Auburn students stayed behind the rope and did not test the constables' willingness to employ their batons.

After restoring order, the umpire called time for the first half. The Auburn crowd loudly demonstrated their approval for their team's first-half performance and dominance over the lauded Sewanee eleven.

In the locker room, most of the Sewanee eleven stretched out either on benches or on the floor. Henry and Joseph moved quickly from one to another, applying ice or liniment. Scrubs ladled Tremlett Spring water into tin cups and served them to the starters.

Patch and Woody sat on the floor with their backs against a wall. Woody ruminated about his failure to break through the Auburn interference and stop their first score. The first touchdown of the season, after ten shutouts. If they lost the game, it would be his fault.

Patch said, "How's the ankle?"

Woody looked blankly at Patch. "I'm sorry. What?"

"Your ankle. How is it?"

"No worse than at the beginning of the game. No oil for the furnace, though."

"You may not have much fuel, but you've got plenty of sand."

Woody smiled. "You too."

The two friends directed their attention to Coach Lourie, who was addressing the team. "I'm not sure why Sam Smith has lost his nerve. He's got a reputation as a fair man. When he refereed the Princeton-Virginia game last year, he called it evenly. But count on more of the same during the second half. And when they gouge, grab hair, or jab in a scrum, give them a hard sock in the gut. Just try to make sure Sam Smith can't see you do it. He'll make the poor-sportsman calls on us and leave the instigators alone."

Brownlow said, "Coach, forget about the referee, can't you see the awful condition we're in?"

"Of course I can. I've been in a locker room beat-up and numb."

Brownlow grumbled, "We've been getting kicked and abused for a damn full half of football."

Ham said, "They're taking it out of us, Coach. We've never seen this kind of stuff."

Coach Lourie said, "So should we forfeit? We can go to the train right now. Or do you want me to put the scrubs on the field to finish out?"

Turl stood up and hit a locker with the side of his fist. "Y'all, we will do or die. We've said that many times to each other. Today, it surely is true. We will do or die."

Prayer Bear said, "God gives us nothing we can't manage. We will not fail God, our school, our families, or each other. If they have to scoop us up off the field this evening and throw us on the train like sacks of corn, so be it. Like Turl said, 'Do or die.'"

The Sewanee football team jogged from the locker room back onto the field. No one spoke until, loud enough for all of his teammates to hear, Patch said, "I've never craved a fight more than right now. Here we go, Tigers!"

Auburn returned the second-half kickoff to their 36-yard line and ran four successful sweeps, moving the line of scrimmage to the 50-yard line.

Turl shouted, "We stop them here, Sewanee, right here!"

Prior to the snap, the Auburn halfbacks moved up to flank Hugo at arm's length. "Hike." The quarterback took the snap and set the ball on the ground behind him. One Auburn halfback picked up the ball, put it on his outside hip, and ran wide to the left while the other halfback pretended he had grabbed the ball and feigned that he had it on his back hip. He bolted toward the right end of the line.

Confused, some of the Sewanee eleven went right and some went left. Kimbrough, who had clearly seen which halfback had the ball, stood in the runner's path. As Kimbrough lunged at the ball carrier, the Auburn halfback cut hard to the center of the field. He ran twenty yards through an empty backfield before Brownlow caught and tackled him from behind.

Auburn was on the Sewanee 30-yard line. They bucked the Sewanee left side for two yards and the right for two more yards. It was third down, one yard to go. Auburn's supporters chanted *fight, Auburn, fight!*

Hugo looked to the sideline, where Coach Heisman was tying his shoe. As directed, Hugo set his team in formation for a field goal attempt. Auburn's fullback kicked the ball hard but was too far under it.

Coach Heisman pounded his fist into his palm. "Hell, he skied it!"

End over end the ball fell until it dropped a yard in front of the goalpost's crossbar. Sewanee took possession of the ball on their 26-yard line.

Ham pitched to Kimbrough, who ran wide to the right. Patch tried to block Auburn's Poke Roberts to the inside, but Roberts punched Patch just below the sternum, knocking the wind out of him and dropping him to his knees. Roberts launched himself at Kimbrough's shins. The nearby players heard a snap.

Facedown on the ground, Poke cried out and held his right collarbone. Kimbrough was down and in a fetal position, rocking back and forth while clutching the ball in one hand and his left shin in the other. Henry, Coach Lourie, the Auburn trainer, and Coach Heisman ran onto the field. Joseph chipped at an ice block, wrapped the shavings in a towel, and sprinted the ice pack to Henry.

The trainer held the ice pack on Kimbrough's shin while Coach Lourie harangued the referee. "What the hell is going on here? Are they going to have to pull knives on us before you call a foul?"

"Tend to your player, coach, and then go back to your sideline."

"If you don't start policing Auburn, I'll pull my eleven off the field."

Coach Heisman helped Poke off the field, and the team's trainer walked him to the locker room.

In the crowd, two Montgomery doctors were sitting together. One said to the other, "Broke his clavicle."

"Yep."

They left the grandstands and went to attend to the injured Auburn player.

Prayer Bear and Otay held Kimbrough under his arms as he walked gingerly to test his leg. "All right, I'm ready." After they let go, he walked on his own, then jogged ten yards and back. "I'm fine." Kimbrough pointed to a spot just below his left knee. "I'll have a Sewanee purple bruise here in a bit, that's all."

It was second down, with seven yards needed to reach a first down. Turl asked Kimbrough, "Can you punt?"

Kimbrough took a few practice kicks in the air. Each time he planted his left foot, it felt like a nail was driven into the top of his shin. "How far do you want it to go?"

Turl said, "How about Atlanta?"

The Sewanee Tigers lined up, and Ham signaled for a punt. Kimbrough dropped back, caught the snap, and punted the ball thirty-two yards. Hugo ran up and made a basket catch. Brownlow form-tackled him at the Auburn 44-yard line.

For the next five possessions, both the teams failed to make first downs and punted on second or third down. Even with his injury, Kimbrough was a superior kicker to Auburn's and eventually had Auburn backed up to their 16-yard line.

Hugo mostly called buck plays and engaged the Tigers in mass pushing matches, movable mounds advancing and retreating. Possessing the football for nine minutes, Auburn drove the ball thirty-four yards.

Turl called his teammates into a huddle. "They're too fresh. No more scrums—dive at their legs."

It was third down and Auburn had the ball on the 50-yard line with one yard to go for a first down. At the snap, the Sewanee linemen cut the opposing linemen down at their knees. Patch hurdled fallen bodies, landed, sprang, and pounced on Hugo. Auburn lost two yards, and the ball went over to Sewanee.

Six minutes remained in the game. It was dusk. The Sewanee scrubs were all standing on the edge of the sideline. Joseph stood on the bench imagining several different ways his Tigers would score a touchdown. The referee gave the teams sixty seconds to water their eleven. The Sewanee starters lined up at the barrel of Tremlett Spring water.

Play resumed. Down five points, Sewanee had the ball at midfield.

Patch lined up deep in the backfield, and Ham pitched him the ball. Patch ran left. The Auburn right end overplayed the Sewanee speedster, so Patch slanted inside and passed him. An Auburn halfback was an arm's length away from Patch, who cut outside and angled toward the Auburn sideline.

He was sure he could outrun the defender and turn the corner, but the halfback was fast, too, and Patch was running out of field. A step before the boundary line, he made a sharp turn upfield. The Auburn halfback shoved him with one hand. Patch staggered but stayed in play. As Patch ran in front of his opponents' bench, an Auburn scrub slid his foot over the sideline and tripped him. Patch landed with the ball between his stomach and the ground.

Ham helped Patch stand up. Winded, Patch tried to say, "Trip."

Ham said, "Dip?"

"Trip."

"I can't understand you. Just calm down."

Laboring to breathe, Patch watched the referee jog into position for the next play as the umpire established the line of scrimmage. He grabbed Ham's arm. "No foul?"

"For what?"

Patch scanned the line of Auburn scrubs, searching for a tell, but they all looked past him or met his gaze with a poker face. He shook his head and walked away.

Four minutes remained in the game, and dusk was approaching darkness.

Ham ran up to Turl and said, "I'm not sure we've got a thirty-four-yard drive left in us. How about Kimbrough drop-kicks?"

"No tie, dammit."

"What should I call?"

Turl closed his eyes, opened them, and said, "Double fake kick—right end."

The two went to their positions. Ham called out, "Kick!" Kimbrough backed up ten yards. Auburn shifted their formation. Three of their backs moved up to the line, and Hugo dropped back into position to receive the punt. "Rising tide 38, rising tide 38, hut!"

Otay didn't snap the ball, and Kimbrough ran up to his regular position, five yards behind Ham. Auburn's backs returned to their regular positions, behind their linemen.

Ham shouted, "Hut!"

Again, Otay didn't snap the ball, and Kimbrough ran backward to his kicking spot. Auburn's backfield repositioned into their punt return formation.

John Heisman squinted. "What the hell is this?"

Without a signal from Ham, Otay snapped a perfect spiral back to Kimbrough. The Sewanee fullback held the football tilted down in front of him but didn't start his kicking approach. Patch pulled left and circled toward Kimbrough. An Auburn halfback from each side angled toward Kimbrough, who turned and handed the ball to Patch. Turl, Prayer Bear, and Brownlow formed a column of protection, and Patch ran alongside the interference.

Auburn's Hugo tried to blast through Patch's line of blockers. He bounced off Prayer Bear and Brownlow, then tried to break through again. They leveled him. The Auburn right end circumvented the interference and grabbed Patch's jersey from behind. Turl pivoted back and lowered his shoulder into the defender's stomach. The Auburn end grunted, folded at the waist, and dropped to the turf.

The three guardians turned and faced the Auburn rush, and Patch accelerated to the goal line. Sewanee ten, Auburn ten.

Heisman walked over to Montgomery's chief constable, standing behind the coach and rope barrier, and said, "Thomas, in case Sewanee makes the extra point, do you have another fifteen men around here who could escort Sewanee and the officials to safety?"

"Already have twenty of my men moving in that direction. No riot on my watch, John."

"Good man."

In growing darkness, the Sewanee eleven ran down the field and set up for the extra-point kick. Kimbrough tried not to limp, but the injury had spread beyond its initial nickel-sized area.

Ham held the football in place for Kimbrough. Determined to ignore the throbbing, the kicker approached the ball. A hot sensation enveloped his shinbone when he planted his left foot. Without a solidly planted left leg, Kimbrough struck the ball with less than his usual force. The kick began low. An Auburn tackle reached toward the sky and came within a hand's length of batting down the football. The ball wobbled toward the goalposts and dropped over the crossbar, giving Sewanee eleven points to Auburn's ten.

Insisting that the ball had fallen toward the field of play, Auburn supporters booed and jeered in response to the point awarded to Sewanee.

Auburn raced to midfield to line up to kick to Sewanee, but at the Auburn goal line, the referee and umpire conferred.

The umpire, Joe Joslin, said, "Can't play football in the dark, and I surely can't umpire in the dark."

"You want to see the Auburn folks rush out onto the field again? We'll have mayhem, Joe."

"We have no choice. This game is over. It's in the rule book—no play after dusk."

"The rule book also says we can call a draw regardless of score, due to nightfall or excessive fighting."

"Nope. We don't want a scandal, which is what we'll get if we take a point from Sewanee."

"Big risk with the crowd."

"Umpire's decision." Joslin nodded at the Sewanee sideline. "Don't fret. Those gents with the sticks are going to take us out of here along with Sewanee."

Sam Smith walked to the Sewanee sideline. He looked at the twenty constables lined up there, then said to Coach Lourie, "Game over, coach. Too dark. Your boys win."

"Best call you've made all day."

On the other side of the field, Joe Joslin approached John Heisman, who removed his spectacles. "Joe, by my watch, we've got two minutes left in this game, and by my eyes we've got enough light to play out the time!"

"Too dark, coach, too dark. The players out there look like ghosts. Sewanee wins by one." The umpire turned and walked toward midfield, where the two teams waited for instructions.

Coach Heisman followed him. "You want to be the man who decided this game instead of allowing the teams to do it?"

"Too dark!"

"Come on, they could fumble the kickoff and we could kick the winning goal."

Joe turned and faced Coach Heisman. "John, just how do you expect me to judge that field goal? Too dark!"

The Auburn coach reached down, grabbed two fistfuls of grass, and stormed back to his sideline.

Joe Joslin reached midfield and said, "I need the captains." Turl and Hugo stood by the umpire, who told them, "This contest is concluded due to darkness. Sewanee is the victor. The score, Sewanee eleven and Auburn ten. Well-fought match, men."

Despite their disappointment, the Auburn team showed no bitterness toward Sewanee. The members of the two teams shook hands. Hugo said to Turl, "Y'all go on to Atlanta and beat Carolina. I want our one loss to be against the champions of the South."

"We will oblige you."

As word spread that the game was over and Sewanee had been awarded the victory, Auburn supporters started climbing down from the grandstand. Those at ground level began pushing toward the field. The constables, with their nightsticks out, surrounded the Sewanee entourage and the two game officials and escorted them away from the field. Two dozen drunk, belligerent

Auburn students followed, heckling the group all the way to the train station.

The Mountain Goat slowly pulled out of Union Station, starting a seven-hour haul to Atlanta. Half an hour outside of Montgomery, most of the passengers were asleep.

Kimbrough was not. Lying on a lower berth, he tried to ignore his shin injury, which throbbed and stabbed. The laudanum Henry had given him earlier had barely lowered the pain.

Henry checked on the fullback. "How are you, Mister Kimbrough?"

Kimbrough pointed at Henry's medical case. "I think I need some more magic out of your bag."

"The dose should start easing your pain shortly. I'll come back here in just a bit, and if your bruise is still keeping you awake, I'll give you more."

"I've got to sleep, Henry."

Knowing Kimbrough's high threshold for pain, Henry gave him an additional drop of laudanum.

Three berths down, Joseph was attending to Prayer Bear, whose face was badly scratched. From the time the Mountain Goat had left the train station, Henry and Joseph had cleaned and bandaged abrasions for ten of the eleven, and now it was Prayer Bear's turn. Henry watched Joseph dab an alcohol-soaked cotton ball on the guard's wound.

"Joseph Hill, you little devil. You've set my face on fire."

Using a dry cotton ball, Joseph absorbed rivulets of alcohol that ran down Prayer Bear's cheek.

Affectionately, Prayer Bear lightly tapped Joseph's shoulder. "Both of you tormentors get on to bed. This team's going to need a lot of doctoring over the next three days."

Henry pointed at Prayer Bear. "Try to sleep with the left side of your face on the pillow so that scrape can breathe."

"That's my normal side anyway. Now y'all leave me in peace to my nighttime devotion."

"Have a good sleep, Mister Embree," Joseph said.

"You too, young man."

At the back of the train, Henry pulled down Joseph's berth.

Joseph reached under one of the seats and slid out Henry's anatomy book. "Henry, I'm not sleepy yet."

"Well, I am." After extending the book to Henry, Joseph sat down. Henry sighed, then sat next to him. "Let's study about Mister Kimbrough's bad shin." After scanning the table of contents, Henry turned to the chapter on the lower extremities and found a sketch of the skeletal structure of a leg.

Pointing to the shin area, Joseph asked, "How do you say this word?"

"You can say it. It's just another Latin word. Remember, a lot of their endings sound the same."

Joseph slowly said, "Fibula."

"That's right."

Joseph ran his finger down the drawn fibula. "It's skinny. What's this bigger bone do?" Joseph slowly pronounced *tibia*.

"It connects the knee to the ankle bone."

"Mister Kimbrough got his tibia broken?"

"He's got a deep bruise."

"What's that?"

"Swelling. Broken bones don't swell up. He's got more pain than he's letting on, a lot more."

Henry and Joseph continued studying bones, but within ten minutes, Joseph was asleep. Henry pulled a blanket down from Joseph's berth and covered him with it. Soon after, Henry put the book under his seat, closed his eyes, and fell asleep.

This left Patch as the only person awake in the Pullman car. After discarding six attempts at a letter to his father, he was reading the seventh to himself.

Dear Father,

I should have written you much sooner. It has been a lack of nerve, not a lack of respect, which has held me back. By now, I am sure that you and Grandfather have learned of my recent indiscretion. Please know how very sorry I am to have forced both of you into such an uncomfortable and undeserved light.

My only solace is that the entire Anglican leadership holds both of you in the highest regard and will not allow the sins of the son to visit upon two such men. Again, my deepest apologies to you, Grandfather, and Mother (whom I am sure you have guarded from this scandal).

Please allow me to comfort your mind to some degree. It is, beyond question, highly inappropriate for me to have been alone with Miss Fontaine. But I am duty bound to defend Miss Fontaine against the crude rumors circulating. At no given moment, past or present, has there been an iota of lascivious conduct between your son and Miss Fontaine. Even in seclusion together, the notion of improper behavior never entered my mind.

For the first time in my young manhood, I have opened my eyes and heart to a woman's inner beauty as a deeper, more profound sister to her physical beauty. My time with Miss Fontaine facilitated my growth. It is my greatest hope that one day you will meet her. Upon such meeting, you will discover that she reflects the greatest aspects of her fine family.

We have been fond of each other during my entire period at Sewanee. Never before had we been in seclusion, yet the longing to be alone together overpowered our sense of propriety. We succumbed, ignoring the possible consequences and what was fitting for a lady of Miss Fontaine's caliber and grace.

All I can do after straying from God's will is repent and ask for His forgiveness, which I have done. And of course, I ask you, my dear father and the rest of my loving family, for forgiveness as well.

The purpose of the remainder of this correspondence is to declare to you my plans for the future. The news I am about to present will further upset you and Grandfather, though years from now you both will see the wisdom in my following choice.

My affection for you and Grandfather is immeasurable. I take great pride in your eminent positions in the Church, yet I cannot follow the path that the two of you have set before me. After I graduate this summer I will not be attending the seminary at Sewanee or anywhere else. This may be a cold and shocking revelation, but perhaps not. I can imagine that the aspects of my personality that are ill-suited for the cloth have been apparent to you and Grandfather for some time.

This decision to not pursue the vocation of priesthood rests on bedrock, which is my honest and complete understanding that I will never have the fervor required to serve and lead a flock. Moving through life from this point onward, I will always remain faithful to the highest values of a Christian man. I simply cannot carry the mantle of a church leader. The impulse and desire to do so are absent from my nature.

With admiration and adoration,
Patch

Chapter Eighteen
Friday, December 1st, 1899, Atlanta, Georgia

The Atlanta chapters of the Sewanee and North Carolina alumni clubs hosted both teams at the Kimball House for Friday and Saturday night. The alums also paid for accommodations for Henry, Joseph, and the North Carolina trainer, who stayed at Atlanta's upscale hotel for black people, The European.

The Tigers reached their rooms at 3:00 a.m. and had to be roused for lunch at noon. After they ate, they joined Henry and Joseph in the Kimball House gymnasium for sponge baths, rubdowns, and wound care.

That evening in the hotel's dining room, the alumni clubs held a dinner in honor of the two teams vying for the Southern championship. The seating was arranged so North Carolina players would sit with Sewanee players at each table. The opposing coaches and student managers sat together.

There were toasts to respective opponents, their states, their schools, their alumni clubs, the game of football, and the South. Every player, on both teams, had a one-drink limit of either scotch or bourbon. Additionally, everyone got a glass of champagne for the final toast of the evening, given by the president of the North Carolina Atlanta Alumni Club: "A toast to these young men who are from all over the southland. Young men who will battle each other in front of thousands tomorrow. Young men who will compete for the glory of their schools and classmates. May the contest be robustly athletic, physical, and gentlemanly. May God look over all of you and deliver you through the match without serious injury. Cheers!"

At 9:00 p.m., both teams were in their rooms. Woody and Patch lay in their beds within reaching distance of each other. Patch reflected on how this was the way they had slept in boarding school, now at Sewanee, and even on trips.

Patch said, "You know, we're like brothers."

"Of course."

"Brothers tell each other everything, no secrets."

"Not all brothers are complete confidants."

"You tell me a secret you really would rather not tell me. Then, I'll do the same."

Woody remained silent. Patch decided that if Woody didn't want to share a secret, he would still share his.

Woody cleared his throat and closed his eyes. "Since I met Lillian, I can't get out of my mind an image of her bare-chested."

"That's your secret?"

"Yes."

"You're going to worry yourself to death, Woody."

"It's an egregious sin."

"No, no. You're wrong. It's natural for boys and men—we're made this way. It's Darwin. It's how the species continues."

"How frequently do you do it?"

"A lot. I can't prevent it. None of us can. Some Texas guy might have watched her play tennis today and undressed her with his eyes."

Woody rolled over and faced Patch. "Why would you say something like that?"

"Because you're fretting about nothing. Nothing. You are always worrying yourself into melancholy. And Lillian, imagining her without clothes is especially natural for you. She wants to be on your arm."

"The Bible instructs us to have pure thoughts."

"Woody, the Bible is a golden bucket with holes."

"That's borderline blasphemous."

"Do we take multiple wives anymore? Do fathers stone their sons as punishment for the son cursing the father?"

"Oh, God, make clean our hearts within us. And take not thy Holy Spirit from us.' What do you think that is a prayer for?"

"To help us be kind."

There was silence for a few minutes. Then Woody said, "Your turn. Your secret."

"I have sent a letter to my father—"

"Declaring your intentions to marry Cecilia Fontaine?"

Patch paused. "No." He paused again. "Declaring my intentions to not enroll in seminary."

Woody clasped his hands behind his head and drew in a long breath. "How do you think this will affect him, and your grandfather?"

"I haven't heard the calling. I can't be a priest, much less a bishop."

"Maybe in seminary God will speak to you."

"He spoke to you at Saint Mathias."

"He did, yet it has been in seminary where I have felt God's grace the most."

"We both know he's showered me with clemencies. If a secular life displeases him, his grace will be there, as always."

The young men lay in silence for a time. Woody said, "Are we going to drift apart now?"

"Woody, we will always be brothers, just not in the priesthood. I look forward to sharing secrets with you for years to come."

"May the peace of the Lord be always with you."

"And also with you."

Chapter Nineteen
Saturday, December 2nd, 1899, Atlanta, Georgia

Alfie and Coach Lourie sat alone on the Sewanee bench an hour before the Sewanee–North Carolina kickoff time.

Coach Lourie said, "We're going to have to rent a boxcar to tote our share of today's gate back to the Mountain."

Alfie pointed across the field. "You see that fat fellow over there?"

"Yep."

"He's Carolina's manager. When we telegraphed back and forth in the spring, we convinced each other that this game would be for the championship."

"Even if you had been wrong, a match here would guarantee bountiful revenues."

"First telegram I sent him simply had a suggested date and the word *Atlanta*. His response was *agreed*."

At 1:00 p.m., the temperature was fifty-one degrees and there were no clouds in the sky. The grandstands and bleachers at Atlanta's Piedmont Park were filled to capacity. The ends of the playing field were lined with luxurious carriages carrying fans of the game in addition to partisans. Behind the roped-off sidelines stood around three hundred on each side. Spectators also stood on a hill forty yards from the field and on the rooftops of some nearby buildings. People traveled from as far away as Mobile and Richmond to attend this match. Many members of the crowd had seen the Sewanee and Auburn battle two days earlier in Montgomery.

Ten of the Sewanee eleven were set to play despite injuries and aches accumulated over the season. Kimbrough was unsure whether he could join them. He'd woken up that morning in severe pain. He wondered if Coffey was good enough to face Carolina.

In front of the team, Kimbrough had refused to wince or hobble, but in the locker room a half hour before kickoff, he went to Henry and said, "It's not good."

"Much worse than it was, isn't it?"

Kimbrough nodded.

"You know you'll make it so you can't walk if you try to play on it?"

The star fullback and kicker closed his eyes and did not respond.

"Please roll down your sock, Mister Kimbrough." Just below his knee, Kimbrough's shin had a lump the size of half a walnut. "I'm going to just put my finger on it. I won't push, all right?"

"Go ahead." Henry gently laid his index finger on the lump, and Kimbrough involuntarily jerked his leg. "You wrap it and I'll be fine."

"Mister Kimbrough, wrapping this leg's not going to help you at all. We've been icing it for two days and it keeps inflaming."

"Give me a shot, then."

"You need to show coach this before I do anything." Henry called to Joseph and asked him to get Coach Lourie.

The Sewanee coach was on the field talking to the North Carolina coach, his Princeton teammate and friend J. G. Reynolds.

Joseph ran up to the coaches. "Pardon me, coach."

"Just a minute, Joseph." Coach Lourie looked back at Coach Reynolds, and Joseph moved away from the coaches, out of earshot. "How about this—facing off against each other for a championship?"

"A lot of stars had to be aligned."

"Yes, indeed. All right, J.G., what's the bet?"

"If Sewanee wins, drinks on me. If we win, drinks on you."

"Why such a pittance? I heard that Heisman is around here looking to lay ten dollars on Carolina."

"Is he offering a spread?"

"Not sure."

"Unless he gives you ten points, I'd hold onto your cash." Enjoying their nascent rivalry, they both laughed. "Hobie, I'm telling you our boys are ready for your eleven, ready and hungry for a championship."

"Is that right, J.G.?" They chuckled. Coach Lourie put his hand on his friend's shoulder. "Excuse me, coach. I have to see what's got our assistant trainer all in a lather."

"We'll wager the bar bill. All right?"

"I look forward to emptying your wallet."

They both grinned, and Coach Lourie walked over to Joseph. "All right, Joseph, what's on your mind?"

"Henry and Mister Kimbrough need you, quick."

Inside the locker room, Coach Lourie and Joseph found Kimbrough surrounded by Turl and Henry.

The coach saw Kimbrough's shin. "Oh, hell!" He looked at Henry. "Can he play?"

Kimbrough said, "Unless I'm not breathing, I'm on that football field."

Coach Lourie said, "How do you plan to manage that?"

With his palm up, Kimbrough waved his hand above his injury. "Give me a shot of cocaine, right into the purple."

Henry said, "You'll pass out as soon as I stick you."

"You've got smelling salts."

"Coach, Mister Kimbrough won't be able to walk after the cocaine wears off."

"How long will the shot carry me?"

"About three to four hours."

Kimbrough said, "Sounds to me like a football game and a trip to the hotel."

Henry said, "Not the hotel, the hospital."

Turl went down on a knee and began tightening the laces of one of his boots. "You're not doing it, Kimbrough. You've already given us twenty games' worth of running, kicking, and punishing the opposition. You've been our Hercules. I'm not going to allow you to cripple yourself."

"I'll be fine in a few months. Right, Henry?"

"I can't make you any promises, Mister Kimbrough. All I can say is that right now using crutches and regular icing is what's best."

Kimbrough said, "I've always liked long odds, I'll take a shot."

Henry shook his head and looked at Coach Lourie, who said, "Listen to Henry. The cocaine will drop you, and you'll land on a bed of rocks."

"When it drops me. I'll take the pain. I'll ice it until it's a mere memory."

Turl and the coach went outside, where they found Alfie leaning against the building and reading a newspaper. "Listen to this: 'It is indisputable that the gridironers from the small Tennessee school, alternately referred to as Sewanee and the University of the South, have swept across the Southern football landscape dominating opponents in an unprecedented manner. However, they have finally spent themselves'—"

"Old news, Alfie!" Coach Lourie interrupted. "Have you seen Kimbrough's leg?"

"Yesterday."

Turl said, "Well, today it's even worse. Critically worse."

Alfie rolled up the newspaper and stuffed it in his back pocket. "Let me wager a guess. He wants a shot of cocaine so he can get on the field."

"Henry's dead against it," said Coach Lourie. "So am I."

"The final decision is up to you, Turl. I wouldn't want to be in your position. He could permanently damage his leg if you allow him to play. On the other hand, if you compromise his glory, it could damage his heart, permanently."

Alfie went into the locker room. Ten minutes later, Turl and Coach Lourie walked through the door. The room became silent.

With his hands on his knees, Turl stared into Kimbrough's eyes from a foot away and said, "Out on that field is an ambulance carriage. When I decide your time is up on the field today, whether it's one minute in or near the end, you will be carried to that carriage and go to the hospital. Do I have your word, as a Christian man, that you will not protest any of that?"

"I will do exactly everything you listed."

"Go ahead, Henry. This man has earned his destiny."

Coach Lourie cleared out the locker room except for Henry and Kimbrough. Outside the locker room, Coach Lourie asked the team for their attention. "After today's game ends, you will be the football champions of the South. You will have achieved this and more by completing an undefeated season over twelve games with eleven shutouts and five wins in six days, which you executed traveling over three thousand miles. Not Yale, Harvard, Wisconsin, or my beloved Princeton has even approached the accomplishment you will complete, today, here in Atlanta. And I doubt any team ever will—"

Kimbrough screamed.

Finn said, "Goddamn!"

Coach Lourie's voice cracked as he tried to continue his pep talk. He cleared his throat and said, "The butterflies in your stomachs will escape with the first jarring hit you give or take, but don't forget these dancing harbingers of triumph. Keep them near to your heart throughout today's contest and, hell, for the rest of your lives."

As Kimbrough's teammates walked to the field, Finn jogged up to Patch and said, "How are those broken ribs of yours?"

"Bruised, not broken, and fine. For weeks now."

"I was thinking. Maybe about halfway through the second half, your ribs get, I don't know, sore."

Patch stopped and stared at the black eye he had given Finn. It was faded but still noticeable. Patch felt an impulse to hit it again. "What are you implying? You worm."

"I've got to play in front of my daddy today, Patch. Sitting on the bench the whole game—the humiliation would be too much to bear."

Patch felt Finn's desperation and a modicum of pity for him. "All I've got to say is root for us. We take a good lead, and coach might put you in."

"Maybe that's all you've got to say, but I've got more. If you don't come out of the game, I'm going to share with everyone what I saw you and your precious Cecilia doing in the cabin."

Patch grabbed Finn's jersey. He looked around to see if anyone was watching them. No one was. Patch pushed his scrub and let go of his jersey. Finn barely kept to his feet. "You didn't see anything, because there was nothing to see."

"I don't know, Patch. Do you really want her name further besmirched?"

"Go ahead, Finn, spread your filthy rumor. It and a hundred others have already been passed around." Patch walked away and then ran over to join the other starters.

Fifteen minutes later, Kimbrough came out of the locker room and practiced his punts and dropkicks, while his teammates warmed up. He felt only a twinge of discomfort when he planted his left foot, and he enjoyed powering through the pain. His kicks had loft and length. Almost every one of them was a spiral, eliciting *ooh*s and *ahh*s from the crowd.

Alfie and Coach Lourie stood and watched.

Coach Lourie said, "Heisman is looking to lay ten against us. Are you in?"

"How about two apiece for us, and we both chip in three for the boys?"

"Yep. Sounds right."

Coach Lourie pointed to the north end of the field, where Auburn's John Heisman was leaning against an opulent carriage, talking with the Georgia Tech coach.

As Alfie walked up to the two men, he heard Coach Heisman say, "The South isn't ready for a Harvard or Princeton, but I would enjoy seeing my eleven against, say, Pop's Indians or even Stagg's Maroons."

Alfie removed his hat. "Good afternoon, coaches."

"Good afternoon," they both replied.

"Mister Heisman."

"Yes. Mister Melville, correct?"

"Yes sir."

"Interested in another match with my eleven?"

"This will be our last stop, sir."

"I suppose twelve is a good number. What's on your mind?"

"I heard through the grapevine you're looking for the other end of ten dollars against Sewanee."

"Yes, I am, sir. Are you game?"

"I'm your man, coach."

They shook hands.

At 2:15 p.m., North Carolina kicked off to Sewanee. Kimbrough marked the turf on the Sewanee 22-yard line, caught the ball, and punted back to the Tar Heels. Their fullback fielded the ball and marked at the Tar Heel 35-yard line. He punted back to Sewanee.

Marking for fair catches and punting was the game's action for the next four plays. Both teams' kickers sent spirals tracing long arcs through the air. With each spectacular punt, the crowd cheered.

Sewanee was gaining a four- to six-yard advantage with each kick, so North Carolina dropped out of the duel with Kimbrough and, from their 15-yard line, began bucking the Sewanee line. North Carolina's strategy paid off. The Tar Heels earned seven consecutive first downs and advanced the line of scrimmage to the Sewanee 45-yard line.

Turl signaled for the backs to line up in the gaps between the Tigers' linemen. North Carolina's fullback tried to plunge through the Sewanee line but was stopped for no gain.

To back the Tigers up deep into their own territory, the Tar Heels punted on second down. Their kicker hit the ball solidly and sent Kimbrough back to the goal line. The Sewanee fullback reached for the football, but it slid through his hands and bounced off his chest. At the Sewanee 10-yard line, the Tar Heel quarterback, Clay Cansler, fell on the ball. Kimbrough downed him there.

On first down, Sewanee was offside, so the umpire moved the ball half the distance to the goal line. The Tigers jumped the snap again, and the ball was placed two and a half yards from the goal line. The Sewanee faithful started chanting *iron, iron, iron.*

Cansler took the snap and dove off his center's hip. With his fullback pushing him from behind, he moved the ball forward two yards. It was now second down and the ball was at the one-half-yard line.

The North Carolina quarterback pitched the ball to his fullback, who waited and then fell in behind the other backs as they escorted him on a direct line at Woody. At full speed, Turl crashed through the protection and locked his arms around the runner's torso, stopping him. The two gridironers were at a standstill when Woody hit the ball carrier at his waist. Together, Turl and Woody pulled him down for a two-yard loss.

It was third down, and North Carolina's fullback was set to attempt a field goal. The ball was snapped. Prayer Bear shot through the gap between the Tar Heel guard and tackle and caused the fullback to rush his kick and drill the ball into the back of the Tar Heel center. The Sewanee crowd bellowed the *iron* chant.

Sewanee gained three first downs, mostly running mass sweeps. North Carolina stopped the Tigers at the Sewanee 24-yard line, forcing a third-down punt. Feeling no pain, Kimbrough launched the ball from his foot with ideal timing and sailed it fifty yards.

Lourie said to Alfie, "He's putting on a show, a marvelous show."

"You know about Wisconsin's Aussie fullback? He scored a sixty-two-yard dropkick in a blizzard last year."

"Pat O'Dea, the Kangaroo Kicker."

"I think our man might be the O'Dea of the South."

"He's playing like it's his last game ever."

Finn, standing near Alfie and the coach, spontaneously sang an ode to Kimbrough to the tune of "Margery":

> *To this brave lad forever we shall proudly sing.*
> *He is the boy we love and in the games we play,*
> *We'll cry, "Kimbrough kicks far and high."*

Alfie grinned at Finn. "That was superb. After we win, I'll take you around to the writers for the big papers. Don't forget those lines."

On first down and from their 26-yard line, Carolina ran for eleven yards, but Sewanee held their opponent to three yards on the next two plays. Instead of a third-down attempt for a first down, the Tar Heels chose to punt.

Fielding the kick, Kimbrough marked for a fair catch on Sewanee's 30-yard line and caught the football. A North Carolina end, who didn't see Kimbrough make his mark, tackled him, so the referee penalized North Carolina fifteen yards.

Kimbrough lined up for his ninth punt of the first half. Otay snapped him the football. Kimbrough firmly planted his left foot, let go of the ball, and struck it with his right foot.

He smiled as he watched the football sail and spin. It flew in a tight spiral, moving slowly through the sky. It reached its apex and, instead of descending, cruised parallel to the field. The display hushed the crowd as the gravity-defying object captured the spectators' full attention. Standing at the Tar Heel 15-yard line, the North Carolina quarterback backpedaled to receive the punt, but it soared over his head and landed in the end zone.

To Coach Lourie, Alfie said, "Fifty-five yards! The power!"

"The elegance."

The umpire placed the football on North Carolina's 10-yard line. There were eight minutes left in the half.

Turl huddled his team and said, "We force a punt here and we get a short field. So dig in."

Sewanee's eleven struggled to stop the Tar Heels' offensive attack. North Carolina's line hit the Tigers hard. Their runningbacks ran fearlessly, bent at the waist, pumping their legs like track sprinters with their heads low. Averaging four to five yards a carry, North Carolina slowly erased the edge that Kimbrough had provided his team.

Turl gathered his teammates. "Cut 'em in half, boys!"

On the following plays, Sewanee's eleven carried out Turl's instruction, each aiming a shoulder at a Tar Heel's thighs, sliding under their opponents' forward-leaning torsos. On first down at midfield, North Carolina gained a yard and another one on second down.

Henry said, "Here we go, Tigers. Here we go!"

The scrubs added their voices to Henry's. The Sewanee crowd cheered:

> *Rah rah ree, who are we?*
> *Sewanee, double e!*
> *Rough, tough, we are the stuff.*
> *We play football, never get enough!*

With three minutes remaining on the first-half clock, North Carolina lined up. Cutting through the din of the crowd, Cansler called out, "Blue sky, blue sky, tobacco!" and dropped back to punt. "Hike!" Their center snapped him the ball.

From the right end spot, Patch feinted to the left, and the Tar Heel end took the fake. Patch skirted around him and had a direct line to the punter. He launched himself at the spot where he expected the ball to come off Cansler's foot. The Sewanee gymnast was fully extended, a yard off the ground, his fingers spread and his thumbs touching. The North Carolina quarterback kicked the football. With both hands, Patch pinned it to the turf.

Woody ran to his roommate, helped him up, and said, "Magnificent, Mister Mercer, outstanding!"

The scrubs' enthusiasm sent some of them onto the field, so the umpire shouted at Coach Lourie, "Get them off the field, coach!" Coach Lourie, Peck, and Alfie wrangled the scrubs back to behind the sideline.

Sewanee had the ball on North Carolina's 40-yard line. It was too far for a field goal or dropkick. With two minutes remaining in the half, Turl told Ham to call a *Halfback Cross Right*.

Ham pitched to Turl, who waited for Ham, Brownlow, and Kimbrough to push behind Woody and Prayer Bear. The two linemen and three backs bulldozed a path through the Tar Heels. Turl followed the Tigers' wedge. After he gained four yards, a Tar Heel jumped on his back. The Sewanee captain and his escorts drove another six yards before North Carolina stopped the Tigers' forward progress.

With the Tar Heel still on his back, Turl bent over and pressed the football to the ground. "Down! Down!" Turl buckled under the weight of the tackler. Several North Carolina players dove on top of their teammate and Turl. The referee blasted staccato chirps with his whistle. Prayer Bear roared as he and other Tigers ripped Tar Heels off the pile and freed their captain.

Turl tossed the ball to Ham on the North Carolina 25-yard line. Sewanee scrambled into field goal formation. Ham placed the football in position. "Go!"

Kimbrough approached and struck the ball. It flew end over end until, with a few yards to spare, it cleared the crossbar.

The umpire said, "Time. First half over! Sewanee five, North Carolina zero."

As the team walked to the locker room, Coach Lourie asked Henry and

Turl to stay behind. "Henry, Kimbrough's limping a bit. His pain's creeping back, isn't it?"

"I'd say it is."

"Other than a shot, what can you do for him?" asked Turl.

"Not very much," Henry said. "I'll prop his leg up and have Joseph ice his shin."

Turl and Coach Lourie exchanged glances.

"Should numb the pain a bit. For a while."

Coach Lourie said, "Thank you, Henry."

"You're welcome, coach. Captain." Henry started to walk away and stopped. "Of course, Mister Kimbrough won't let on, so . . ."

"All three of us will watch him closely. Don't hesitate to speak up," Turl said.

"All right. I won't."

In the locker room, Finn sat down next to Coffey. "How do you feel?"

"Fine. How do you feel?"

"Pensive."

"Yeah. I think we need about a twenty-point lead for them to sub us in . . . Have you figured out what you're gonna say to your father?"

Finn pressed the sides of his head and quietly said, "No."

"I wish I could help you, in some way." Coffey tightened his boot laces.

Finn watched him for a moment. "Why are you bothering with that?"

"What?"

Finn looked over at Kimbrough, who was lying on a training table with his leg propped up. Joseph was holding an ice bag on the fullback's shin. "I get it. You're thinking Kimbrough may not hold up."

Coffey gave a subtle nod.

"Look, Coff. You can help me."

Coffey stared at Kimbrough. "No. I won't do that. You've played five times as much as I have this season. And I'm his sub. I have my honor to think of."

"You could tell them that your legs have knotted up—tight as drums."

"Sorry. I won't be part of any scamming. This is the championship."

"Then—then after fifteen minutes your legs knot up. We split the half."

"Finn, they made me his scrub, and I owe him my best." Coffey stood. "You should figure out what you're going to say to your father." He patted his friend on the back and walked away.

Peck sat down next to Finn. "What were y'all talking about?"

Finn looked past Peck and said, "Nothing, Pecker." He stood and exited the locker room.

For the first twelve minutes of the second half, neither team was able to move the ball past midfield. Both defenses held strong, only occasionally allowing first downs, and the North Carolina and Sewanee offenses played conservatively, punting on every third down.

Gradually, Kimbrough's punts were losing distance. When his fourth punt of the half traveled only twenty-five yards, Henry turned to Coach Lourie. "He's in too much pain, Coach."

"I need to get him off the field." Coach Lourie called out, "Coffey, come here!" The scrub jumped up from the bench. "Go in for Kimbrough and tell Turl to take over the kicking."

Coffey said, "Y'all might have to drag Kimbrough off the field."

Coach Lourie sighed. "So be it."

After Kimbrough caught the next North Carolina punt and marked the turf, Coach Lourie yelled to the umpire, "Time out! Substitution!"

The umpire blew his whistle and said, "Dead ball! Dead ball!" Kimbrough went ahead and punted, shanking the kick. "Substitution, Sewanee."

Coffey ran up to Turl. "I'm in for Kimbrough. Coach wants you to do the kicking." The captain called Prayer Bear over, and the two approached Kimbrough, who shooed them away. As he took a step backward, his left leg buckled. On his next step, he fell to the turf. Prayer Bear and Turl lifted him up and helped their star player off the field, Kimbrough hopping on his right leg.

The rest of the Sewanee eleven clapped in unison. The North Carolina eleven began to clap, along with those on both sidelines. The crowd cheered.

Alfie ran to the ambulance carriage. Winded, he reached it. "Get to the Sewanee side!"

Lifting himself onto the wagon bench, the driver said, "Hang on from the back!" Alfie jumped onto the rear runner and gripped the carriage's two back handles. "You on?"

"Yes!"

At the middle of the field, the umpire shouted, "I need the captains." Turl and Cansler gathered around the official. "The game will resume once the ambulance has loaded the injured player and left the field. Go inform your coaches."

"Sir, are you going to extend the time?" Cansler asked.

"Yes." The umpire looked at his watch. "Noted."

The ambulance carriage arrived behind the Sewanee bench as Henry cradled Kimbrough's leg and lowered it into a tub filled with Tremlett Spring water and chunks of ice.

Heads turned toward the carriage. Kimbrough looked straight ahead, and Coach Lourie stepped into his line of sight. "It's time to go to the hospital. And after the game, we'll all be there with you."

Kimbrough turned his head to the side. "It's best I stay here."

Turl reached the sideline and patted Coach Lourie on the arm. "Game starts again after they carry Kimbrough out of here. Time will be extended."

Coach Lourie hadn't taken his gaze off Kimbrough. "The longer you delay, the longer time Carolina gets to rest."

"The sooner you tell the umpire that I'm staying, the sooner we finish them off."

Turl sat down next to Kimbrough. "You gave your word as a Christian gentleman."

"Please release me from my oath. Let me see us finish this."

Turl responded, "None of us will ever know a man with your grit. You refuse defeat. Going to the hospital is not defeat, it's—"

"Where is Henry? Henry! Where are you?"

"I'm standing right behind you, Mister Kimbrough."

Alfie led the two ambulance workers to Kimbrough. They were carrying a stretcher. "Gentlemen, this is Kimbrough Lowndes. The greatest football player of all time. Please treat him as such."

"Henry has given me laudanum, and my shin is starting to numb in this arctic bath. They will do the same at the hospital. Won't they, Henry?"

Henry shook his head. "Doctors need to see your leg, Mister Kimbrough."

"And they will when this game is over, and these men take me."

Prayer Bear came off the field and walked up to Kimbrough. He placed his hand on Kimbrough's shoulder. "Lowndes, you're being stiff-necked, aren't you? You need to get to the hospital, and we need to get to beating these Tar Heels. So, we can carry you and stuff you in that medical wagon, or you can go peacefully."

"I was thirty minutes from finishing on the field of battle. You understand. All y'all do." He pointed to the ambulance workers. "They'll load me up as soon as we become champions of the South."

No one responded. Kimbrough placed his hand in the water and swirled it. "They don't have Tremlett Spring water at the hospital."

Turl rubbed his chin while staring at Kimbrough's submerged lower leg. "I wouldn't want to miss our finale." He shook Kimbrough's hand and tugged on Prayer Bear's jersey. "Come on, Mister Embree. For God, school, and our mighty Achilles."

As they ran onto the field, Prayer Bear grumbled, "Invoking pagans does not please the Lord, captain."

"All right. Our mighty warrior."

Turl and Prayer Bear approached the umpire. "They'll take him to the hospital right after the game," Turl said.

The umpire barked, "Let's play football!"

Eight yards back in a punting position, Turl took the snap, faked a punt, and ran around Patch, who had hit the North Carolina end across from him, then slid off to run interference for Turl. The captain gained twelve yards before a North Carolina halfback punched the ball out of his hands and dove on the football.

North Carolina was on the Sewanee 46-yard line. On first down, the Tar Heels bucked the Sewanee line for six yards and a first down. On the next play, they fumbled the football over to Sewanee.

From Sewanee's 40-yard line, Ham pitched to Brownlow, who bobbled and then fumbled the ball. North Carolina recovered it.

Over the next fifteen minutes, Sewanee fumbled and turned the ball over to North Carolina two more times. The Tar Heels dropped the football twice, losing it once.

Both teams' running attempts, whether hitting the line or drifting outside the ends, turned into scrums with all twenty-two players pushing and pulling. Neither offense managed to break a runner free, but the Tar Heels were able to move the ball to the Tigers' 27-yard line—two yards farther than the North Carolina placekicker's longest successful field goal of the year.

With two and a half minutes left, the Tar Heel quarterback held the ball in place, and their kicker booted it. After the football reached its highest point, it began to curve left until it passed a foot outside the left goalpost. The football went over to Sewanee.

Running behind Prayer Bear and Woody four times in a row, the Tigers ground out two first downs. Then Ham pitched to Patch, who gained four yards around the left end before being pulled down. On second down from the Sewanee 41-yard line, Ham tossed to Turl, who unsuccessfully tried to plunge directly behind the Tigers' center. Sewanee gained no yardage on the play.

It was third down and one yard to go. A first down would allow the Tigers to run out the clock and become the undisputed football champions of the South.

Turl had to make the most critical decision of his football career—push for the yard or punt. He looked over at the sidelines to see if Coach Lourie was sending him a signal. Instead, the umpire caught Turl's eye. The official subtly shook his head and said, "Let's go, Sewanee, line up!"

Turl dropped back eight yards and stood in position to punt. His teammates looked back at their captain. Prayer Bear smiled at Turl and said, "Let's get under this punt, Tigers, it's going to be a good'n!"

Otay snapped the football, a perfect and swift spiral back to Turl. The Sewanee front seven kept the Tar Heels from crossing the line of scrimmage as Turl took two steps and kicked the ball. It was a high punt.

Alfie said, "He skied it?"

Coach Lourie said, "No. It's high but it'll carry."

Standing next to them, Henry yelled, "There you go, Captain Turl!"

Cansler stood on the North Carolina 40-yard line, where the football fell into his outstretched hands. Patch, Ham, Brownlow, and Coffey had blasted through the Tar Heel blockers. Arm's-distance apart, they galloped toward the punt receiver, who paused, wrapped both arms around the ball, and hesitantly ran toward the four Tigers. He veered in the direction of Brownlow and Coffey. They both lowered their shoulders to tackle the runner. Just before contact, the Tar Heel jumped into the air and turned sideways. Brownlow and Coffey both grazed him with a hand, while Patch and Ham ran past him. The quarterback cut to the right and saw a wide-open field in front of him. Patch and Ham turned around and chased the ball carrier. Patch was the closer of the two, but he was twelve yards behind Cansler, streaking toward the goal line to tie the game.

Joseph said, "Go, Mister Patch!"

Patch was now within five yards of the runner. Henry said, "Mister Patch is a racehorse!"

At the Sewanee 17-yard line, Patch was two strides behind the Tar Heel. In his palm, the umpire had his pocket watch open as he and the referee, from twenty yards behind, followed the two-man chase. When Patch crossed the 12-yard line, he dove, swiped at the runner's ankles, and caused him to stagger and land facedown on the turf. Patch sprang to his feet. The quarterback began to stand up, but Patch pounced on his prey's back and downed him on the 4-yard line.

The umpire stopped and looked at his pocket watch. "Contest over. Sewanee Tigers five, North Carolina Tar Heels zero. Fine match, gentlemen, all shake hands!"

People from the grandstands and behind the end zones ran onto the field, eventually covering most of the gridiron. Ham was the first to reach Patch. Next was Otay Carter, one of the slowest runners on the Sewanee team. Otay hugged the slightly built Patch, lifting him off the ground and squeezing him, while Ham vigorously shook the hero's hand.

The other Sewanee players, along with their coach, trainers, and manager, reached the celebration in the end zone. Brownlow and Coffey carried Kimbrough on their shoulders. His face was pasty, and his body was limp. His head occasionally lolled.

Otay put Patch down and said, "Patch Mercer, don't you know we're goin' to have a riotous time in Ole'lanta tonight!"

Alfie jumped on the center's back. "Spending John Heisman's money all night long!"

Otay and Patch guffawed, while their teammates embraced, tackled, hoisted each other, and shouted. Several let loose rebel yells.

Turl stepped away from the scene and covered his eyes to hide his tears. After he blotted them, he noticed Woody on a knee with his head bowed. Woody looked up and smiled at Turl.

On his shoulders, Prayer Bear carried Joseph and marched alongside Kimbrough and his bearers. Several Tigers created a loosely formed wedge and guided the procession through the jubilant mass on the field.

The 1899 Southern Football Champions gathered together in front of the Sewanee supporters who remained in the grandstand. Along with the Sewanee faithful on the field, the Tigers sang their school's alma mater.

After his teammates paraded Kimbrough Lowndes in front of the grandstand, they carried him to the ambulance carriage. Perspiration made his skin shine and his hair wet. Woody grabbed Kimbrough's arms and Prayer Bear cradled his legs, and the two Sewanee linemen placed him on a stretcher.

In a weak voice only Woody could hear, Kimbrough protested, "I'm not going in there. I'm raisin' Cain with y'all tonight. By God."

A Sewanee cheer faded as Turl climbed in to ride alongside his teammate. The people in the grandstand and on the field stood quietly. Alfie, Coach Lourie, Henry, Joseph, and each player lay a hand on the ambulance before it pulled away.

Looking for his parents, Finn scanned the crowd on the field and in the bleachers. Coffey approached him and put his arm over his shoulder. "I saw them step into one of the fancy carriages."

"Where is it?"

"It left."

Finn took a deep breath and sighed. "Good."

He grinned at Coffey. They watched the ambulance carriage turn down a street and disappear. Finn remembered his impromptu ode to Kimbrough and began to sing it.

> *To this brave lad forever we shall proudly sing.*
> *He is the boy we love and in the games we play,*
> *We'll cry, "Kimbrough kicks far and high."*

Finn sang the ditty a few times. His teammates and others nearby soon grasped the lyrics and sang along. After a few minutes, the singers' voices reached a crescendo and the ode ended.

There was a moment of calm. Beaming, Prayer Bear looked at the faces of his teammates. "For this life and the next," he said, "y'all are my brothers."

Patch locked arms with Prayer Bear. The team joined them, creating a circle and locking arms. Prayer Bear said, "Leave a gap for Turl and Kimbrough." The circle opened, and the Sewanee Tigers chanted:

> *Everywhere we go*
> *People want to know*
> *Who we are*
> *So we tell them*
> *We are the Tigers,*
> *The mighty, mighty Tigers!*

Epilogue

Kimbrough Lowndes

Exactly one week after he led his teammates to victory in the Southern Championship game, doctors amputated the lower half of Kimbrough Lowndes's left leg. A significant area of his tibia and its surrounding tissue had become necrotic.

Kimbrough spent the following winter and spring at his parents' farm outside Memphis. For the first several weeks, he drank whiskey every night until he had drunk himself to sleep.

In April, he started wearing a prosthesis, a Palmer leg, and within a month, he was hunting every day—killing and dressing deer, geese, and doves.

In the summer of 1900, Kimbrough returned to Sewanee and graduated with honors. He lived with his parents in Memphis and dedicated himself to helping his father manage the family's cotton transport company. Over the next fifteen years, Kimbrough grew his business skills and his passion for commercial competition. He enjoyed the thrill of risking capital over rails, rivers, and seas.

The United States entered World War I on April 6, 1917. Kimbrough quickly petitioned for a naval commission. Within two months, Kimbrough received a letter from the Department of the Navy denying his request: *DISABLED* was stamped at the bottom of the letter. He would have been the fourth person in his family to serve in the U.S. Navy.

Kimbrough spent the next fourteen days in his room except for meals and the first hour of each day's dawn, when he walked a quarter mile to the Mississippi River. There he would remove his prosthesis and lean out and grab a low-lying, thick tree branch—from which to lower his body into the fast-moving water. Chest high in the river, he would count to eighteen hundred ninety-nine and then lift himself out of the river. On the fifteenth day, he emerged from his room with a new sense of purpose.

During the summer of 1917, German U-boats increased their attacks on enemy nations' merchant vessels. During Kimbrough's sequestration, a German U-boat sank *The Copious*—a merchant ship in which Lowndes Cotton Shipping held a fifty percent interest. In response, Kimbrough persuaded his father to allow him to arm the family's other transatlantic ship, *The Jackson*, with depth charges.

Kimbrough sailed on *The Jackson*, delivering cotton to European ports and guarding the cargo and crew from German U-boat attacks. During its wartime passages, *The Jackson* encountered six U-boats and sent them all away by releasing depth charges. Although *The Jackson* never sank a German U-boat, these detonations produced hydraulic shocks that rocked the submarines and damaged two of them. On May 7, 1918, a German U-boat chased *The Jackson* off the coast of Portugal and sank Kimbrough's ship with a torpedo. There were no survivors.

At Sewanee, a portrait of Kimbrough hangs in Saint Luke's Hall. On the bottom frame of the painting is a gilded plaque: *Kimbrough Dunlop Lowndes, '00, captain of industry and the sea, and the ore of the 1899 Iron Tigers.*

Woodward Partridge "Woody" Barnwell

In Galveston on April 24, 1900, Woodward Partridge Barnwell married Lillian Hillyard Lewis.

Lillian toured on the national tennis circuit, and a month after her wedding, she qualified for Wimbledon. Although she lost in the first round, she, her parents, and Woody stayed through the championship match and toured northern Europe.

On September eighth, the young couple and Lillian's parents embarked upon their journey back to Galveston on the RMS *Galane*. Six weeks from their departure, Woody was due to report to a parish outside of Cincinnati, where he would serve as the congregation's priest.

While they were at sea, the Texas Gulf Coast was hit by a hurricane that produced a storm surge of twelve feet and destroyed 3,600 homes on the city island of Galveston. Approximately six thousand residents were killed, among them Woody's mother and father, sister, two uncles, and eleven other close relatives.

Woody blamed himself for his family's deaths, believing that God spared Lillian's family because of her pure heart and mind compared to Woody's poisonous and sinful soul. For years, Woody's faith in God's infinite grace waned.

In 1921, Woody was asked to leave his sixth parish, the church council citing his disconnection from the parishioners and his uninspired performance of the sacraments. Woody knew he was finished as a clergyman.

Lillian had continued her tennis career until their fourth child was born and then devoted herself to her children and life as the spouse of a priest. For twenty-two years, she labored to make Woody happy. They had moments of joy and lightness, but melancholy and anxiety invariably possessed Woody.

On Tuesday, December 14, 1923, Woodrow Partridge Barnwell checked into a hotel and killed himself with a revolver. At the start of Sewanee's 1924 spring semester, the *Sewanee Purple* printed an article remembering this "beloved servant of the Church and soldier of the gridiron." After detailing the churches where Reverend Barnwell served, the article continued, "He was a starting guard on the Sewanee football squad that took the South by storm in 1899, a team of gridiron warriors who forever set the standard to which all football teams will always aspire."

Patch eulogized his friend. In his tribute, he read an excerpt from a letter Woody had sent him a few months earlier:

A quarter of a century later, I cling to what you, our teammates and I accomplished during that unforgettable season. On the train, recouping on the Mountain, and fighting foes on football fields across the South with you and the others were some of the greatest moments of my life.

I pray that all who were part of our epic crusade remain Iron Tigers until the end of their days, just as our heroic fullback and brother Kimbrough Lowndes did, may he rest in peace for eternity.

Deacon Telfair "Prayer Bear" Embree performed the funeral rites for his teammate.

The *Sewanee Purple* article concluded with an appeal to the men of Sewanee: "On your next trip to The Mountain, please visit the Lourie-Melville trophy room in Jenkins Hall to pay tribute to priest, husband, father of four, and football hero Woodward "Woody" Partridge Barnwell and his fallen comrade, our Achilles, Kimbrough Dunlop Lowndes. Above the eighteen ninety-nine Southern Championship Trophy is the Sewanee team photograph of that same year. Search for the faces of these two Iron Tigers and say a prayer of thanks and wish peace upon them."

A year after her husband's suicide, Lillian moved herself and her children to Austin, Texas, where her parents had resettled after the Galveston hurricane. Woody and Lillian's oldest, Thomas Barnwell, attended the Sewanee Seminary and became a priest. At the age of sixty-one, he became the Archbishop of Texas.

Henry Jordan, Joseph Hill, and Telfair "Prayer Bear" Embree

Henry blamed himself for Kimbrough's amputation but eventually, encouraged by Prayer Bear and Dr. Robert Cromwell, recommitted himself to becoming a doctor.

Dr. Cromwell provided $200 for Henry's medical education and secured another $1,400 from other doctors, enough for Henry's entire medical school education. In 1901, Henry began his studies in the Department of Medicine at Central Tennessee College. He graduated three years later and took a position as an assistant surgeon at Provident Hospital, a teaching hospital established in Chicago for the city's black population.

After trading letters for years, Henry and his friend Deacon Telfair "Prayer Bear" Embree were finally reunited when Deacon Embree visited Henry in Chicago, during Henry's fifth year at Provident Hospital. Deacon Embree attempted to persuade Henry to return to Tennessee and help establish medical clinics in remote Cumberland Mountain enclaves.

Henry agreed, under the condition that he remain for another year at the Chicago hospital, so he could mentor twenty-five-year-old Joseph Hill during Joseph's first year as a medical student at Provident.

Once Henry joined him, Pastor Prayer Bear, as his parishioners called him, focused on building medical clinics near the five Episcopal missions he had established. Despite their confidence in Prayer Bear and the priest's obvious attachment to Henry, the parishioners of the Cumberland Mountain chapels were deeply suspicious of Dr. Jordan. For almost a year, Pastor Prayer Bear had to accompany his friend to the satellite parishes. Henry's resilience, personality, and passion to care for everyone, however, slowly endeared him to these people deep in the Cumberland hollers.

Dr. Jordan and Deacon Embree built and staffed four clinics. In 1928, Telfair Embree became Archdeacon Embree, but he remained Pastor Prayer Bear to his people in the Cumberlands.

The two friends eventually retired. Henry and Prayer Bear lived out the rest of their lives as bachelors in Havana, Cuba. They spent most of their time fishing together in the Gulf of Mexico.

Alpheus "Alfie" Melville and Coach Hobart "Hobie" Lourie

Alfie finished his liberal arts degree at Sewanee and graduated in the summer of 1900. That same year, Coach Lourie took a job as football coach at his alma mater, Princeton.

Alfie went home to Mobile and became an assistant publisher for his grandfather's magazine, *The Southern Gentleman.* Hobie Lourie coached at Princeton for five seasons. During the off-season, he sold advertising and copy edited for the *Philadelphia Inquirer.*

In 1906, Hobie Lourie retired from coaching and joined Alfie in Mobile for a new venture. As co-owners, the two men published a biweekly magazine, *The Varsity,* which covered college baseball and football east of the Mississippi. In the fourth year of the publication, the partners expanded their reportage coast to coast. By 1912, *The Varsity* had become the country's most popular collegiate sports publication.

In 1913, after years of financially supporting candidates for federal office, Alfie ran for the U.S. Senate, with Hobie as his campaign manager and, after the election, as the Alabama senator's chief of staff.

Late in Senator Melville's first term, the United States entered World War I. Alfie used his influence to secure officer commissions for himself and Hobie in the American Expeditionary Force. Hobie joined the war as a captain and Alfie was a colonel.

From September 1918 until the Armistice in November, they commanded troops and fought in the Meuse-Argonne Campaign, the deadliest in American history. Up and down the Hindenburg Line, the combatants blasted each other with artillery and poisoned each other with mustard gas.

When the war officially ended in January 1919, Colonel Melville and Captain Lourie banded together with two fellow officers and two enlisted men to bring the war's principal German war criminal to justice. Without orders, they plotted to kidnap the German kaiser, Wilhelm II, who had abdicated three days prior to the German surrender and fled to a cousin's castle in the Netherlands.

With falsified passports, the renegade unit entered Dutch territory on January 27. Hours later, they reached the village of Amerongen, near the castle where the kaiser was staying.

By claiming to have a private letter for the former kaiser from American General John J. Pershing, Alfie gained entrance to the castle. When the estate's owner demanded to see the letter, Alfie informed him that he did not have the letter on his person but it was close by. German Imperial Guards escorted Alfie out of the castle.

Alfie joined his fellow Americans in the U.S. military vehicle. Pulling away from the castle, the men faced sixty villagers. The royalists were carrying torches and marching up the road toward the castle. Worried that the mob would attack them and turn them over to the Dutch authorities, the Americans sped down the hill and eluded the villagers. An hour later, Alfie showed his coconspirators a pewter ashtray bearing a German coat of arms and the initials W.E., which stood for Wilhelm Emperor. Alfie had stolen it from the castle.

Until late in life, Alfie often brooded over his failed mission and twisted the misadventure into a tale of a U.S. skirmish with the kaiser's soldiers. He thought the heroic publicity would be valuable if he ever ran for the White House or the Alabama governor's mansion. He never pursued either.

Alfie Melville and Hobie Lourie returned to Mobile. Within two years, both bachelors married women from Mobile society, and the couples soon began having children. Hobie became a successful shrimp exporter, while Alfie purchased three newspapers and invested heavily in publicly traded stocks.

When the stock market crashed in 1929, to meet his margin calls, Alfie mortgaged his home, which had been in his family since 1869, and sold his newspaper businesses. However, these funds were not sufficient to keep Alfie and his wife solvent, so he borrowed money from Hobie Lourie.

Soon after, Alfie became managing editor of the *Mobile Herald* and repaid his friend over the following eleven years.

The former Sewanee football coach and the manager retired in their late sixties. They fished on the Gulf, played pool at the Midtown Billiards Club, and celebrated at each other's children's weddings and grandchildren's christenings. They also attended Sewanee homecoming games, where they spent time with other Iron Tigers.

Finn Grayson, Thompson Quinn Peck, and James Bristol Coffey

After graduating from Sewanee's medical school, Finn, Peck, and Coffey became residents at Atlanta's Hardy Hospital. Three years later they started a medical practice in Midtown Atlanta. Dr. Grayson, Dr. Peck, and Dr. Coffey were general surgeons. Over a four-year span, they became the surgeons of choice for established Atlanta.

Peck and Coffey married Atlanta natives, and Finn married a second cousin from Augusta, Georgia. Within two years of their weddings, the three doctors were fathers.

The former college glee club members renewed their passions for singing by joining their church's choir. They also played on the Atlanta Young Men's Christian Association football team and, in 1910, scrimmaged against Sewanee. Finn served on the Atlanta YMCA board of directors and eventually became the organization's board president. Coffey donated his time as an active member of the Georgia Medical Board, while Peck was director of the All Saints Episcopal Church choir and a football coach at the Atlanta boarding school he had attended.

Mmes. Peck, Coffey, and Grayson were active volunteers at All Saints Episcopal Church, and they were also in leadership positions in the Atlanta chapter of the United Daughters of the Confederacy.

In 1915, the doctors and their wives viewed a new movie that was generating a national controversy: *The Birth of a Nation*, a vindication for devoted Southern supporters of the Lost Cause.

Later that year, on Thanksgiving evening, Finn, Peck, and Coffey stood at the summit of Georgia's Stone Mountain with eighteen other men. All of them wore white robes and pointed hoods. The group burned a sixteen-foot cross, said prayers, gave speeches, and declared the establishment of the second Ku Klux Klan.

The three men resigned from their volunteer positions and focused on recruiting other physicians and politicians to join the Klan.

In 1918, Thompson Quinn Peck volunteered to join the U.S. Medical Reserve Corps and served as a medic. The forty-year-old doctor was killed when artillery fire struck the ambulance he was driving during the Battle of Cantigny.

James Coffey also died in 1918. He, his wife, and their ten-year-old son died from influenza during the pandemic.

Finn Grayson was a member of the Klan until he died of lung cancer in 1940. At the time of his death, he and his wife had six children and eleven grandchildren. His grandson, Atlas Spotswood Grayson, was an Episcopal priest who was a supporter of and participant in the civil rights movement. Another one of Finn's grandchildren was Joseph Hall, a U.S. congressman from Virginia who voted against the 1964 Civil Rights Act.

Titus Scott "Turl" Turley

After graduating from Sewanee in 1900, the Iron Tigers' captain returned to his hometown of Brazoria, Texas. There he took care of his father, who was dying of tuberculosis and refused to be hospitalized.

A few days after his father's funeral, Turl was invited to take a junior executive position at the family's oil refinery in Houston. Turl quickly mastered the various executive functions at Turley Petroleum. By the beginning of his third year at the company, he oversaw contract negotiations.

Turl played football and baseball for the Houston Downtown Athletic Club. A pitcher, Turl discovered that he enjoyed baseball more than football and became consumed with the game.

In 1905, Turl resigned his position at Turley Petroleum, intending to play professional baseball with the hope of later becoming a big-league manager. Turl tried out for the Houston Buffaloes at the pitcher and first baseman positions, but the manager told Turl he was not ready for the professional level and should keep playing club baseball.

Every day, Turl read the Texas League box scores published in the *Houston Chronicle* and tracked each team's pitching statistics. He tried out for the Temple Boll Weevils, one of the two worst pitching teams in the league.

The manager, Stub Lee, decided that Turl needed a better curve ball but was impressed with Turl's pitch velocity and batting skills. Turl joined the team on July 18, 1906.

That first season, Turl pitched twelve times for his team. The following year, re-signed by the Boll Weevils, Turl started thirty-five games and won twenty-one of his appearances. He had the best pitching record in the league.

At the end of the last game of the season, a Cincinnati Reds scout offered Turl a contract to play for the Reds.

Turl won twelve games in his first year with Cincinnati, lost nine, and hit the third most RBIs on the team. His second year, he had six wins, thirteen losses, and was the team RBI leader. The following year, at winter workouts in Florida, he tore a tendon in his throwing arm. At the start of the major league season his arm had not healed enough to pitch. Because he was such a strong hitter, the Reds put him in the lineup at first base. Turl played two more years for the Reds and had the tenth most RBIs in the National League both years.

In January 1911, Stub Lee announced his retirement as manager of the Temple Boll Weevils. Turl immediately contacted the owner and asked him to consider hiring Turl as the new manager. The owner was hesitant to hire Turl, who had no coaching or managing experience, but Stub offered to mentor Turl and prepare him to become the Boll Weevils' manager for the 1912 season.

After two mediocre seasons with Turl as the manager, the Boll Weevils won the Texas League in 1914. Just before Christmas of the same year, the owner of the Chicago Cubs called Turl and asked him to join the Cubs as their new pitching coach. Turl declined the offer. He managed the Boll Weevils until 1926. During Turl's fifteen years as their manager, the Boll Weevils won five Texas League Championships.

Turl met his wife in Temple, Texas. They built a house there and had one child, a daughter. After retiring from baseball, he moved his family to Houston. When Turl's uncle retired as chief executive officer of Turley Petroleum, the board of directors hired Titus Turley to take over.

The former Sewanee football captain died of natural causes at the age of seventy-six. Five of the 1899 eleven traveled to Turl's funeral.

Benjamin Harold "Patch" Mercer

Patch graduated from Sewanee and immediately left the country for a tour of Europe, North Africa, and Palestine. His plan was to travel for two years. While abroad, Patch practiced abstinence for almost the entire first year of his travels. His chaste streak ended in Marseilles, with a cabaret performer.

In Algiers, he was introduced to a French-Algerian woman, Rosemonde. Over several weeks, they became fond of each other. Soon after, they traveled together to Palestine.

One morning in Jaffa, Patch awoke with a high fever. For six days, he remained in bed, alternating between sweating and shivering. He could hear the sea outside his window, and his mind wandered to memories of swimming in the Atlantic while growing up in Savannah. As the fever waned, he realized he had to go home. Patch told Rosemonde that he hoped they would meet again. She felt the same way. He escorted her back to Algiers and returned to his native home of Savannah.

Patch reacquainted himself with his family and old friends.

One fall evening, Patch announced to his mother, father, and grandfather that he was going to St. Louis to find Cecilia Fontaine and ask her to marry him.

Cecilia's aunt, in St. Louis, informed Patch that Cecilia had left for New Orleans four months prior. Cecilia had inherited a luxury hotel from her grandfather and was operating it. Patch went to New Orleans and sat in the lobby of the Hotel Saint-Oliver. When Cecilia saw Patch, she asked him what had taken him so long. He admitted it was cowardice and stupidity, took an engagement ring from his breast pocket, and asked her to be his wife.

Eight months later they were married in Saint Martinville Parish, Louisiana. Woody was Patch's best man, and the other groomsmen were Turl, Kimbrough, and Ham. Woody and Lillian's son Thomas was the ring bearer.

Patch and Cecilia lived in the Saint-Oliver's penthouse. Cecilia ran the hotel, and Patch was a cotton broker at the New Orleans Cotton Exchange. The Mercers, intrepid and frequent travelers, took day, regional, and cross-country trips in a two-seater biplane.

Flying was a constant in their lives. The one year that was an exception was 1918, when Patch flew reconnaissance missions over France, Germany, and Belgium for the American Expeditionary Force. Patch attributed his safe return home from war to divine intervention.

After Woody's death, Patch went into semiretirement. He spent mornings at the cotton exchange, where he would make a few trades, read the *Times-Picayune,* and visit with friends. Then it was back to the Hotel Saint-Oliver to lunch with Cecilia. Afterward, he went to the veterans' hospital to tend the spiritual needs of men who were permanently disabled. Each trip he took a pocket-sized Book of Common Prayer that Woody had given him before Patch left to serve in Europe.

Patch would read prayers to these men. That was how he memorialized and, in spirit, spent time with Father Woody Barnwell.

The Iron Tigers' Legacy

In the summer and fall of 1899, twenty-one young athletes from a men's college of 300 students won twelve out of twelve football games. During this season, the team from Tennessee traveled west on a train for nine days, covering 2,500 miles. On this Southern grand tour, Sewanee won five games in six days. Additionally, the Tigers scored 322 points and allowed only 10.

These student-athletes shared a rare type of brotherhood, endured an arduous journey, and achieved glorious triumphs. With esprit de corps as exemplary as the Sewanee players, Student Manager Alfie Melville, Coach Hobie Lourie, Trainer Henry Jordan, and Assistant Trainer Joseph Hill took care of the team members. And the mighty Mountain Goat and her engineers delivered her Sewanee passengers safely and punctually to all nine of their away games.

Today, in the Lourie-Melville Trophy Room on the Sewanee campus, one can study the artifacts and details of this incomparable and never-to-be-repeated season. Today, over a century later, the most popular poster on the school's dormitory walls is a blow-up of the 1899 team picture. In large print, below the team's photo, are two words: *Iron Tigers.*

The End

Acknowledgments

My soulmate champions me, protects me—mostly from myself—and fills my life with grace, beauty, and humor. Whatever good lies within me, she brings it out and places it before my eyes. No one is perfect, but she is perfectly original. Beyond these wonders, she reads, proofs, and edits my manuscripts several times before anyone outside our household sees them. Hilary, they say trees cannot grow to the sky, but my gratitude and love for you shade the redwood forest and will forever climb.

Someone said that all children are wonderful because every mother has at least one. My mother, too, thinks I'm wonderful. She holds strong in her conviction and expresses her love in many ways, including focusing her keen eyes on my drafts. Thank you, Mother, for all you have done for me and our family.

Soon after I entered college, I started a lifelong friendship with Roger Easa Harb—the big brother I never had. In addition to serving as a beta reader for this book, Roger, a marketing marvel, was a consummate advisor throughout this project and cocreator of the Iron Tiger podcast and YouTube trailer. Promoting Iron Tigers is not our first commercial venture together, nor will it be our last. Roger, I cherish our collaborations and friendship. You are a prince, and all who know you are better for it.

For being generous with your time, insightful suggestions, and great spirit, I thank you Kelly, Caroline, Coach, Pamela, Jeanette, Shannon, Alexis, and Roger. My beta readers—how blessed I am to have your guidance and friendship.

Sally Boyington, a brilliant editor and fellow writer, worked with me on *Iron Tigers* for one year. I accepted the vast majority of her suggestions. When I rejected one, the next day I would typically recognize that she was spot-on, and I'd make the change. Sally taught me how to be a better novelist. She's as excellent a writing coach as she is an editor. Because she was invested in my progress, I began to trust her early in the process, and my trust became second nature soon after. Thank you for being by my side and rooting for me and the Tigers, Sally. I wish you nothing but success as a novelist, editor, and fiddle player!

For his patience, creativity, and generosity, I am grateful to Momodou Lamin Barrow, my website and cover designer, dear friend, and an iron tiger through and through.

In matters of the Episcopal liturgy, practices, and beliefs, the Rev. RJ Powell, chaplain at Tyson House: Episcopal-Lutheran Campus Ministry at the University of Tennessee, Knoxville, gave me much guidance.

One of my most important sources was Wendell O. Givens's *Ninety-Nine Iron*, a nonfiction account of Sewanee's famed 1899 football season (University of Alabama Press, 2003). Mr. Givens's research was extensive and detailed, covering the team, its players, its opponents, particulars of the trip, and the world of late 1890s Southern football. His book is engaging and a pleasure to read.

A primary source on which Mr. Givens and I relied heavily is the reporting of Luke Lea, the 1899 Sewanee Tigers' manager. For all of his team's games, Mr. Lea wrote meticulous reports—complete with play-by-play details and color commentary. When the entourage reached a train station, Mr. Lea wired his accounts to the editor at the Sewanee student newspaper, *The Sewanee Purple*. His reporting survives today on the original pages of the *Purple*.

Without Mr. Givens and Mr. Lea, *Iron Tigers* would be a novel, not a historical novel.

Iron Tigers has several protagonists, including the team itself. I spent five years riding the train with the Tigers, the fictional and actual young men, and, from a variety of points-of-view, watching them battle their opponents. When they weren't away playing a game or partying in New Orleans, they were home on the Mountain, their beloved Sewanee. I spent years exploring Sewanee's historical moment at the turn of the century—campus life, atmosphere, academics, religion, race and class dynamics, and architecture.

I discovered layered portrayals of this time and place in *Sewanee Perspectives: On the History of the University of the South* (2008), a collection of essays narrating essential aspects of Sewanee's first 150 years. I leaned heavily on Woody Register's "Remembering Ninety-Nine Iron: A Historical Perspective on the Legendary Football Team That Won Five Games in Six Days"; Jon Meacham's "Sewanee, History, and Memory"; Gerald L. Smith and Sean T. Suarez's "The Loveliest Village: Gown and Town in Sewanee, 1860–1910"; and Waring McGrady's "College and Church: The Official View." Much thanks to these historians who took their exhaustive research and turned their discoveries into fascinating accounts of their topics.

Other books that informed and colored *Iron Tigers* include Dave Revsine's *The Opening Kickoff: The Tumultuous Birth of a Football Nation;* Michael Oriard's *The Art of Football: The Early Game in the Golden Age of Illustration;* Fielding H. Yost's *Football for Player and Spectator;* David M. Nelson's *The Anatomy of a Game: Football, the Rules, and the Men Who Made the Game;* Samuel Ernest Bilik's *The Trainers Bible;* and Fuzzy Woodruff's *A History of Southern Football, 1890–1928.*

Discovering archived materials from the late 1890s such as *The Sewanee Purple,* Sewanee course catalogues, photos, and graduation programs was an exciting part of this journey. Writers take our curiosity to archivists, and they lead us to documents, books, images, and maps—historical records that provide answers and generate more questions. The best archivists, with quiet passion, adopt our interests as if they are their own. This is what Matt Reynolds did for me over a five-year period. Matt was the associate director of Sewanee University's Archives and Special Collections. He led me to research questions I had not considered and to the materials to explore these questions. Matt greatly contributed to my research endeavors. Tragically, Matt Reynolds passed in 2022. May his family and friends always find comfort in his memory. Thank you, Matt.

In the Sewanee archives I learned a great deal about Sewanee's black community during the late nineteenth and early twentieth centuries. At that time the university's black employees were referred to as servants. One servant was critical to the success of the 1899 Iron Tigers: Cal Burrows, a garbage collector and athletic trainer. The student body had affection for their team's trainer and gratitude for the invaluable care he provided the Iron Men—tending to their battered bodies throughout the season. But Cal Burrows, as a black man and a servant, was expected to show deference and unwavering loyalty, and the students' love for him was thus conditional and paternalistic.

Despite his significant role in the Sewanee season of 1899, historians have found no information regarding Cal Burrows's life after 1899. Henry Jordan and Joseph Hill, my book's fictional trainers, represent Cal Burrows. Through them I express the life of Sewanee's black servants at the turn of the century and the skills and responsibilities of athletic trainers. Henry and Joseph also embody African Americans who followed vocational dreams that the Jim Crow South warned them not to pursue. The narratives of such Iron Men and Women are still missing from our history books—just like the absent records of Cal Burrows.

White Southern colleges began the process of integrating the descendants of Black slaves 75 years after the United States abolished slavery. In 1966, Sewanee admitted Nathaniel Owens as the college's first Black undergraduate student. He was recruited to play football, and as the first Sewanee Black football player, he is the final protagonist of the Iron Men's epic tale and his life the denouement. Judge Nathaniel Owens retired from a Georgia district court bench in 2017.

Thank you to all my friends who checked in on my progress and encouraged me along the way. You're in my heart, Abraham, Alexis, Jay, Abhay, Caroline, Rick, and Ruth; Evan, Gina, Ashton, Matthew, John, Mel, Michelle, and Vinny at Gourmet's Market; Ben, Heather, Evan, Donna, and Mary Kate at the Knoxville Westside YMCA.

Regardless of what any college football team has accomplished or will ever accomplish, none will exceed the endurance of the 1899 Sewanee Iron Men. I am forever indebted to and appreciative of these men of phenomenal grit, these brothers:

<u>Starting Eleven</u>

Ormand Simpkins—fullback, kicker, liberal arts student

Henry Goldthwaite "Ditty" Seibels—right halfback, captain, law student

Ringland Fisher "Rex" Kilpatrick—left halfback, law student

William Blackburn "Warbler" Wilson—quarterback, law student

William Henry Poole—center, seminary student

Henry Sheridan Keyes—left guard, medical student

John William Jones—left tackle, seminary student

Bartlet et Ultimus Sims—left end, medical student

William Stirling "Wild Bill" Claiborne—right guard, seminary student

Richard Elliott Bolling—right tackle, medical student

Hugh Miller Thompson Pearce—right end, kicker, liberal arts student

<u>Substitutes</u>

Ralph Peters Black—liberal arts student

Preston Smith Brooks, Jr.—liberal arts student

Harris Goodwin Cope—law student

Andrews Cleveland Evans—liberal arts student

Daniel Baldwin Hull—law student

Joseph Lee Kirby-Smith—liberal arts student

Landon Randolph Mason—medical student

Floy Hoffman Parker—liberal arts student

Albert T. Davidson—liberal arts student

Charles Quintard Gray—liberal arts student

<u>Support</u>

Cal Burrows—athletic trainer

Billy Suter—coach

Luke Lea—student manager, liberal arts student

Finally, it is wholly fitting to end these acknowledgments where I started them. Thank you, my amazing Hilary.